Losing

Gemma

Losing
Gemma

Katy Gardner

RIVERHEAD BOOKS, NEW YORK

Riverhead Books
Published by The Berkley Publishing Group
A division of Penguin Putnam Inc.
375 Hudson Street
New York, New York 10014

Copyright © 2002 by Katy Gardner
Book design by Tiffany Kukec
Cover design and photography by Ben Gibson

First Riverhead trade paperback edition: April 2002

Visit our website at www.penguinputnam.com

Library of Congress Cataloging-in-Publication Data

Gardner, Katy.
    Losing Gemma / Katy Gardner.—1st Riverhead trade pbk. ed.
        p. cm.
    ISBN 1-57322-933-4
    1. British—India—Fiction. 2. Female friendship—Fiction. 3. Young women—Fiction. 4. Backpacking—Fiction. 5. India—Fiction. 6. Death—Fiction.
    I. Title.

PR6057.A6316 L67 2002
823'.914—dc21

                                                                2001057884

PRINTED IN THE UNITED STATES OF AMERICA

10   9   8   7   6   5   4   3   2   1

For Graham

Acknowledgments

Many thanks to Clare Conville, Louise Moore, Emma Parry, Wendy Carlton, Venetia van Kuffeler, Graham Alborough, Nina Beachcroft, and Mary Bardbury. Finally, thanks to Karen Khera, with whom I made my own first (and very happy!) journey around India.

Preface

AFTER Gemma's funeral, I returned to my parents' house, climbed the stairs to my bedroom, and lay down on the floor as if I would never get up again. It was the worst day of my life, and I wanted the walls to cave in, to be crushed under a detritus of bricks, Blu-Taked wallpaper, and curling, teenage posters: my whole childhood—the one that we had shared—collapsing over me just as our history had buried her.

So I lay there and waited, but nothing happened. The gentle English sun worked its way across the walls, the late evening light faded, and slowly the room became dark. I grew chilled and my bones began to ache; eventually I could hear my mother, tapping on the door.

There was nothing more to say and nothing more to do, that was why I could not move. Even after Gemma's death I had failed her: I should have read out one of her poems or made some kind of speech, but all I could do was sit at the back of the church next to Steve and my parents, my hands locked so tightly together that my knuckles turned blue. I did not look up for I could not bear to see the curious glances of the old school crowd, the dull despair in her mother's eyes. I knew what everyone else thought of me, the kind of things they had been saying.

My best friend was dead, you see. And it wall all my fault.

THIS is the story of Gemma and me: how I lost her, I suppose. I don't usually tell it to anyone but myself; I save it for the darkest moments: the long hours before dawn or the unexpected panics that creep up silently, mugging me from behind. That's when I repeat it again and again, revisiting each small detail as if by the telling of it I might change the past. This time though, things are different. This time the past has already been erased.

I'll start at the place I thought was the beginning but now know was near the end. I was pretty full of myself back in those days; I thought life was a cinch, that everything I did was charmed and charming. I was twenty-three (name: Esther Waring, B.A.: University of Sussex; passport stamps achieved so far: Morocco, Egypt, and Israel), the year was 1989, and I was perched on the edge of my seat, several thousand feet above the shanties of Delhi. I liked to think of myself as a traveler back then, a lover of movement and excitement, but, ironically, I hated planes. As the wheels touched down I was clutching the worn acrylic armrest of the Air India Boeing 747, trying to look nonchalant but secretly praying. For a few anxious moments I'd been unable to see the runway, even though we were clearly about to land. I peered horrified at the rapidly approaching ground, relaxing only minimally when I glimpsed the rusting carcasses of abandoned planes and suddenly—coming to meet me—an expanse of tarmac. There was a thump, an agonizing rush of speed and lingering doubt (would the brakes work?), and then the plane finally came to rest outside Indira Gandhi International Airport.

The moment we were on the ground my fears evaporated; in retrospect they seemed ridiculous, even slightly shaming. Fear of flying from a global, backpacking babe like me? It was pathetic, a symptom of my chronic need for control. I unclicked my belt, reaching impatiently for my bags. Gemma was still dithering around, groping under her seat for God knows what, but I was unable to wait. Jumping up I pushed my way into the aisle.

The line shuffled slowly forward. When I finally reached the exit I paused, momentarily blasted by the hot air and reek of aviation fuel. Then, shielding my eyes against the dazzling afternoon light, I swung my bags around my shoulders and clanked down the metal steps.

Gemma, who never pushed herself anywhere, let alone into a line of impatiently shoving passengers, didn't appear for at least another five minutes. I waited in a state of frustrated excitement on the tarmac, blinking up at the white flanks of the jumbo until I saw her small rounded frame appearing from its stale-breathed jaws. Her face was screwed up against the light, and she looked dazed, as if unsure of where she was going.

"Poly, you plonker! Over here!"

At the sound of her old nickname she started and glanced up, her expression relaxing as she located my face in the crowd; when she finally reached the bottom of the steps her voice was breathless, her face flushed.

"I lost my passport! It fell down the side of my seat . . ."

"Yup, Poly Styrene, Queen of Kohl is about to conquer the Orient."

"Shut it, Siouxsie Sioux."

She stuck out her tongue and we touched hands, a fleeting gesture that seemed to sum everything up: partners in crime, old friends through thick and thin. Then, linking arms, we climbed onto the airline bus.

The Arrivals lounge was a vast hangar of a building which echoed to the sporadic stamping of passports and the squawk of malnourished sparrows. We waited at the end of a long line to be processed by the sour-faced immigration official perching humorlessly at his desk ahead of us. Besides the Indian families, with their kohl-eyed, frilly dressed toddlers and endless luggage, and various sharp-suited businessmen, the flight had been filled with disappointingly suburban types. A quick inspection of the logo on the nylon bags of a group of middle-aged women informed me that they were part of a Sunnyworld Spectacles of India Tour. Watching them, my heart momentarily drooped. I craved travel, not tourism, you see, and back then the distinction seemed terribly important. For everything I had planned and everything I believed myself to be, I wanted for us to be in a place for the adventurous minority, not some soft option for people like my parents. Catching Gemma's eye, I glanced at the women and pulled a face. Gemma opened her mouth, her tongue lolling like an idiot, and crossed her eyes.

More promisingly, the guys behind us were chatting loudly about "Asia." I kept glancing covertly over my shoulder, checking them out. I knew the sort well: travel bores who'll regale one with tales of hardship and daring for hour after hour, laboring under the illusion that it made them "interesting." Both were vying to be the Best Traveled: one was talking authoritatively about how he planned to cross the Himalayas into Ladakh; the other had an interest in temples. After a while I grew irritated by the competitive tone of their conversation. Turning around, I eyed up a young studenty type reading Hermann Hesse, more out of habit and boredom than any real desire to flirt.

He remained buried in the book. Gemma, too, had dropped to the floor and was picking at her nails and glancing anxiously around. She would be thinking that the latrines nearby smelled disgusting and worrying about where we were going to spend the night, I thought as I watched her sigh heavily and flick a morsel of dirt from her nails. Dear, muddle-headed Gemma, with whom I was about to embark on the journey of my dreams: she so often got unnerved and discouraged by situations that I relished with glee. Now that we were finally here I would have to help her cope.

Two hours later we dragged our rucksacks from the luggage carousel and walked through the smeared glass doors of Arrivals. For a moment we were overtaken, British flotsam bobbing in an unstoppable torrent of bodies and luggage and grasping hands. Drivers waved signs in our faces and touts pushed hotel cards at us while at least three porters attempted to pull our rucksacks from our backs. All around us families were being reunited, the long gone British exiles falling weeping into their relatives' arms as garlands of golden tinsel were placed over their heads. Beyond the sweep of airport concrete the sky gashed red, the last rays of sun reflecting from the glistening, expectant faces of the crowd. Crows hopped around our feet, pecking at the remnants of a spilled bag of chancchuri. The air was suffocatingly hot.

My plan had been to find a taxi, haggle the driver down to ten dollars—a rip-off according to the *Lonely Planet* guide, but considering that it was our first night I was prepared to compromise—and ride into Connaught Circus. Back at the main entrance to the airport I had dismissed what felt like an endless supply of drivers, but now the place was suddenly deserted. The Sunnyworld drones had climbed onto their shining tour buses, the returned migrants ushered reverentially onto the minibuses hired to return them in splendor to their villages, and the backpackers gone God knows where. Gemma and I stood alone by the side of the road, unsure what to do next.

Isn't it incredible how those apparently minute, split-second decisions can change the course of a life? If we had gone with one of the touts, or asked the backpackers how best to get into the city center, or even done the unthinkable and visited the Tourist Information Office, everything might have been different. But in those days I would never have taken such diminutive action. I was too proud, too keen to prove my credentials as a Traveler: to take the cheapest and most authentic route to everywhere and everything. That was how I'd backpacked around Europe the summer before, how I'd visited North Africa with Luke, the guy I went out with briefly in my second year, and how now, in this year off that I'd dreamed of for so long, I was planning to "do" India. Gemma, whose foreign adventures consisted of a holiday to Majorca with her dad and his new wife and an aborted three months au-pairing in Belgium—neither of which experiences I could honestly count as "travel"—had little say. Perhaps I was naive; I was certainly bossy.

And so, rather than following the other passengers onto an air-conditioned bus or hailing a taxi we suddenly found ourselves alone at the side of the road. And what I realize now is this was the first of my many mistakes, for it was then that we were noticed.

"Look, you stay here, and I'll investigate—see if there are any buses or anything."

Unhooking my rucksack from my back and dropping it at Gemma's feet, I walked swiftly away, swiveling my head around as I searched for suitably "local" looking buses. With the exception of a silver four-wheel-drive vehicle parked immediately opposite, the car park was deserted. It was almost dark now, and I could feel a line of sweat trickling down the small of my back. Although it tickled, I was pleased it was there: it was right that I should be slightly dirty and sticky with the heat, I thought, it showed that I was well and truly in the South.

I crossed the road, peering through the gloom at a solitary bus on the other side of the concourse. I'm ashamed to admit that despite my total ignorance of Hindi, I made a pretense of examining the sign on the front, as if by staring at it for long enough its destination would seep osmotically into my consciousness. With the unpromising exception of the driver, who was wrapped in a shawl and lying asleep at the wheel, the bus was empty.

Perhaps I should not have left Gemma alone like that, I thought with a jolt: after all, it was the first time she had been outside Europe. I remembered her expression of fleeting panic as I'd set off and imagined her perched on top of the rucksacks, as easy prey for the men who hovered outside the airport in the hope of sex or an easy scam. By now they would be circling for the kill, asking "What country?" and "Please, madam, where is your husband?"

I looked back, hoping to reassure her with a wave, and saw to my surprise that she was no longer alone. Squatting in the dust next to her was another traveler: a tall guy, with long, dirty yellow hair, bright orange drawstring pantaloons in the style of German hippies, and a tasseled leather bag which he had placed on the floor by his feet. Leaning on the railings opposite, apparently overlooking the scene, were two girls. Both had their backs turned toward me, but one was notably skinny, with a long black braid appearing from a beaded headscarf and a red dress, its hem trailing in the dust. The other was broader, with a large behind and lumpy looking legs. She kept turning her head away and shaking it with what could only be irritation. I remember looking at them, and thinking vaguely that something was wrong. Perhaps it was the way they were watching the hippie, as if they knew him but for some reason were not permitted to join him, or perhaps it was just that they were having an argument. Whatever it was, I only glanced at them for a second or so.

I raised my hand and was just about to shout: "Gemma!" when a taxi swerved into my path, its horn blaring in triumph at having found the remaining two passengers from the London flight.

TWENTY minutes later we had reached the outskirts of the city, the initially deserted airport road becoming crowded with scooter-rickshaws and motorbikes and overladen Tata trucks. I gazed awestruck from the taxi window. We were traveling through the blasted hinterland of outer Delhi but the landscape seemed gloriously exotic to me, the smoky evening light heavier and hotter than anything I had ever experienced, the air fragrant and filled with promise. About ten minutes into the journey we had passed a flock of vultures picking at something dead on the tarmac; a few miles later we nearly hit a mangy cow idling in the middle of the road. The driver braked hard, then slowly circled around the animal, humming to himself. Gemma and I gawped at each other then burst out laughing. It was too dark now to see what lay beyond the dull orange glow of the highway lights, but outside the cab I could hear cicadas and the distant yowl of jackals.

We sat in silence, our rucksacks on our laps. All I could think was that finally I had made it. I wanted to roll the window down, push my head out, and take it in with great greedy gulps but despite my love of excessive gestures something held me back. Perhaps it was Gemma, whose stolid presence always restrained me from my wilder moments. Even when we were kids and I was about to do something stupid, like pocket sweets from the newsagents, or ring up a teacher and do heavy breathing down the phone, she would look at me and frown and for just a moment I would hesitate. Glancing at her across the back seat I realized that in the fuggy warmth of the night air she was on the brink of sleep; her eyes kept flickering closed, her mouth loosening as her face relaxed. When the taxi bumped over a particularly large hole she opened her eyes and sat up straight, shaking her head.

"Bollocks. I'm tired. Is it something in the air?"

"Didn't you read about it? It's a special gas they use to drug the foreigners so they can rip them off."

She stared at me.

"Duh!"

"Well, you shouldn't have guzzled all that booze on the plane!"

"It was free!"

We were silent again.

A few miles further on I said: "So who was that guy you were talking to?"

"What guy?"

She gazed at me.

"A hippie? With orange trousers and all that hair? He was sitting next to you? Jesus, Pol? What planet are you on?"

She shrugged, her face fighting and then succumbing to a huge yawn.

"Planet jet lag, I guess."

We were passing a mosque now, its pillars hung with sparkling lights like the fairy castles we used to dream of when we were seven. Gemma stared at it for a moment, her eyes widening.

"It's a mosque," I said in explanation.

She frowned again, then yawned and closed her eyes.

Me and Poly Styrene—that juvenile nickname she had never truly shaken off—had been best friends since our first day at school and that was the way we still were. We might have grown up, moving on from our pubescent skirmish with bin- and eyeliners, progressing through Ska and New Romantics and Dexys up through school until I went off to university, and she moved out of her mum's and into her flat over the Alliance and Leicester, but as far as I was concerned, the sisterhood we had found as little girls was going to last forever. It was part of my badly digested undergraduate feminism, plastered over my consciousness with a capital F. Men weren't important, or at least, they shouldn't be. What mattered—I convinced myself—was the solidarity of women. Sure, we might have had our tense moments, our times of unspoken conflict, but wasn't that just part of the intricate fabric of friendship, weaving us ever closer and more colorfully together? The mosque disappeared and the taxi came up to and then blatantly skipped a set of flashing traffic lights. When I next looked at Gemma she was asleep, her head bumping the taxi door, a silver thread of drool trickling from her mouth.

As I gazed at her, I was overtaken by a rush of affection. There was something so sweet and trusting in the way she fell asleep at every available opportunity. When we were at school she had a habit of dozing off in the middle of lessons and later, in the days of pubs and all-night parties, she was always the first to succumb, curling up in the corner under her coat as we cavorted around her inert body. I was the opposite: too awake, my mind always buzzing. Sometimes I would lie with my eyes wide open all night, waiting for the sky outside my curtains to lighten, for another day to bring me closer to what I thought of as my "real," adult life.

And now, finally, I was here. After all those months of planning and saving, I had escaped the tedium of Britain. Unlike my college friends with their deathly city jobs and sad, hemmed-in plans, I was, I told myself with the triumphant optimism of the very young, a career-path refusenik. Not for me the daily trudge to the office. No, I was different. I was going to hurl myself at the world and see what happened.

2

THE taxi dropped us at the end of what I know now to be Jan-path. Temporarily dazed by the rushing traffic we stood by the side of the road clutching our backpacks and trying to get our bearings. We were standing on a large arterial road, which led into a wide circle of smart shops, restaurants, and airline offices. It was after nine now and the pavement was littered with sleep-ing bodies.

I gazed around in excitement. Behind me a boy was squatting in front of a tray heaped with silver-foiled leaves, aniseed seeds, and betel nuts. Further down the pavement a group of ragged children were tugging at the arms of passersby. As I stared across the road I suddenly noticed a turbaned man squat down in front of a wicker basket. Pulling off its lid, he waved his hand over the top like a puppeteer until the jerking body of a long brown snake poked its way over the top.

"Bloody hell, we've just walked into a Merchant Ivory film!"

Gemma blinked at me. She looked stunned, her mouth hang-ing slightly open, her arms folded nervously around her waist.

"Do you think it's still poisonous?"

"Sure. You won't find any real live *bitey* snakes around *here.*"

"Ha fucking ha."

Tossing her head, she pulled the *Lonely Planet* from her bag and started to thumb through it.

"We really need to work out where we're going," she was muttering. "It says here there's a youth hostel somewhere near . . ." She frowned, concentrating hard on the book.

"Relax! Let's just soak up the scene . . ."

Glancing to the right, where the stream of 1950s-style Ambassador cars and scooters had stopped at the lights, I grabbed her hand and began to pull her across the road. For a second or so it remained empty. Then from the opposite direction a tidal wave of vehicles suddenly poured around us. For a moment we stood paralyzed in the middle of the maelstrom, clutching each other in horror.

"What do we do now?"

I stared into Gemma's small startled eyes. In the traffic roaring toward us, there was just about to be a sudden lull.

"Just go for it!" I screamed.

Gripping each other's hands tightly and yelling at the top of our voices, we ran for our lives. By the time we reached the sidewalk we were shaking with terror and laughter. Perhaps it was too much for Gemma, who was now gasping by the side of the road, her hands on her knees, but I felt as if I had jumped out of a plane and landed on my feet.

"Yo! We did it!"

Gemma looked up at me, raising her eyebrows sarcastically.

"Within an inch of their lives, the intrepid explorers breasted the raging torrent."

"But what a way to go!"

There was a pause, then Gemma said quietly, "Perhaps we should've just let that taxi driver take us to his cousin's hotel."

I glanced sharply at her face, but from its benign gaze I decided that this was intended as a question rather than a criticism. Since I was the more experienced traveler, I'd naturally assumed that she was going to leave the practicalities to me.

"I don't think so," I said dismissively. "They're all on a percentage, these guys. Come on, let's try this one."

We turned down a side road which intersected the main arc of buildings and immediately saw a series of neon hotel signs and, sitting on the sidewalk, a group of backpackers. I smiled at Gemma reassuringly.

We started to cross again, this time peering in every direction before stepping off the curb. As we reached the other side I nodded at the group, a couple of men and a thin, tanned woman with bare feet and anklets. They looked as if they had been on the road a long time, I remember thinking enviously, long enough to shed their old Western selves entirely. I wanted to be like that, too, with dusty feet and slim brown wrists encased in lines of sparkly bazaar bangles. I wanted to be an old hand, someone "with experience," who had done and seen it all, not a fresh arrival, straight off the London flight and clutching her guidebook. Most of all, I wanted to be different from everyone at home.

I glanced back at Gemma. Embarrassingly, she still had the *Lonely Planet* out and was frowning and waving it around in front of her, like a tourist at the Taj Mahal. Ignoring her I gestured toward the first hotel, a grimy looking place advertising rooms for fifty rupees a night.

"What about here?"

Gemma looked at me doubtfully.

"It doesn't mention it in the book."

"For fuck's sake, Gem. Forget the bloody book."

I turned on my heels and was just about to proceed purposefully up the steps of the hotel when a figure who had suddenly come out of the swing doors lurched down the steps and blundered into me, knocking me backward. With the weight of the rucksack on my back, I fell hard onto my backside.

"Jesus Christ!"

I felt a sharp stab of pain in my elbow and for a moment was disoriented. It seems stupid now, but my immediate concern was that the other backpackers might have seen and all attempts at traveler cool would be ruined.

"Are you okay?"

For a moment I saw Gemma's face peering down at me. Then her eyes flicked away, focusing on something to her left.

"What?"

Looking past her I glimpsed the fast disappearing back of my assailant: a thin woman weaving almost drunkenly along the sidewalk. She kept starting to run and then checking herself and slowing down, as if aware that she was being watched. Something about the way she moved, perhaps her uneven gait, or the slumped, almost crushed shape of her back, made her appear either very stoned or very scared. She was wearing a long cotton petticoat, the sort worn by Indian women under their saris, and a skimpy top.

"Jesus!"

I pulled myself up shakily. It'd been a harder fall than I'd first thought and my arm was stinging. Looking down I saw that my elbow was bleeding and the side of my hand was badly grazed.

"What's *she* on?"

Gemma rested her hand on my shoulder, her eyes wide.

"She might at least have stopped . . ."

We stared at the woman's back for a little while longer. After about thirty seconds she reached the end of the road and turned into Connaught Circus.

"She looked Indian . . ." Gemma eventually said.

"Nah, she's a Westerner. Probably stoned."

"Perhaps she's had too much of that Indian gas you were telling me about."

Turning round, Gemma put her foot on the first step.

"Wait."

I gazed into the late evening haze, watching as the crowd closed around the woman. There was something bothering me.

"What?"

"Nah, it's gone."

Pulling my rucksack higher onto my back, I turned and walked unsteadily up the steps.

WE were given a room on the third floor: a small cubicle with two string charpoy-beds and a shuttered window overlooking the bricks and pipes of the opposite building. It was just what I had imagined: as far from the floral, en suite suburban horrors of the package hotel as possible. There was virtually no furniture: on the wall above the beds was a narrow ledge, containing a guttered candle stub and an empty cigarette packet; opposite the window, a bare wooden table, its soft wood indented with graffiti. On the ceiling a fan clattered noisily. Gemma had turned it to "full" the moment the proprietor had left and now it was working itself into a frenzy, the heavy metal hub shaking so violently that the fan seemed in danger of spinning off the ceiling and decapitating us. The "bathroom" was across the corridor, a rusty shower and a filthy hole which, after a cursory inspection, even I, with all my half-baked bravado, had decided was best avoided.

Gemma threw her rucksack onto the floor next to the farthest bed—an unstable-looking construction of wood and ropes— and flopped down.

"Thank God for that. I thought he was going to say they were full."

I perched on the edge of the bed and started to fiddle uncomfortably with the top of my bag. My hand was still throbbing. Lying opposite me, Gemma was staring across the room. She was brooding, I could tell from the glum shape of her mouth, the pensive glaze of her eyes. Determined to snap her out of it, I stood up and waved my hand jauntily in front of her face.

"Is the accommodation to your taste, memsahib?"

She smiled distractedly. "Quite divine."

"As you can see, our luxurious suite of rooms caters to the modern tourist's every need."

There was a long pause and then, to my relief, she sat up.

"If this is a super-deluxe room I dread to think what 'budget' involves," she said slowly.

"The roof, probably."

"I've got to have a shower. I feel really yucky."

"Have you seen it?"

Glancing at me, she suddenly closed her eyes and fell backward, her body hitting the taut rope base of the bed with a soft thud.

"Whatever. I'm knackered."

She lay there for a few minutes, her eyes closed, her breathing deep and regular. For a moment I thought she'd fallen asleep again, but then she sat up, opening her eyes wide and yawning as she looked across the room.

"Christ, this is uncomfortable."

We stared at each other. Suddenly her mouth started to twitch, as if she was desperately trying to repress a huge bubble of mirth. Just looking at her made me smile. Thank God, I was thinking; she's not sulking after all.

"What? What's the matter with you?"

"Oh, come on, little Miss Anthropology. Look at this bloody place!"

She glanced at me again and the laughter escaped with a great spluttering raspberry.

"And so, our brave lady explorers face their first night in the wilds of India . . ."

She collapsed with the onslaught of another explosion. I

pursed my lips and fluttered my eyelashes in my famous imper-
sonation of Mrs. Crewe, our A-level English teacher; an old, in-
fantile joke we still found funny.

"Gemma Harding, I do hope you're not taking the piss."

"It's like fucking *Colditz!*"

"Well, I think it's . . . *delightful.*"

"A stylish example of late 1980s minimalism."

"All mod-cons, including, for your own convenience, a de-
lightfully designed communal cess pit!"

And so it went on, us with the giggles on our first night in India.

After we'd recovered we sat on our beds, chuckling and wiping our faces. I gazed across the room at Gemma: her cheeks
pink with heat and laughter, her damp hair flopping in her eyes.
Her features were as familiar to me as my own. I'd grown up
with them and knew every contour and expression by heart;
she just had to jerk her head or bite her lip and I knew exactly
what she was thinking. It was true that she was never going to
make it as a Hollywood nymphet: her face was too round, her
nose too knobbly, and her legs too short, but I liked how she
looked. It reminded me of my childhood, of bicycle rides down
country lanes and camping out on cool summer nights.

She, however, was never satisfied. Her hair and her weight
were the two great enemies, and ever since I could remember
she'd been waging campaigns against them. Over the last few
years she'd been experimenting with the former, cropping it into
the spiky post-punk style of the moment, and dying her fringe
unlikely colors: pink and orange and most recently, bright purple. She'd also taken to painting black eyeliner around her eyes,
a procedure which—as I had tried to point out—had the unfortunate effect of making them appear smaller rather than more
alluring. Yet despite these attempts she looked the same to me:
her round, podgy face stubbornly shrugging off the slightest
overtures of sophistication.

Then there was her figure. Her body was the traditional English shape: thick legs and hips, a slimmer waist, and small round tits. And, as she was always complaining, her legs were too short. The long pencil skirts everyone wore in the mid eighties made her look as if she was swathed in cheap curtain material whilst drainpipe jeans were, to be honest, a dumpy disaster. So she was constantly on a diet. But however much she starved herself on low-calorie yogurts and apples, or, for a really terrible month or so, a diet consisting solely of bran and orange juice, her frame remained the same. Her legs were still too short and her hips too wide; rather than transforming her into a svelte imp, the weight loss made her face sunken and her knees bony.

At this point I should probably come clean. It's not the sort of thing one is supposed to say, but I think we both knew that one of Gemma's main problems was the way *I* looked. It's faded now: I'm too thin and my face is gray and drawn, but as Gem and I used to joke at school, if we put her brains and my bod together we'd have the ideal combo. I don't think it mattered when we were kids, but later, when the school discos and parties and boyfriends started, it somehow became important. I remember one time in particular; we were getting ready to go to some stupid youth club disco aged about fourteen. Standing together in front of the long mirror in my parents' bedroom, I suddenly saw myself as a stranger might. I looked almost like a model, I realized with shock and an unfamiliar pride. Virtually overnight, my long legs had turned shapely and my waist had tucked in sharply below my new, blossoming bust. I piled my curly hair onto the top of my head, stuck out my chest, and pouted, like a page three girl.

"Bloody hell. You look really tarty."

Jerking round, I saw that Gemma was standing behind me, watching my performance. Despite the outrageous clothes, lipstick, and mascara, she still looked like a podgy little girl. I think I must have laughed, or said something back, but from then on there was a perceptible shift between us. Something neither of us fully understood had changed.

Of course we were just little girls dressing up, but we took it so seriously. Suddenly our appearances had become vital and we would spend long afternoons trailing around Top Shop and Miss Selfridge trying on clothes we had no money to buy. I could chart our history from what we wore: a genealogy of fashion statements—mistakes and triumphs—taken on and discarded as the years ticked past. When we were thirteen we had pretended to be punks in hastily improvised miniskirts and ripped tops, pink satin winklepickers, and black kohl, painted awkwardly around our eyes. I tottered around in stilettos; Gemma had a pin which gave the appearance of going through her nose. It was around then that I started to call her "Poly Styrene," after we saw the real thing, plump and punkily clad on *Top of the Pops*. I, in contrast, was named "Siouxsie Sioux," but it was a token gesture, for despite Gemma's attempts to shake off the image, her name somehow stuck; it summed up a nervous, neurotic quality that even the ripped miniskirts and black lipstick could not fully mask. "Clean my teeth ten times a day," I used to sing at her. "Scrub away, scrub away, scrub away."

Later, of course, we moved on from punk. I had my beloved black ra-ra skirt and my Madonna-style lacy gloves, stained brown at the tips from the cigarettes I learned to smoke. While I donned dangly earrings and New Romantic frilly shirts, Gemma veered toward Student Goth, with black ankle boots and leggings, her army surplus greatcoat, and long violet tasseled dress.

But I'm jumping ahead: her grungey phase came later, around the time she started smoking too much dope and dropped out of school. Before that, we'd both tart ourselves up to the nines. We spent hours getting ready, experimenting with makeup and hairspray and fishnet tights. Then, pretending we always dressed in such a way, we would set off for the sad discos and youth clubs we frequented, with that frightened, fluttery feeling in our tummies. We'd spend the evening pretending to ignore the boys in the fifth form, while waiting desperately to see if they'd ask us for a dance: all that giggly, nerve-racking, competitive crap. In retrospect I can see that Gemma found it really hard. She'd spend hours getting ready, then sit miserably in the corner all evening chewing her hair while I got chatted up. "My sex life is carried out vicariously!" she announced after one event. Not fully understanding, I just winked at her and smiled.

The problem for me was that once I'd got them, the boys at school embarrassed me with their fumbling attempts at seduction and clumsy protestations of love. University was largely the same. I don't know why, really, but I'd pile up these pathetic, hangdog admirers in the same way that Gemma accumulated books. I always enjoyed the first phase: the being chased, the first kiss or first few weeks of passion, but then I'd grow dispirited and somehow impatient with the whole endeavor. Nobody ever seemed right, and I certainly didn't relish becoming part of a clingy, predictable coupling. What I wanted, you see, was excitement and change. Aged nineteen or twenty there seemed simply too much of life to experience to spend it with some gauche youth. Besides, I told myself, I was not looking for a man. As was the fashion back then at Sussex, I declared myself a feminist.

I stared into Gemma's face, smiling at her with affection. Of course I'd never have told her, but I preferred her with her old, mousy hair and bulging tummy. I wanted her to stay just the same as always: my cuddly, constant bestest ever best friend. Whenever I returned home for the holidays and discovered yet another attempt at self-transformation—her hair color changed again, or some new health food fad—I always felt secretly irked. It's childish, I know, but it made me feel left out.

"You know what?" I said. "I think we should work out our route."

I stood up, stretching and clicking my knuckles.

"Give us that book."

Gemma pulled the *Lonely Planet* from her bag and started to flick through it.

"I was reading about Goa and Kerala on the plane," she said. "They sound amazing."

"No, look. Let's do it this way. Let's ask the gods."

I had planned it all, long before the trip included Gemma. I would travel according to chance, a real adventurer, journeying to wherever fate decreed.

"Whatever page it lands on, we'll go there first."

I looked across the room at her uncertain face.

"Go on, it'll be much more of a laugh."

Plucking the guide from her fingers, I stood ceremoniously in the middle of the room, then tossed it high above my head. It flew upward through the fan-stirred air, its pages fluttering wildly as a myriad of possibilities flicked past. At the zenith of its flight it paused. Then suddenly it came crashing down onto the bare stone floor, our fate decided.

I could have stopped it, of course I could. I could have caught the book, turned the pages with my own hands, and changed it all. But innocent of everything that was to come, I let it fall.

The book landed at Gemma's feet; its pages splayed and bent back like the wings of a squashed beetle.

"Go on then. Pick it up and see."

She picked it up and laid it on her lap. For a moment she was silent, her forehead furrowed in concentration as I hopped at her side.

"So what does it say?"

She sighed and turned the page, still unwilling to comment.

"Where is it?"

"This is really interesting . . ."

"Come on, Gem! Give it here!"

"No, wait. I'm going to read it out to you. Ready?"

I nodded impatiently.

"Okay, here we go . . . Agun Mazir, Orissa. 'This little visited town situated in the heart of the forests of eastern Orissa is best known as the site of the shrine of Pir Saheb Nirulla, a Sufi mystic who is said to have burnt to death there in 1947 . . . ' "

She broke off and studied the book.

" 'The town has been a centre of pilgrimage for the last forty years . . . ' God, this is really weird . . ."

"What does it say?"

"This guy, this Pir Saheb blokey . . . he burst into flames when he was meditating or praying or something, and now all these pilgrims come to the shrine thinking it's going to heal them or get them a job or whatever . . ."

I'd had enough of listening. I leaned over and plucked the book from her hands.

"What do you mean, he burst into flames?"

"It was a miracle. Look, read that bit at the bottom. He was a hermit, living in the jungle, and he spontaneously combusted . . ."

" 'The truth behind the myth,' " I read out, " 'is hotly contested by local historians . . . while devotees to the shrine insist in the miraculous nature of Pir Saheb Nirulla's combustion, others have a more prosaic and grim explanation, citing the partition of India and violence between Hindus and Muslims as the real cause of his burning.' "

Gemma blinked at me.

"Blimey."

"Anyway, that's where we're going. It sounds wild."

There was a pause. From the look in Gemma's eyes, I thought she was about to demur.

"Is there anywhere to stay?" she said quietly.

"Let's see . . ." I scanned the book hastily for information.

" 'The town has only one hotel, catering solely for devotees who travel from all over India to visit the shrine. . . . There is also a tourist bungalow, which is reached by a path leading into the forest to the north. Cost . . . forty rupees . . . single, air-conditioning . . . ' blah, blah . . . sounds fine. Let's do it."

I put the book down and stood up. I guess I should have told Gemma about this part of the trip before we left Stevenage, but somehow, in all the rush to get our visas and jabs and everything packed, I'd forgotten. Glancing at her face I sensed that she was still not wholly persuaded.

"How do you get there?"

"Train to Calcutta, then another train to Orissa, then bus it. Go on, Gem. It'll be really fun. It sounds like it's totally off the beaten track and we don't just want to go to all the usual predictable places, do we? We can do Goa afterward."

I glanced at her doubtful face. It was so much part of my fantasy that I hadn't even considered she might want to do things differently.

"We don't have to always ask the book," I said patiently. "But since we did I think we should go where it says. Perhaps there's a reason why it opened there."

"A reason?"

"Yeah, you know. Fate."

She stared at me. She looked hot and unhappy, an expression she often assumed at clubs and parties when she was supposed to be having fun. I would spot her sometimes, dancing half-heartedly on the other side of the room, and just for a moment, when she thought no one was watching, she'd stare down at her feet, her mouth drooping as if she were close to tears. Now she paused, as if making up her mind. Then pushing her hair out of her eyes, she shook her head and laughed.

"You win. Let's go for it."

LATER that night we climbed the hotel's wide stone stairway to the top floor, and following the sound of laughter and a guitar opened a fire door to the roof. The view was stunning. From the eighth floor we could see across Connaught Place to the wide thoroughfare of Janpath, its steady traffic melted to a single, molten line of light. Beyond this was a sparkling mass of streets and houses, interspersed by sudden patches of blackness—the bustees where the electricity did not reach. Above us the violet sky was encrusted with a million stars.

"Wow!"

I took a deep breath of the warm night air, and stepped through the door. The roof was scattered with sleeping bags. Immediately opposite the door a small group of travelers were sitting with their legs hanging over the edge of the building as they talked and smoked. A little further on a young Western guy with a shaved head and a lunghi was playing the guitar. The air smelled of coconut oil and marijuana.

As the door opened a couple of heads turned. I smiled ingratiatingly as if gatecrashing a private party. I was hoping no one would guess how recently we had arrived.

"Looks like you were right about the budget rooms," Gemma muttered. "The place is crammed with crusties."

"Sshh! They'll hear."

We made our way to the other side of the roof and sat on the edge, peering down at the street below. The vendors and beggars had gone now, the pavement covered by the dark shapes of sleeping bodies. Despite Gemma's remarks, my entire being pulsed with excitement. This was *exactly* what I wanted: the romantic hippie squalor of a flophouse roof under an Indian sky.

"Isn't it amazing? I can't believe we're actually here."

I sighed ecstatically. Pulling a face, Gemma produced two cigarettes and a packet of matches from her shirt pocket.

"I need a fag."

"Where did you get the matches?"

"Someone left them on the ledge."

She took out a match and struck it against the side of the box. It flared brilliantly for a brief second then went out. When she struck a second the sizzling head flew off the end of the match and into my lap.

"Ow!"

Finally she produced a flame, lit both cigarettes, and passed one to me, our own little ritual.

"Bugger me, it's hot," she said, leaning back on her elbows.

"What did you expect, Blackpool?"

"Sarky."

She pinched my arm affectionately.

"You know something?" I said. "This is what I've dreamed about doing for years."

"What? Sitting in the dust and listening to a bunch of hippies croon Bob Dylan?"

"Nah. You know—this." I gestured at the scene below. I suddenly really wanted her to understand, to share my enthusiasm. "It's fantastic, isn't it?"

She didn't even look down, just sniffed and said, "Hmph." She's just *scared* of it, I told myself; she's not used to this kind of scene, she finds it intimidating.

"Gem," I said gently, laying my hand on her arm. "We're going to have a real ball here."

She nodded, looking into my eyes and smiling.

"Yeah, yeah. I know. Just so long as you don't start singing 'Blowing in the Wind' at me."

"It's a deal."

We sat for a while in companionable silence, smoking and looking up at the sky.

"So what do you think Steve would think of it?" Gemma suddenly said. "You know, I'm already really missing him."

I shrugged uncomfortably. Steve's views on India, or indeed anything else, were not something I wished to discuss. To deflect her attention I turned and stared into her face, raising my eyebrows meaningfully.

"You know what this reminds me of?"

"What?"

"Your roof at home . . ."

"Oh Christ!"

Gemma clamped her hand over her mouth in mock horror. For a moment we stared at each other, then, at exactly the same time, we started to laugh.

It was the summer before secondary school, just before Gemma's dad left and she moved with her brother and mum into the semi in Stevenage. We were still little girls: our chests flat and our skin smooth, but something within us had started to stir. It wasn't as if we didn't *know* about sex; we did, in graphic detail—Gemma's brother's subscription to *Fiesta* had taken care of that. No, it was more that we'd never connected this embarrassing, exciting, and slightly nasty knowledge with ourselves. It was true that I'd experienced vague longings, a sense of desire I channeled into unfocused fantasies involving Roger Daltry, whose tight-trousered photo spreads adorned my sister's room. I'd also enjoyed a long and arduous correspondence with a French schoolboy which stopped only when he arrived for the exchange program and I discovered that he was a foot smaller than me and picked his nose. In the spirit of adventurous competition Gemma had kissed a twelve-year-old boy who lived down her road, but all she reported back was that it had made her lips sore.

So I guess it must have been to do with sex, in a warped, prepubescent way. It was certainly not something we would have dreamed of doing a year later. It involved us taking off our underwear—why, I've totally forgotten—and then climbing out onto the flat roof opposite Gemma's parents' bedroom. All summer we'd been using the roof as an urban tree house, a place to regroup and discuss strategy in the small war which had blown up with a group of local boys. Today, however, we pulled down our underwear, and leaving them tucked down the side of the radiator, climbed solemnly onto the roof. It was a hot day in August; even now I can remember the warmth of the asphalt on my bum as we sat on the edge, our legs overhanging the hot plastic drainpipe, pulling our skirts higher and higher over our thighs as we exposed ourselves to the elements.

I was the first to do it. Still half sitting, I lifted my bottom and peed over the drain, just as a boy might. The golden liquid gushed down the pipe: wonderfully and intriguingly wicked, an effect heightened by the fear that Gemma's father might suddenly appear at the window.

After that first thrilling experimentation, peeing from the roof became a regular event. Later we moved onto more serious things: spliffs stolen from Gem's brother; our virginity-losing competition when we were fifteen (Gemma won, but only because her mum was always at work so she had somewhere to do it); the thrills and spills of underage drinking. But for a while our shared peeing was our delicious secret. Now, over ten years later, we lay on our backs in the Indian night, staring up at the stars and laughing. After a while we were silent, watching our cigarettes glow red in the darkness and listening to the boy with the guitar. He had started to strum "Stairway to Heaven" now.

Gemma raised her eyebrows at me.

"I wish someone would take that bloody thing off him and break it over his head."

"Fascist."

"Well, it offends me!"

I laughed. I was content with almost anything, but Gemma took her music very seriously, amassing a huge collection of records by bands I'd never heard of.

"I mean, have we fallen into a naff seventies' time warp here or what?"

She sighed in exaggerated disgust. After a while she yawned and added sleepily: "I really think we should complain to the authorities."

"Yeah, yeah, yeah."

There was another long pause. When I next looked I saw that her eyes were closed, the cigarette dangling dangerously from her fingers. Leaning over her prone body, I pulled it gently away and stubbed it out on the side of the roof.

"So then," I said quietly. "Tomorrow Calcutta and then onward to Mr. Combustion. Okay?"

"Uh-huh."

"I was thinking. We ought to leave our traveler's checks and important stuff locked up here. It says in the book you can do it at the railway station. Then we don't have to worry about it getting stolen when we're on the road."

"Mmm."

"Gem? Are you asleep again?"

But this time there was no reply.

3

WHEN I opened my eyes the next morning Gemma was sitting up in bed reading.

"What's the time?"

"It's five A.M. at home, eleven in the morning here in sunny Delhi."

"Jesus! We've got so much to do!"

Vaulting out of bed, I threw my clothes on and started to push my gear into my bag.

"Money change, station, tickets. Then outta here."

"What's the hurry?"

"You don't want to just stay put, do you? That bloke at Sussex who did India last year said we should get out of Delhi as soon as we could."

She shrugged. "Fine. Whatever."

We cashed £100 worth of traveler's checks at the hostel and checked out, lugging our rucksacks back down the steps and along the sidewalk. It was nearly midday now, and far, far hotter than the evening before. Under the unforgiving glare of the sun, the grand arcades of Connaught Circus looked dirtier and more battered, a bit like Oxford Street in the Tropics. We gazed around, dazed by the heat. The sidewalks were filled with traders selling sugar-sweet posters of Vishnu and Michael Jackson, badly printed novellas for a hundred rupees, and cheap Balinese batiks. All around us people hurried past: businessmen in tight safari suits, glossy ladies in stiff saris and high heels, scruffy, skinny men in dhotis or shorts with tiffin tins on their heads; groups of wealthy, overweight teenagers in jeans and trainers. The circular road was crammed with traffic; the petrol fumes made us cough and cover our mouths with our hands.

I stared avidly at the scene, soaking it all in. It was the pace of it that I liked the most: the frantic onslaught of vehicles from every direction; the honking of horns, and ringing of bells; the sheer velocity of people piled into cars and rickshaws. Goggling in amazement, I watched as four young men balanced precariously on the back of a single bicycle sailed past. "Hey baby!" they shouted. "What is your country?" Perhaps I should have given them a snooty stare, but I just waved and laughed. We were surrounded by raw pulsating energy, as if life was somehow closer to the surface than in the cold closed North, and it made me want to shout out loud with joy.

"Let's get a rickshaw."

Putting one foot into the road, I flagged down one of the phuttering yellow and black scooter-rickshaws that shimmied past in the heat. As it veered sharply toward us Gemma gawped at me as if I was suggesting she ride to the station by unicycle.

"You *are* joking?"

"Why? It'll be fun."

"Sure it's fun, if fun involves being crushed alive by ten-ton trucks."

Ignoring her, I piled our bags inside. The driver flashed me a toothy smile. Like most rickshaw drivers in Delhi he was a Sikh, with a bright green turban, a silver bangle on his wrist, a resplendent beard, and reflector shades. His dashboard was decorated with tinsel and sparkling religious effigies; his fingernails were hennaed red.

"Station, please!"

He grinned, then still looking over his shoulder at us, did a U-turn in the middle of the road. Gemma screamed in horror; I instinctively closed my eyes, an elated rush of adrenaline pouring through my veins. For a terrifying second I could hear horns and angry curses and smell the petrol fumes of the traffic streaming around us. When I opened my eyes I saw that we had joined the far-side lane and with thousands of other vehicles were hurtling in the direction of the old city.

As we neared the station the streets became progressively more narrow and crowded. Now we were competing with ox-drawn carts, dark, sweat-shiny men carrying piles of pots or bricks on their heads, scooters conveying whole families, and a marketful of vendors whose wares spilled from the broken sidewalks onto the streets. From time to time the rickshaw would lurch over a particularly deep pothole and then we'd bounce uncontrollably, our heads bumping the tarpaulin roof of the carriage. Perhaps it was not the most comfortable way to travel, but it felt like a fairground ride, and I adored it. The driver drove at breakneck speed, only slowing when the crush of traffic became impassable. Then, within seconds, thin—often tiny—hands would push their way inside the rickshaw, their palms outstretched for change.

Gemma clung grimly onto her bags. I could see that she was nervous, but was too engrossed to do anything more than vaguely squeeze her hand.

"Isn't it amazing? I love it!" I remember crying out at one point. She just stared at me as if I was mad. When we finally jerked to a halt in front of the huge, earth-red station, I leaped up enthusiastically, pulling my rucksack over my shoulders and reaching into my money belt for the four ten-rupee notes the book had said the journey should cost. Behind me, Gemma was still fussing with her bags.

"Come on, let's go and find the ticket office."

Turning to the driver I handed him the money, nodding at him and smiling. He looked down at it, frowning. Very slowly he tucked the four notes into the chest pocket of his oily shirt, then turning back to me, held out his hand.

"One hundred rupees," he said.

I spun around in surprise.

"You what?!"

"One hundred rupees."

"You must be joking! It only costs forty to the station . . ."

He stared at me impassively.

"That's what it says in our guide," I said firmly, then blew my authority by blurting: "You're ripping us off! You should've had your meter on!" My voice sounded unnaturally high, as if I'd suddenly become six again and was about to be denied something terribly important, like my rightful share of a bag of sweets or some special treat.

"No, madam, meter is broken." With a jerk of his chin the driver indicated the twisted face of the meter. "We agree one hundred rupees."

"We did not!" I felt ridiculously close to tears. I think I might have even stamped my foot.

Next to me, Gemma had put her bags down and was looking at me anxiously.

"Esther . . ."

I ignored her. I could feel my face burning puce. I knew it didn't really matter, not in the great scheme of things, but I felt like such a fool. I'd thought I could handle everything and now, on my very first excursion, I was being humiliated. And in front of Gemma, too.

"Bastard!" I hissed.

I gestured in the direction of the other scooter-rickshaws waiting on the concourse.

"Ask them! They'll tell you how much it costs!"

A few of the drivers were beginning to saunter in our direction.

"Look," Gemma said quietly. "Just give the guy the extra money. It's less than a quid."

"But that's not the *point*!"

"What is the point then?"

I turned to look at her. She was gazing at me stubbornly, her mind made up. I took a deep breath. It was clearly time to establish some basics.

"The point is," I said slowly, "that you can't let them rip you off. It just puts up all the fares for everyone else."

"So?"

"So, I . . ."

I stopped. The driver was glaring at me. Next to him, Gemma was chewing her nails and frowning.

"It's the whole principle of the thing," I said lamely. To be honest, by this stage I'd forgotten what the actual principle was.

"What? That's *crap*! It's only about fifty p. Just give him the money."

There was a long silence in which a large lump seemed to be forming in my throat. I bit my lip, aware that people were turning to look at us. Why couldn't Gemma simply agree with me? Why did she always have to be so obstinate? At our feet a small crowd of children had accumulated, their hands outstretched. Gemma folded her arms, her eyes glinting with determined resistance. This was not really about us being ripped off by the rickshaw driver, I was thinking. It was about her and me.

I swallowed hard.

"All right, then," I whispered. "Take your sodding money."

Peeling another sixty rupees from the wad of cash folded in my pocket I flung it at the driver and strode quickly in the direction of the station as Gemma hurried behind me. My whole head, from the top of my scalp to the base of my neck, felt as if it had caught on fire.

We walked into the station, staggering slightly from the weight of our packs and looking around in vain for the ticket office. Even I had not been prepared for the pulsating energy of the place: the crowds of people streaming around us; the red turbaned porters with piles of suitcases on their heads; the sleeping bodies stretched out on oily platforms; the cries of pedlars; the screech and wheeze of braking trains; and the hum of a thousand voices. I could smell the oil of the engines and the sweet reek of urine; as we passed a stall selling peanuts and chancchuri, the whiff of roasting spices made my empty belly gurgle. Above us a loudspeaker crackled unintelligibly; somewhere in the distance I could hear canned sitar music. At our feet the most determined of the children, a small girl with bare feet and a bright red flower behind her ear, was still pulling at Gemma's elbows and crying out: "Baksheesh, memsahib!"

I gulped. I kept telling myself it was all part of the adventure, but the incident with the rickshaw driver had left me shaking with anger and humiliation. What prats we were, I thought furiously. And I wished the little girl would leave us alone, too. She must have sensed that Gemma was the softer touch because she'd grabbed hold of her hand, making it impossible to shake her off without using considerable force.

Gemma trotted beside me, her face taut.

"What shall we do now?" she whispered.

"Find the ticket office," I replied curtly. I stared at the mass of bodies ahead of us, willing it to separate and the ticket office miraculously appear. To be honest I was more than a little unnerved. Why did the task of negotiating our way across the station and buying a ticket suddenly seem so difficult?

Gemma sniffed miserably. It was typical of her, I thought

with irritation. Just now, when I needed her to keep her head together she was going to throw a nervous fit.

"What am I going to do about this kid? Oh God, please go
away . . ."

She stopped, looking down at the child mournfully and shaking her head.

"No!" I said firmly, more to Gemma than to the girl. "No
way!"

"Let's just give her something . . ."

"It just encourages them!"

Gemma looked at me, her eyes red and watery. I think she
was on the verge of bursting into tears. Suddenly she rummaged
in her money belt and pulled out a crisp one-hundred rupee
note.

"Here!"

For a second the girl just gazed at the money. Then, as if
afraid it might suddenly disappear, she snatched it and ran into
the crowd. I stared at Gemma's sweaty, flustered face in disbelief.

"What did you do that for?"

"I just wanted her to go away!" She smiled at me weakly.

"Jesus, Gem! A hundred rupees is a shitload of money here!
If you do that it buggers up the whole economy!"

"So what? It made her happy, didn't it?" She shrugged, dis-
missing all my firmly held convictions with one small muscular
movement.

"You're mad," I said.

We walked in silence toward a large electronic Departures
board. Underneath this a crowd of people were clustered
around a line of metal grilled booths. The money didn't really
matter, I was telling myself; it wasn't worth a fight. I'd just have
to explain all these things to Gemma later. After all, I *had* written a dissertation on the effects of tourism on local economies in
my final year, I *did* know what I was talking about.

"Perhaps we get the tickets there," I said lightly.

Gemma walked slightly faster, her face set. I could tell from the pout of her mouth and the appearance of that sullen little line between her eyebrows that she was sulking, but I was determined not to get drawn in. So, I had snapped at her, I thought with exasperation, but she shouldn't be so sensitive. It didn't *mean* anything. As we approached the booths I saw that amidst the apparently formless crowd were actually three discernible lines.

"Is this the line for tickets?"

The man at the end of the shortest line nodded enthusiastically.

"Yes, yes, this way please."

He gestured to another, far longer line.

"Not here?"

He nodded.

"No, madam. This is for first-class only."

We stood in the line for many long minutes. There seemed to be no rationale for what took place ahead of us. People pushed in, or carried out complicated transactions which involved another three officials and much gesticulating, but other than us, no one seemed to object or grow impatient. From time to time the official at the booth would slip off his stool and disappear altogether, and Gemma and I would tut and strain our necks as the time ticked past, our annoyance at each other conveniently displaced onto the line.

"Jesus Christ!"

"Why can't they have some sort of system?"

It took about an hour to reach the front. When we did, I took a deep breath, leaned across the counter, and announced to the balding official: "Two tickets for Calcutta, please. And when's the next train?"

He glanced up from his ledger book, barely acknowledging my presence.

"Not here," he said. "The tourist office is that way. You must buy your tickets there."

With a flick of his head he gestured toward the other side of the station.

"You've *got* to be joking!"

We stared at him in disbelief, but he was no longer interested, his attention transferred to the next customer.

"That's completely *bonkers.*"

"Oh well . . ." I took a deep breath. "I suppose it's all part of the adventure."

Something unreadable flickered across Gemma's face. For a moment I thought the sulk was about to reappear but then she laughed out loud, a sharp yelp of unexpected mirth.

"Yo! Esther and her great adventure! Let it commence!"

Two hours later we had procured two second-class seats to Calcutta on the Bengal Express, which left at six P.M. After another half hour of being directed to the wrong place we found the lockers, where we secured a bag filled with Gemma's books, the traveler's checks, and our air tickets. There were two keys, one for each of us. We put the rest of our cash and our passports in Gemma's money belt. Now, with nothing else to do but wait, we took up our places on platform 10.

Gemma sat huddled by her backpack, *Middlemarch* opened on her lap. I don't think she was actually reading it; she kept staring into space, her face tight and grumpy. I, however, had forgotten about the rickshaw and the beggar girl and was feeling much better. I gazed around, beginning to relax. The platform was filled with people, many of whom had laid blankets and mats on the concrete and were cooking food on portable stoves. Others slept, apparently undisturbed by the mayhem caused each time a train arrived, when everyone would push and shout as if their lives depended upon boarding: first the porters, who chased the train along the platform and jumped aboard, then, following close behind, a wave of passengers laden with boxes and cardboard suitcases and vast canvas bags.

By now we'd been in the station for over five hours, and I was yearning for our journey to begin. I kept threading my way to the edge of the platform and gazing hopefully into the haze. Six P.M. came and went. I wandered over to a stall selling provisions, bought biscuits, bottled water, and a copy of Indian *Cosmopolitan*. I was beginning to feel that we had been there forever.

Then, just as I was glancing through an item on dating agencies in Bangalore, I realized that something was finally happening. All around us people started to stir. The family sitting next to Gemma were packing their belongings; the porters, who had been squatting around a game of cards, were standing, straightening their turbans, and arranging their dhotis.

I peered down the track. Far away, in the shimmering distance, I could see movement. At first it was just a small dot, then gradually the train grew closer until finally it was upon us: the bullish face of the engine shunting past the platforms, followed by carriage after rusty carriage, a metallic, bellowing monster.

"It's here!"

Grabbing our rucksacks we pushed through the surging crowd. I'd already memorized our carriage and seat numbers, and now we ran alongside the train, trying to work out where we should board. When we saw a white-gloved official standing in front of the first-class carriages, we waved our tickets at him, gesticulating that we were lost. He glanced up wearily from his paperwork. He was a thickset man, his black hair heavy with Brylcreem and his spectacles so strong that his magnified eyes goggled at us unnaturally.

"Which carriage?" I mouthed slowly, pointing at my ticket and then the train.

He stared at us in irritation.

"Yes, yes! Please show me your tickets!"

"You speak some English?"

He blinked, then said imperiously: "Your carriage is the third one after this. Please on no account give money to porters unless they have an official badge of identification and make sure you beware vagabonds in the night."

Flicking his eyes back to his list, he waved us away like bothersome flies.

We found our seats easily after that, pulling ourselves and our backpacks aboard the train and pushing our way along the carriage. The second-class compartment consisted of rows of wooden benches and, directly opposite our allotted seats, the latrine: a stinking hole in the floor.

Judging by the crush of people surrounding us it was clear that we would have little room for sleep. It didn't matter, I thought with renewed excitement; we could spend the whole night talking and smoking and watching the lights of India slide past: real hardcore travel. I glanced reassuringly at Gemma, who was perching on the edge of her section of the bench and easing her shoulders out of the backpack. She looked nervously around the carriage.

"How are we going to sleep here?"

"Does it matter? It'll be fine. Just relax."

Finally releasing herself from the pack, she started to push it under her seat. I turned to my own rucksack, hauling it up onto the luggage rack and groping vacantly through its nylon pockets for a padlock so I could secure it to the railings.

"That's funny." Gemma turned round, blinking in surprise. "I thought my money belt was here."

"What do you mean?"

"I thought I put it in the top . . . it must be in the main part . . ."

Pulling the rucksack back onto the dusty carriage floor, she began to rummage through its contents. As I watched her, tremors of anxiety began to build inside me; when we'd been sitting on the platform I'd seen it tucked into the top, I remembered. Why couldn't she find it now? Gemma's fingers scrambled with increasing determination through the books and clothes and packets of medicine she'd insisted on bringing.

"Have you got it?"

"No . . ."

"Come on, Gem, it must be somewhere."

"It's gone!"

My stomach lurched.

"It can't be . . . I saw you put it there!"

Heads had begun to turn, a wave of interest slowly breaking along the benches that surrounded us as people turned in our direction.

"But it isn't!"

I could no longer bear it. I grabbed the bag from her, desperate to be doing something, anything but stand and watch her passively.

"Gemma, you halfwit! It has to be here!"

By now I could feel the eyes of the entire carriage upon us. From the benches opposite a large military-looking man with a handlebar mustache and a somewhat incongruous knitted tank-top had risen to his feet as if about to join the search.

"It's got our passports in it!" I screamed.

From the platform, a whistle blew. There was a jolt, and we started to move. Gemma fell to her knees, peering desperately under the bench. Along with the tank-topped sergeant major we had been joined by an elderly lady in a white sari, who, as Gemma had stood up in despair, had grabbed her hand and was squeezing and clasping it to her bosom in an effort to comfort her. On the bench opposite two young men were searching under their own seats although it must have been obvious to all concerned that the belt could not possibly be there.

Gemma had started to cry now, the tears making slimy tracks down her dusty cheeks. I stared at her in horror. I suppose I should have been more supportive, but all I could think was that because of her our trip was about to go belly up. How could she have been so stupid? The belt must have been stolen, or perhaps simply dropped onto the platform. Whatever had happened, by now it would be gone. Why was she always so careless?

With another jolt, the train moved forward again. Slowly, beyond the window, the platform began to move. With the third jerk, I jumped up and grabbed Gemma's arm.

"Oh my God, Gemma, we *have* to get off! We can't go to Calcutta without any money!"

Panic-stricken, we pulled at our packs and began to run along the aisle. The train was gathering speed, the section of the platform where we'd been sitting already slipping quietly past the window. We'd almost reached the carriage door, but now the train was moving too fast to make an exit anything other than suicidal.

As the final section of the platform whizzed past, I turned around. I think my predominant emotion was that of being drained: everything, all my plans, had suddenly been unplugged by Gemma's muddle-headed stupidity.

"We're fucked," I whispered. "We're totally fucked."

"It wasn't my fault, Esther, I . . ."

I didn't let her finish.

"Wait . . ."

Gemma turned, following my gaze.

"What is it?"

"Look . . ."

At the other end of the rocking carriage, a figure was moving purposefully toward us. At first I thought it was one of the holy men I'd noticed waiting with their orange robes and shaven heads on the station platform. But as the swaying figure grew nearer I realized that I was wrong. It wasn't a priest, but a young Western woman, with short blond hair, tanned skin, and long skinny legs.

As she finally reached us she smiled and held out her hands, as if making an offering. Gemma's mouth had fallen open, the color returning slowly to her cheeks.

"She's got it," she whispered.

4

LATER, after we'd stopped thanking her and returned to our seats, the woman told us how she'd seen the belt drop from Gemma's pack.

"I reckon someone must have had a go at it, you know?" she said, squeezing onto the bench next to Gemma. "It was like, just hanging there, like someone had pulled it out? Then I kept trying to catch up with you, but you were running too fast for the train?"

Close up, she was not the miraculous apparition she had seemed initially, the sea of staring faces parting as she passed. Instead, she was just like any other backpacker. It was true that she was notably thin: her clavicle bones too sharp, and her head too large for her slim neck, but after a few months of street dahl and the endless Delhi-belly that such food entailed, weight loss was as much a badge of authentic low-budget travel as browned skin or ethnic clothing. She was wearing a dark red sarong, tied loosely around her concave stomach, a droopy cheesecloth top, and leather flip-flops. Apart from the plastic bangles around her wrist, she had no jewelry. In many ways she looked like my fantasy of myself: a true traveler, her soft Western edges eroded by months or even years of vivid Third World Experience. As she pushed her fingers through her scrubby hair I noticed that her ears were peppered with a long line of holes. She told us her name was Coral, she was Australian, and she'd been in India for the last couple of years.

"You guys had a close shave there," she said, grinning at us as she pulled her feet up under her skirt. "Perhaps your gear looks too new, you know?"

I grimaced.

"Yeah, it could be that. It could also be Gemma being a total twat. I mean, come on, Gem, why didn't you tie the money belt around your waist like everyone else? Duh! That's the whole bloody point!"

Gemma shuffled her feet uncomfortably.

"Oh, don't look like that! I don't mean it. I love you really!"

Leaning over, I gave her a loud, smacking kiss on the cheek. Coral gazed at us. Perhaps it sounded harsh to an outsider, but we always teased each other; it was part of our friendship.

"She's never been to a Third World country before," I added.

Coral glanced at me and smiled. Her face had the slightly sunken look of someone who naturally should have been more plump; her eyes were the watery blue of a young baby, her nose slightly snubbed.

"I carry all my stuff in this old thing. Like, it's been around a bit?"

She nodded at her own bag, a scuffed canvas carry-all, which she had wedged onto the seat beside her.

"But how can you fit everything into that?" said Gemma.

"What is there you need? You've gotta travel light. What you don't have you can borrow, or whatever . . ." She trailed off.

"I just don't know how to thank you enough," I said, then started to laugh. "Oh my God! I sound just like my mother!"

"It's no big deal." Coral flashed me another smile. "Where are you guys heading, anyway?"

"Calcutta."

"Nice one."

Gemma and I glanced at her.

"Why, where are you going?"

She shrugged lazily. "Wherever."

"But you must have known that this train was going to Calcutta . . ."

"I don't think so, honey." She grinned again. "I just jumped on to catch you up, then off it went."

Gemma goggled at her. I tried to look nonplussed, as if I traveled like that all the time.

"You mean you don't have a ticket?"

"Nah."

"But supposing you get chucked off?"

"No worries. There's just one word you need here."

"Which is?"

"Baksheesh!"

We laughed, shuffling over to make more room for her. To be honest, we were so relieved to have the belt back that we would have smiled at anything.

"Do you always travel like this, then?" I said as she pulled a paper packet of bidi cigarettes from her bag. I didn't want to appear naive, but I was fascinated; it certainly put my book-throwing ritual in perspective.

"Me? It depends."

Gemma was still staring at her.

"Aren't you scared?" she said. Coral pulled a tiny bidi from the packet and leaned back, showing off her smooth brown throat.

"Get outta here! What's there to be scared of? This is the most friendly place on the entire planet. Do ya want one?"

We both took a bidi, lighting them from Gemma's matches

and puffing curiously. They reminded me of my twelve-year-old experiments with Woodbines; the unfiltered tobacco made my head reel and my eyes water.

"Whew!"

"But don't you get lonely?" Gemma was saying now. Her face had the utterly engrossed, almost dumbfounded expression of an infant watching something amazing and new, like a truck, or a cow in a field.

"Nah." Coral laughed lightly. "There's always loads of people to hook up with. Anyway, I'm used to it. I've been on the road a long time. I did Southeast Asia before."

"Wow," I said. "That must have been fantastic."

"Sure it was. You should check out Cambodia. It'll blow you away."

Next to me, Gemma was peering down at her bidi.

"Fuck this thing. It keeps going out." Throwing it on the floor, she looked up at Coral again. "I mean, I don't think I'd have the guts."

"It depends what's inside, here . . ." Coral tapped her forehead. "Like if your thoughts are strong, then so's your heart?"

"I don't think I'm that good at strong thoughts," Gemma mumbled. "I keep trying to whip them into shape but then they go all weak and wobbly on me." She snorted. Next to her Coral's face suddenly became serious.

"Well, you could learn to make them stronger," she said. "I mean, like, you don't have to always stay the same, do you?"

I thought she might laugh, but Gemma gazed into Coral's face, her eyes intent.

"Don't I?"

"No way. Hey, the world's an open book. You can do exactly what you like."

We were quiet for a while after that. Gemma pulled her book from her backpack, hunkering down on her seat and holding it in front of her like a shield. Coral produced a Walkman from her bag and plugged herself in, her face dreamy. On the surrounding benches, the other passengers dozed.

I stared out of the window, my thoughts slipping from the compartment to the blurring countryside beyond. As the half-built suburbs gave way to red fields and scattered villages, I felt the unpleasant haze of anxiety and frustration with which we had started the journey dissipate, just as fog lifts and clears in the dawning day. In its place grew swelling joy. Outside, the sun was setting, slipping low and crimson into the lunar landscape. In the mud-bricked homesteads fires had been lit, the smoke rising in fraying tendrils against the violet sky. As we jolted along I could see people moving around their compounds: women in brightly colored shalwar kameez squatting on the ground or leaning over the fires as they prepared the evening meal; men lounging on charpoys; small children who screamed with pleasure when they saw the train, running beside the tracks in a vain attempt to jump aboard. From time to time we passed a camel, or a couple of swaggering oxen pulling a cart. In the east, a single star had appeared.

As the sky darkened and the air cooled I wrapped my arms around my knees and closed my eyes. For almost as long as I could remember I'd been planning my escape. Over the last few years I'd felt increasingly as if I was biding my time, waiting for my real life to begin. It was true that I'd thrown myself at my degree in Sussex with an enthusiasm unrivaled by most of my peers. I loved to see how ideas fitted together, to bury myself in all those different worlds. Yet over the last year my joy at discovery had been offset by the need to get results, to produce long and painstaking dissertations, to fill my head up for exams. And now I needed to breathe again. What could books really teach me, I'd started to wonder. What I needed was real life, not libraries; what I was desperate for was a new challenge.

I pulled my sweater around my shoulders and finally began to doze. Despite my pretense to Gemma about being unfazed by the string beds, I'd hardly slept the night before and not at all on the plane. For a moment, just before my thoughts blurred, I pictured Coral walking down the aisle of the train. Then my hair flopped across my face and I fell asleep.

5

When the carriage grew so dark that she could no longer make out the words on the page, Gemma looked up from Middlemarch to find Esther slumped against the window and Coral sitting cross-legged beside her, the Walkman still clamped over her head. Putting the book gently down, as if afraid of physically harming the characters with whom she had spent such an intense two hours, she leaned over her backpack and started to rummage through it for a cigarette. She needed something to eat, too, for now that she was no longer so nervous the hunger that had been curling inertly in her belly was finally making its presence felt. She had not eaten all day. Perhaps, she thought wryly, she'd finally lose some weight. Peering inside her bag she noticed with regret that Esther had single-handedly demolished all the biscuits.

She wished that she could stop feeling so jumpy. She was pathetic, she told herself, unable to go on holiday without feeling her whole sense of self start to slip away. And yet she could not help herself. Unlike Esther, who'd been behaving as if she owned the place ever since the frigging airport, Gemma felt as if she was tumbling headlong from somewhere that at least she knew, into somewhere else entirely.

As she lit her cigarette she realized that Coral had taken off the Walkman and was watching her.

"*Do you want one?*"

Coral shook her head, smiling.

"*So,*" *she said.* "*You like to read.*"

It was clearly meant as an opening, but Gemma could not think of anything to say. Coral was looking at her expectantly, as if waiting for her to continue.

"*I guess I'm just a bookworm,*" *she finally said. Before she could stop herself, she added:* "*I was meant to be going to Oxford to do English but I cocked the whole thing up.*"

She swallowed self-consciously. She hated the way she blurted personal information at strangers, but the terror of being thought boring compelled her to do it. Coral was still looking at her.

"*I guess that's why I read so much,*" *she added lamely. It was nonsense of course. Gemma had always read prodigiously, Oxford or no Oxford. To change the subject she said, too brightly:* "*What are you listening to?*"

"*Ah, nothing.*" *Leaning over, Coral stuffed the Walkman into her bag.*

"*What do you think of it so far, then?*" *she said.*

"*What, this?*" *Gemma glanced around the carriage.*

Coral nodded, her eyes still fixed to her face.

"*Well, it's great. I mean, to be honest, it's a little intimidating, you know, when you first arrive and all that . . .*" *Her voice trailed off.* "*I mean, I guess you're used to it.*"

"*Yeah, well, I've been on the road a long time.*"

"*Don't you miss home?*"

Coral's eyes went dull and she looked away. Gemma dragged on her cigarette, blowing the smoke from the side of her mouth and tapping the ash on the floor.

"*I don't think I'm going to either,*" *she suddenly said.*

Coral looked up at her, smiling. "*No?*"

"*Not one tiny iota.*"

They grinned at each other. There was another long pause.

"That's kind of what I'd figured," Coral said.

"Yeah?"

"Sure. You like to hide it, but actually you're, like, much stronger than people think?"

Gemma stared at her. "I don't know about that. It's Esther who's the sorted one. I'm all over the shop."

Still smiling at her, Coral shook her head. "Nah. You don't really believe that."

"Don't I?"

"Sure you don't. I can tell. You just let her think she's in charge. Am I right?"

Dropping her cigarette on the floor and stubbing it out with the tip of her flip-flops, Gemma shrugged. Her face felt unnaturally warm.

"So how come you know so much?" she finally said.

～

WHEN I opened my eyes the world had turned green. It was dawn, and the train was chugging past a vast expanse of padi, the curving terraces divided into a lush patchwork. Although the sun had not yet appeared, the sky had lightened to a soft pink and the fields were filled with people. I stretched and leaned down to rub my legs.

It was distinctly chilly. I shivered, craving a warm mug of coffee and my sleeping bag, and suddenly noticed that Gemma was awake, too, curled up on the end of the bench with *Middlemarch* once more. She must have sensed me looking at her, for she slowly put the book down and looked up.

"Hi."

"You've nearly finished it!"

Despite the racketing train we were both whispering. At the end of the bench, Coral was fast asleep, her head lolling against Gemma's shoulder.

"Natch."

"I don't know how you can read so fast."

"I should have paced myself."

"You can read this if you like."

I nodded at *The City of Joy*, my book about Calcutta. I had devoured most of it on the plane and was nearly at the end. It made the place sound *so* desperate and the self-sacrificing Westerners who'd devoted their lives to the poor *so* saintly that I was vaguely considering ditching the trip and going to work with Mother Teresa. Gemma glanced at it dismissively.

"Looks a bit worthy."

"Nothing can be more worthy than George Eliot."

"Ahah. But at least it's good for the mind."

She grinned smugly and turned another page. Sometimes—especially when we were talking about books or films—I felt as if she was still trying to prove something to me, even though we'd left school and were no longer vying with each other to be top of the class. *Relax,* I wanted to tell her. So you never made it to Oxford; I haven't forgotten how clever you are.

After a while she sighed and put the book down. I could sense her watching me.

"Do you know the first thing I'm going to do when we get to Calcutta?" she suddenly said.

"Have a shower?"

"No, after that."

"Give up."

"Write to Steve!"

I looked down at my feet.

"I've been sitting here, composing what I'm going to say."

"I should write home, too," I said quickly. Gemma ignored me.

"Dearest Steve," she intoned theatrically, "what are you doing stuck in that giant flea-pit commonly known as Stevenage New Town while I'm here, wandering the exotic lands of Asia?" She stopped, narrowing her eyes.

"Did I tell you what he said about me coming here?"

I fiddled with my nails, not meeting her eyes.

"No."

"That he would do anything to be able to come, too. Isn't that sweet?"

"He *is* a sweetie," I said vaguely.

"Do you really think so?"

"Sure."

Looking closely into my face she began to twist at the ring he'd given her.

"What do you think he's doing now?"

"Getting pissed in the Royal Oak with all the other tossers." I smiled at her determinedly. "Anyway, thank God we're here and not there, eh?"

The comment hung quietly between us for a while, like a puff of smoke on a still day. Finally, Gemma picked up her book and carried on reading.

An hour or so later we reached the outskirts of Calcutta. As the train began to slow it sounded its horn plaintively, the cry of a giant lumbering beast coming home.

"Voila. The Black Hole approaches."

I smiled at Gemma wanly, reaching over her and fastening the money belt securely around my waist. Next to me, Coral was soundly asleep, her chin lolling on her chest, her mouth ajar.

"This time *I'll* look after this."

By now the suburbs were becoming increasingly crowded. The railway kept crisscrossing roads crammed with cars and people, and the huts with plastic bag roofs had begun to appear. After another few minutes we plunged into a huge shanty, the huts spreading out around the tracks like a rash.

I stared out of the window in shock. I was prepared for poverty but hadn't imagined it would be like this. All around us were people: picking their way along the side of the tracks; crowding around the standpipes where they washed; sleeping; preparing breakfast in front of their makeshift huts; feeding their children; even shitting—right there in the mud as the train thundered by. No one paid the slightest attention to the Bengal Express as it rolled through their lives; it was as if the railway was such an organic part of their world they'd become oblivious to it: the trains came and went, like the passing of the sun across the sky.

I shifted uneasily in my seat, aware of my privileged gaze into the lives of others. Why had I objected to giving money to that little girl? I thought with a sudden, guilty pang. Wasn't it the very least we could do? As I remembered the desperate way she had grabbed the cash I was filled with shame. Who was I to come here and impose rules about "not encouraging them"? It was just a weak excuse for being mean. I glanced uncomfortably away from the window. I didn't want to admit it, but the slum was filling the carriage with an unpleasant stench. Opposite us, the old woman who had held Gemma's hand in Delhi suddenly stood up and pulled the shutters of the window closed, pressing a handkerchief over her nose.

We were nearly at the station now. Gemma was perched on the edge of the bench, her rucksack a distorting hump on her back. Her eyes slid to Coral.

"Do you think we should wake her?"

"Definitely."

Very gently, she reached out and prodded Coral's thin arm. Her eyes opened immediately.

"Well, hi there. How ya doing?"

She smiled hazily and, standing up, hitched her bag around

her shoulders. It was as if she'd been awake all along, I remember thinking. Either that, or she was so used to traveling by Indian trains that she intuitively knew that her station was approaching, the way a farmer might sense the oncoming rain.

"How did you know we'd arrived?"

"Well, we have, haven't we?"

Not waiting for an answer she turned and walked down the carriage. Gemma and I glanced at each other in surprise.

"She didn't even say good-bye!"

We stared in bemusement at her departing back.

"Did we say something?"

Gemma frowned. "I was going to invite her to eat out with us, or something, to thank her."

The platform was coming into view now, and the carriage filling with porters. As the doors opened and the other passengers spilled out onto the platform, we were swept along by the tide of people and luggage. I grasped Gemma's hand, terrified of losing her. Coral had long since disappeared into the distance.

"Where do we go now?"

"I don't know. Out of here, I suppose."

We followed the crowds pouring out of Howrah Station into the bright morning light. Facing us was a concourse filled with shoals of black taxis, scooters, and an endless stream of hand-pulled rickshaws. Although many were empty others contained two or three passengers and a pile of luggage, their drivers dripping with sweat as they progressed laboriously through the swirling traffic.

"Let's get a taxi," Gemma said decisively.

She stepped out into the road, but before she had even lifted her hand, a battered black Ambassador swerved in front of us. The back door swung open.

"Come on then! I got the transport!" Coral leaned out of the door, grinning and patting the worn leather seats beside her. "What are you waiting for?"

For perhaps a second I hesitated. But, before I could work out why, Gemma had pulled her rucksack off her back and hastily, gratefully, climbed inside.

6

THE taxi nosed its way into the gridlocked traffic, honking its horn incessantly.

"Whew!" Gemma said, turning to Coral. "We thought we'd lost you!"

"Nah. You're not getting rid of me that easily. I was just sorting things out."

Gemma glanced at her and laughed. She seemed so much more cheerful than the day before.

"Bollocks, it's hot."

As she twisted around in an effort to get comfortable, her backside made a sucky, slappy noise against the leather upholstery. There had been no room for me in the back, so I was sitting in the front.

"I'm so sweaty it's like I've wet myself! Look at me! I'm such an old tart!"

In the front seat, my knees bent carefully away from the driver, I smiled weakly. I was relieved that Gemma's mood had improved, but it was too hot for banter. My head was fuggy and my face shiny with perspiration. As the car crawled painstakingly toward Howrah Bridge I could feel a fine layer of dirt descending on my skin; my eyes felt gritty, and when I rubbed my face, my fingers came back smeared black. I slid down into my seat, glaring out of the window. Behind me I could hear Gemma and Coral chatting, but I'd stopped listening. My eyes kept flickering shut but I forced them open; unlike Gem, I did not want to miss a second of our journey.

We passed over the bridge, the waters of the Hooghly stretching flat and oily beneath us. The traffic was moving so slowly that in places we were overtaken by foot passengers who jostled in a long line to cross the water. On the other side of the river I could glimpse a row of tanneries, the leather skins heaped in front of industrial vats, foul smoke wafting across the water and into the car. The stench of boiling skins was disgusting. I wound the window up, breathing through my mouth.

After the bridge we drove through a more residential neighborhood, with large decaying mansions set back from the road. Another few blocks later we turned unexpectedly into a major concourse of traffic, including—to my amazement—red double-deckers. I stared after them. On closer inspection they were nothing like London buses; they were as rusty as old tin cans and so crowded that people were hanging out of the doors and windows and even sitting on the roof.

My thoughts began to drift. I imagined Steve and Gemma sitting together in the pub, then inadvertently pictured the hallway of my parents' house; the coats hanging from their hooks, the Monet calendar above the phone, my mum's china cat hatstand crouching in the corner. I shuddered and sat up straight, shunting the uncomfortable thoughts from my mind. I suddenly realized that I had no idea of our destination.

"Where are we going?" I said, swiveling around to face Coral.

"Just this place I know," she said coolly.

"So you've been here before?"

Before she could reply the taxi braked. We had stopped beside a battered block of flats, the front of which was virtually split in two by a giant crack; damp dripped down the sides like tears.

"It's a friend's," Coral said as she climbed out of the car. "He said I could use it."

"That's great!" Gemma cried, appearing after her from the taxi. "Come on, Esther!"

THE door to the flat opened on to a cramped room filled with boxes. Edging her way inside, Coral stood aside with a flourish.

"Come on in, then! It's a right mess . . ."

Gemma and I followed her into the dark room. With the exception of a National Bank of India calendar turned to March 1981 and a dome dubious red stains splattered at spitting height over the scuffed white paintwork, the walls were unadorned. Besides the boxes, the only furniture was an overstuffed leather armchair, a couple of stools, and a pile of cushions thrown haphazardly in one corner of the bare floor. Peering across the room we could see a narrow kitchen with a Calor-gas stove and various heavy pots and pans arranged on the floor.

"Streuth, we need some air!"

Coral put down her bag and walked across the room, throwing open the wooden shutters, which parted to reveal a wide balcony with a view of buildings and trees.

"You can sleep out here."

She gestured to two lumpy mattresses laid out on the balcony.

"You've got sleeping bags and all that?"

"Sure."

"I'll check out the bathroom. I'm dying for a slash."

She disappeared through a door hidden behind a pile of boxes. Gemma heaved her backpack onto the floor and wandered over to the crumbly balustrade.

"Cool."

I followed her outside. It was surprisingly pleasant, with a refreshing breeze, a view of jumbled back streets and, directly beneath us, a small park filled with trees and scuffed grass. Yet for some reason I could not share Gemma's enthusiasm.

"At least it's free," I eventually said.

A shadow of anxiety passed across Gemma's face.

"Unless she's expecting us to pay . . ."

"No way! She's just being friendly."

"I wish I had her guts, to travel around alone like that."

I glanced at her. Her eyes were screwed up against the light and her cheeks shiny from the heat. She looked wistful, dreamy even. I wished I was a free spirit like Coral, too, but if she had a flat waiting for her here why had she pretended on the train to not know where she was going?

"Thank God she picked up your belt," I said lightly. "The angels must have been looking out for us."

"Good old angels."

We leaned over the balcony, gazing at the view.

"Yikes! I'm soppy with sweat."

Blowing out her cheeks Gemma began to fan herself with her hand.

"You look like an entrant for a wet T-shirt competition," I said, glancing at her plump, sodden bosom.

"Can you smell burning?" she suddenly said.

I sniffed at the air.

"All I can smell is drains. Don't you think you're getting a little obsessed?"

"No way!"

"Perhaps you should go back inside. Coral turned the fan to full."

"It's making me itch."

I frowned at her. I was starting to wish that she would stop moaning about the heat.

"How can it be?"

"It just is. Look—here . . ."

Stretching out her arms, she nodded down at the red patches that had appeared on her wrists. I'd seen it before, on Luke in the Sahara.

"It's prickly heat," I said authoritatively. "It'll go away when you start to acclimatize."

"I just hope this place in Orissa has air-conditioning," she muttered. "Otherwise it's going to be a nightmare."

"Gemma . . ."

I didn't finish the sentence. I sighed, looking away from her to the jumble of buildings and the park. Perhaps it was just the jet lag, but I suddenly felt irritated again, disloyal thoughts bubbling uncontrollably in my mind. Why did she have to whine about everything? Ever since we'd arrived she'd been whinging interminably about the heat. Even worse, she cheered up only when Coral was around. We stood for a few seconds in sour silence.

"Hi, guys, how ya doing?"

Taking a deep breath of the balmy air, Coral stepped onto the balcony. She'd showered and was wrapped in a towel, her damp hair clinging to her skull. In the soft morning light she looked younger and more vulnerable than on the train, her skin so thin that it was almost translucent. She was beautiful, I suddenly realized; it was strange that I hadn't noticed before. She stood, staring over the balcony, her face serene. For the briefest of moments I was reminded of something; I stared at her, trying to grasp at it, but already it had slipped out of reach.

"Great view, no?"

I smiled somewhat forcedly. "That's just what we were saying. Where are we, anyway?"

Coral shrugged. "Down there's Tagore Park . . ."

"Hey, listen," Gemma interrupted her, "it's really brilliant of you to let us stay here."

"No hassle."

"So you've been here before?" I blurted. I'd meant it to sound friendly and relaxed, but my voice was gratingly sharp.

Coral grinned at me. "Did I say that? Jeez, I forget all the places I've been."

Something in her voice put me on my guard. I glanced around at her, but she just smiled and winked. She was teasing us, I realized with relief; that was all it was. Her story about jumping aboard the train had been a *joke*. *Of course* she had known where she was going.

We were quiet for a while. I stared down from the balcony, temporarily mesmerized by a young boy floating a plastic boat over the gray water which gurgled in the drain.

"Look at that," Coral murmured.

She pointed to the labyrinth of roads which unfurled to the east of the park. Following her finger, Gemma and I squinted uncomprehendingly at the tangle of buildings and lanes, then noticed a long line of people walking slowly down the main street toward us. Those in front were carrying something on their shoulders; for a moment they disappeared from view, obscured by a row of tall buildings, then they appeared again, the procession snaking down one of the side streets directly below the flat. Now we could hear the discordant sounds of trumpets and drums and see that the object was white and covered in flowers.

"It's a funeral," said Coral. "Beautiful, isn't it?"

"A funeral? You mean that's a body?"

Gemma stepped back from the balcony, her mouth hanging open. The mourners were passing directly beneath us now: a solemn line of orange-robed priests and white-dhotied men. We could see the tops of their heads and the contours of the corpse, wrapped tightly in its shroud. Following a few steps behind and dressed in red and gold suits as if for a circus was a group of musicians.

"Sure it's a body. They must be going to burn it on a pyre down at the ghats. The river is just on the other side of those buildings."

She pointed to the other side of the park. Gemma had been right about the smell of burning, I suddenly realized: rising into the warm air above the buildings was a cloud of smoke.

"It must be someone pretty special. Look at the amount of people there are . . ."

"You mean they're going to actually burn the body, right there?" Gemma stared after the procession as it turned up the lane, her voice incredulous.

"Sure. That's the power of fire. It's the most spiritual of all the elements. It transforms everything it touches. They say that as the brain explodes, that's when the soul is released."

"Blimey."

"It sounds like a chestnut cracking," Coral continued quietly. "It's like, really transcendent?"

I glanced at Gemma, hoping to catch her eye, but she was still gazing intently at Coral.

"To go to the fire, that's, like, the highest form of purification," Coral was saying now. "Like, sati? That's why I light a candle every night, for my puja and stuff."

She looked in the direction of the river. Now that I knew what it was, I saw black smoke billowing toward us. I was starting to remember an essay I'd written in the second year; something about the relationship between gender and religious ideology, which I'd spent an entire week researching in the library.

"Isn't sati where those Hindu widows had to burn themselves on their husbands' pyres?" I said slowly. "Hasn't it been outlawed for eons?"

Coral cut me off. "It's like the most transcendental act any woman can do," she said authoritatively. "Through sati they break out of the cycle of karma and become gods themselves."

She smiled at me, as if there was nothing left to add. She'd obviously been in India a long time, but I could no longer hold myself back.

"But that's just one way of looking at it, isn't it? I mean, among others?"

Under their tanned sheen, Coral's cheeks paled. "Yeah? Like?"

"Well, some people would say it isn't about gods or spirituality. It's about patriarchy. You know, men burning women to death . . ."

I stopped, self-righteousness rising in my chest like acid indigestion. I was trying desperately to remember the conclusion to my essay, which to my pleasure had been awarded an A+, but my mind had stalled. For a moment, Coral was silent, her face turned to the burning pyre.

"But isn't that just, like, people in the West saying that?" Gemma suddenly said. "I mean, who are we to judge?"

She sounded like the most annoying students on my course, the not so bright ones, who had got hold of the idea of cultural relativity and now repeated it ad nauseum in seminars, as if it was the only answer. They're different, so live and let live, they'd say, and I'd twiddle my fingers and doodle furiously on my notepad. It was so woolly, so bleeding-heart complacent that it made me want to spit. I turned on Gemma, no longer able to contain myself. "What do you mean? Don't you think women in other places should be given the same rights as us?"

She glared at me, her small nostrils flaring. "I don't know," she said in a small, hard voice. "You're the one with the anthropology degree. I'm just a sixth-form drop-out. Remember?"

Coral reached out and put her hand on her arm. "Guys, cool it," she said. "You mustn't let India get to you."

I swallowed hard.

"I'm not letting India get to me," I said quietly. "I just don't agree that sati is transcendental. You've just got hold of some romantic idea about it. And, anyway, it doesn't happen anymore. It's just a cliché that India is like that. It's just foreigners getting off on exotica . . ."

I stopped, aware that I had said enough. I hadn't intended to get so worked up, but Coral's condescending tone had infuriated me and now my heart was pounding and my palms were sweaty from the unexpected confrontation.

Next to me, Gemma was staring at the floor, her hands still flapping in front of her face in a useless attempt to cool herself down. There was a long, heavy silence.

"Let's have a smoke," Coral eventually said. "I've got some great stuff inside."

Gemma and I followed her back into the flat, still not looking at each other. Tucking the towel around her legs, Coral squatted down on the floor. We sat in front of her, like nursery school-children waiting for a story. Rummaging in her bag, she produced a lump of hash and a small pipe. She lit it, closing her eyes and breathing in deeply. After a few moments she handed it onto me.

Around us sunlight fell in bright patches onto the dusty floor; the air smelled of hot concrete and marijuana. I was calming down now; in retrospect my vehemence seemed slightly embarrassing. It was stupid to argue over a bonfire, I thought as I breathed in the pungent smoke. I should relax, not take everything so much to heart. So what if Coral liked the idea of sati? We were going to spend one stoned night with her, not set up home. I passed the pipe onto Gemma. As she took it we smiled sheepishly at each other. I think I might have winked.

"This is the life," Gemma said.

Coral closed her eyes, sighing and smiling to herself. "Sure is."

"So where else have you been, Coral? Where do you recommend?" I said after a while.

"What, in India? It depends what you're into." She opened her eyes, peering into my face as if trying to work me out. "Like, if you're into partying then you've got to check out Goa. Go to Anjuna. It's full of folks like you. You'll have a ball."

I nodded. Gemma looked at me uncertainly.

"Where else?" she said quietly.

"Well, there's the mountains. That's where I go to get my head sorted out."

"Where exactly?"

"Manali . . . up in the heavens."

She laughed, pushing her hand through her wet hair and taking the pipe from Gemma.

"So where are you guys headed next?"

"We've got this plan . . ." Gemma started.

"Orissa," I put in quickly. I didn't want to tell Coral about Agun Mazir; she'd think it was pathetic, a schoolgirl's prank.

"We're going to visit this shrine," Gemma plowed on. "It's Esther's idea. What's the name of the saint, Ess? Nirulla, or something."

"Er, yeah."

"We let fate decide. We threw the guide in the air and we're going to the place where it landed."

She paused, then said: "It's Esther's way of showing how adventurous she is." She giggled, digging me in the ribs with her elbow. I could feel my face flush a deep, treacherous pink. Coral was looking at me carefully through the smoke.

"Cool."

"Of course I'd have been happy with a beach and my book," Gemma was saying slowly. "But that's what Esther wanted to do and it's Esther's gig." She busied herself with the pipe, turning her face away so that I couldn't see her expression. "Like most other things," she added quietly.

"Do you know what," said Coral reaching out to touch her hand. "I think it's going to be your gig, too."

It must have been the lack of sleep or the heat or the effect of the dope, but suddenly I wanted to scream. To stop this from happening I sucked at my lips and jumped up.

"I'm going for a walk," I said. "I need to get some air."

ONCE outside I took a deep breath and turned in the direction of the main road. I walked fast, my body rigid. My face felt tight and puckered; my thumbnails were digging so hard into my palms that it hurt. I kept splashing into the scummy puddles that lay across the lane, but I was so consumed by annoyance and humiliation and hurt that I hardly noticed. How could Gemma have embarrassed me like that in front of Coral? Even she, with all her inexperience, must have known how stupid the Pir Nirulla plan made me look, especially the way she put it. And if she found my ideas so risible, why did she agree to them?

I turned abruptly onto the main road, registering a row of scooter rickshaws waiting in front of a line of shops. It was typical Gemma behavior, I was thinking. Rather than say what she really thought, she pretended to go along with me, then made nasty little digs which implied I'd pushed her into it. She'd never face things full on. Every time we came close to having a fight she'd shy away, like a reluctant gymkhana pony at a gate, eyes fixed to the ground as she cantered resolutely in the opposite direction. Then later, it would all come out, in the most complicated, twisted ways. For me it was so different: fighting was as natural and untraumatic as breathing, my temper extinguished as quickly as it flared. It was like that for everyone in my family:

people spoke their minds and then moved on. We were noisy, rumbustious, always shouting and disagreeing and debating.

I crossed the road and started to stomp toward the rickshaws. Perhaps that was the problem: Gemma's house was always too quiet. Her parents had never argued, or if they did it was furtively, behind closed doors. I walked more quickly, suddenly swamped with guilt at the thought of her horrible, unhappy family. I shouldn't get so annoyed with her, I told myself. I should be patient and kind, keep my emotions controlled. After all, life had always been so much easier for me; it was only fair.

The door slammed with wall-juddering force. Gemma stared at it, but said nothing. For a second or so she assumed Esther would reappear, her face contrite—as usually happened after she lost her temper. Then she heard the crash of the door downstairs and realized she'd gone. On the floor in front of her a small gecko was scuttling toward her hand.

The dope was stronger than the stuff she was used to. Her thoughts were drifting, time speeding and slowing in a way that she liked. The gecko reached her little finger, and started to nibble it.

"What did you mean?" she said after what seemed like a long, vacant gap. "About it being my gig, too?"

THIS time I was not going to wait in line. I walked purposefully toward the booth marked "First Class and VIPs." The clerk sitting inside was young, with a dapper mustache and an open-necked, floral shirt. Staring beseechingly into his eyes, I bit my lip.

"Please, I was hoping you could help."

"Madam?"

"I'm in a terrible fix. I have to travel with my small daughter to Orissa on the next train, which I've been told is full. My husband is meeting us at the other end, and I really don't know what to do."

"A passage for Monday is possible . . ."

"No, no. That's almost a week away. That won't do at all."

I gazed at his mouth, then looked away. Considering the pledge I'd taken last term to the aims and solutions of the University's Radical Feminism Group it was somewhat disturbing how naturally this came to me.

"You see, I don't have an . . . appropriate place to stay here. I've never traveled alone before so I really am forced to throw myself into your hands."

My voice was sounding clipped and high, like a nice English gal in a 1950s film.

"Surely there must be a spare ticket, a cancellation, or something?"

The young man looked into my face and swallowed so heavily that I could see his Adam's apple slipping up and down.

"One moment, madam."

Five minutes later he returned with two first-class tickets for Orissa. The train left the next morning.

7

Gemma lay on her bed, staring up at the sky. She had been dreaming fragmented, angry dreams of her mother and had woken with a start to find herself alone. In the leafy green light filtering through the balcony's railings she could see her back-pack, sandals, and the battered pages of Middlemarch *splayed facedown on the floor.*

She was too hot. She kicked off the sheet that Coral must have spread over her as she slept and stretched out her legs. After Esther had gone they'd talked for hours; as she remembered the things Coral had told her she started to smile. It was good that Esther had stormed off like that. Things were always better without her.

It must have been getting late, for the sky had turned golden and the air had a hazy quality she hadn't noticed before. From the floor below, she could smell onions frying. She placed her hands on the warm cement of the balcony and peered over. If only she could breathe properly, but the air was so hot. She was still itching, too. Glancing down she saw that the rash had spread up her arms and was now encroaching the soft skin between her breasts. She scratched her neck, then reached inside her damp bra, her fingers scrabbling at her sticky skin.

"Just let it happen," she whispered. "Just go with the flow."

Above the sprawling urban landscape the sun was about to set. In the few minutes that she'd been standing on the balcony the sky had burst into spectacular color. Over the rooftops a thin smudge of smoke was rising, the sunset smearing it with the appearance of flames. Just looking at it filled her with fear and excitement for the changes about to come. It was so vivid, so bright, almost too much.

"Hello!"

She jumped, and looked round. Facing her on the other side of the muady lane was a half-built block of flats, steel rods rising from its concrete roof like antennae. As she gazed across to the flat roof opposite she noticed a young woman standing watching her, her hands on her hips. She was wearing a bright pink sari, a shiny yellow blouse, and, tucked behind her ear, a huge white flower. Long black hair swung down her back. She must have been hanging out the laundry, for arranged on a line behind her was a brightly patterned stretch of cloth.

Tentatively, Gemma attempted a smile. The woman paused, unsure, then suddenly grinned. Still staring into Gemma's face she jerked her head enquiringly, then almost seemed to wink. There was a tiny gap between her teeth, her diamond nose-pin glinting in the light.

As they smiled at each other Gemma felt the tightness within her loosen. Her heart lifted a little and as it did the softest shimmer of a breeze shifted her hair around her face. Something about the way her new acquaintance was standing, with such graceful ease and humor, made her want to laugh.

"Namaste!" *she shouted.* "How's it going?"

The woman spluttered, her features collapsing into laughter. For a second or so she covered her face with the end of her sari, her body shaking with repressed hilarity. Then, composing herself, she turned back to face Gemma. Fixing her with her eyes, she slowly pulled her arms up over her head. Gemma could see

dark patches of sweat under her arms and the outline of ribs es-
caping from her blouse. She seemed to be fiddling with her hair.
For a moment Gemma was confused. Then she saw that the
woman had plucked another fat flower from the back of her
head. Still smiling, she walked to the edge of the building.

"Apnar jonno!" she cried, and threw it high in the air.

The flower traveled about halfway between the buildings then
fell sharply, bound only for the ditch. But then suddenly, as if
caught by the angels, it rose on a gust of hot air and Gemma was
leaning far out over the balcony and plucking it from the breeze.

It was a lily, heavy with scent, its white-flecked flesh brushing
her fingers with silvery pollen. Gemma held it in her hands, gaz-
ing at it. It was a sign, she thought; a message from the gods.

～

AFTER getting the tickets I caught another rickshaw to the Vic-
toria Memorial, and sat for a while on the worn grass of the
Maidan looking across at the guano-splattered old queen. I felt
much better, now that I was out and about and organizing, my
anger at Gemma a dim memory. As the day progressed I convinced myself that she hadn't meant to hurt or humiliate me. I
should be more patient, I remembered. It was her first proper
trip away; she was bound to feel nervous. And she'd always
been haunted by fears that I couldn't understand and she didn't
choose to communicate. Even when we were kids she had a ten-
dency to be elusive, sliding artfully away from questions which
she didn't like; more recently I sometimes suspected her of deliberately withholding information. But it didn't really matter.
She hadn't meant to upset me, I told myself; it was just a simple
disagreement over an abstract idea. And it *was* kind of Coral to
let us stay with her. In fact it was a shame we couldn't stay for
longer, but I was sure Gemma would understand why it was
best not to wait another whole week for the train.

After the Maidan I browsed in the shops, then bought myself some chapatis and dhal in a restaurant around the corner. I was soon joined by a portly gentleman who told me his brother had a house in Ealing and his son was studying engineering in York. I chatted with him for a while, then headed back. It was lucky Coral had mentioned the name of the park, I thought as I climbed into another rickshaw. Otherwise I wouldn't have a clue how to get back to the flat; I'd be completely lost.

I arrived back at the apartment block about forty minutes later, so grimy from the pollution that my nails were black and my eyes stung. I paid the scooter driver and picked my way across the garbage-strewn road. It was dusk now and the pavement was alive with people. If Gemma and I had fallen out I had only myself to blame I thought as I reached the entrance of the apartment building. I was being irritable and intolerant; I should try to be a better friend. After all, why should I expect her to be as adaptable as me?

I decided to jog up the stairs rather than take the creaky elevator to the seventh floor. It was an invigorating climb; on each floor barred windows revealed a panoramic view of the twinkling city. When I reached the top I paused to catch my breath. Then composing myself, I turned to the door. I didn't have a key, I suddenly realized.

To my relief, the door was ajar. Pushing it open I quietly stepped inside the flat. Despite the soft light drifting from the balcony the room was almost dark. For a moment or so I stood disorientated by the door, trying to locate the electricity switch. Then suddenly, from out of the gloom, I heard a quiet voice.

"It's like, a blessing? . . ."

Something about the intonation of the words was deeply familiar. My fingers groped over the wall. There was a long pause and then the voice said: "The way I see it, there's a reason for everything."

It was Coral. And, I realized with relief, I'd found the light switch. I flicked it on, composing my face as I looked across the room. The light flickered uncertainly, casting a sick yellow light over the room. Suddenly I noticed Coral sitting in the corner, her hand still clutching the phone.

"Gotta go," she said, glancing up at me and smiling. There was another short pause, then she put the receiver down.

We looked across the room at each other. She had changed into loose cotton trousers and a bright pink cropped top which showed off her flat stomach and, just above the line of the trousers, a tattoo of a phoenix, rising from indigo flames. It looked great, I thought with a rush of admiration and envy; how come I didn't have a tattoo?

"Hi," she said. "Been anywhere nice?"

"Oh you know, just around about the place—exploring the city."

"And?"

I walked across the room, flopping down onto a cushion beside her.

"It's fab. Filthy though. Even my bra's turned gray."

She smiled and nodded at me with her unreadable eyes. In the glare of the bare electric bulb she seemed older again, her eyes and mouth etched with fine, spidery lines which I hadn't noticed before. She kept shifting and changing, I thought, her age and identity impossible to pin down.

"Listen," I carried on. "It's really great of you to let us stay here tonight. You've been a total star, what with saving our bacon on the train and everything."

She shrugged. "It's all part of the service."

"So what have *you* been doing?"

"Ah, you know, just hanging out. I've done so much heavy duty stuff lately it's good to just sit and let it all settle for a bit. Y'know?"

I wasn't sure that I did. I nodded noncommittally. There was a pause.

"Look," I said slowly. "I'm sorry about this morning. I shouldn't have stormed out like that. I was being a real jerk."

"No worries. It's history."

"Was Gemma upset?"

She put her hands around her knees, hugging them close to her chest. "Don't think so. You guys just have to sort whatever it is that's bothering you both, that's all."

I blinked at her, my throat constricting. "What do you mean?"

"Well, there's something going on, isn't there?" She stared at me. "The way you are together," she said. "I mean, even I can see it."

I breathed in sharply. The way she was looking at me was making me feel increasingly queasy.

"There's nothing going on," I heard myself say tightly. "We're just knackered, and Gem's not used to being in the heat, that's all. We're best friends. We always have been."

Coral gazed at me coolly. I had no idea what she was thinking.

"She's been telling me all about how you guys have known each other since kindergarten and how you always hang out everywhere together and everything?"

"Yes?"

"And, like, how you went off to college and . . ."

I swallowed. Perhaps she was trying to be helpful, but she was making it worse.

"What did she say about me going to university?"

"Ah, you know, nothing much. Just that you always get what you want."

My cheeks flushed scarlet. I put my hands over them, trying to cool down.

"Yeah, well, she was meant to be our school's great white hope. Then she fucked up her exams. It's really hard for her."

"That's one way of putting it. I mean what she said was that . . ."

"So anyway," I said, standing up hastily. "Where is she?"

"She went out."

"Went out?"

"Slept all afternoon, then said she needed some air."

"Where did she say she was going?"

"Don't ask me. She said something about some woman she was going to visit . . ."

"Some woman?"

Coral shrugged again. "I was doing my meditation so I didn't really take it in."

I walked slowly across the room to the balcony. From the dusky gloom of the lane below I could see Gemma walking slowly back along the lane. Something about her seemed different, but in the half-light it was hard to work out what. I stepped quickly back into the room.

"I'm going to meet her."

I stood on the sixth-floor landing, staring down the stairwell. After a few minutes the top of Gemma's head appeared several floors below.

"Gemma!" I called softly. I could hear the slap of her flip-flops on the stone stairs and her puffy breath. She didn't reply. Perhaps she was still narked with me, I thought anxiously.

"Gemma!" I called again. "It's me!"

For a moment there was silence, then a woman dressed in a blue-flowered sari with a large white flower behind her ear appeared on the penultimate landing. Her face was pink, her shoulders slightly slumped. She looked up at me almost coyly, then lifted her hand and waved. For a moment I had no idea who she was, then suddenly I realized.

"Jesus Christ! What are you wearing?"

"It's a sari."

With one final step, she reached my level.

"Shit, look, it's coming undone." Glancing down at the material, she started to fuss at the pleats, tucking them in at the front and smoothing them with her hands. She was wearing a half blouse, too, I noticed, and underneath the sari, a long white petticoat.

"Where did you get it?"

"It was brilliant! I was up on the balcony, feeling really hot and bothered and everything and I met this woman—on the roof . . ."

I stared at her. The sari suited her rounded figure, making her seem voluptuous rather than dumpy. With the flower behind her ear and bulging blouse she looked like a Bengali housewife.

". . . and she gave me tea in her house, and then for a laugh, I got all togged up in the local gear. It's great, isn't it?"

"Yeah." I smiled vaguely. To be honest I was irked that she'd had such an interesting time without me. I brushed the unfamiliar emotion aside.

"Look, Gem," I said hastily, reaching out and taking her plump white hands. "I wanted to say sorry. I was in a terrible mood this morning and for some stupid reason I got really pissed off by that conversation about sati. I don't know what got into me. It must be PMS, or something."

Gemma looked down at the floor.

"That's okay. You're just getting hassled by being here and everything. It's normal."

I paused. Being hassled by India was *not* the reason why I'd been annoyed. Could she never take any share of blame? There was a short, uncomfortable silence. Then, repressing my urge to have the last word, I shrugged.

"Whatever. It's crap to fall out."

Putting my arms around her shoulders I squeezed her tightly. "Friends again?"

"Yeah, friends."

It felt odd, hugging someone so familiar who looked so radically different. We stepped apart, smiling and looking into each other's eyes with slight embarrassment. During our embrace the flower behind her ear had been knocked askew. It was wilting, too, its stamen lilting drunkenly, the pollen sprinkled over her hair.

"Your flower's falling out."

Reaching up over her head, she pushed it back into place. Perhaps it was the argument, or her strange costume, but I felt unaccustomedly shy of her.

"Anyway," I said, sweeping the sensation aside. "I've got it all sorted out. I've booked us tickets for Orissa tomorrow morning."

There was another long pause. I sucked at my cheeks. I'd assumed she would be pleased.

"You do still want to go?"

"Yeah, sure . . ."

"No cold feet?"

"No. It'll be fun."

"Then what's the matter?"

"I dunno . . ."

"What is it? Tell me."

She glanced at me, slyly almost. "I suppose I was thinking that we should invite Coral to come with us," she said slowly. "I mean, she's a laugh, isn't she? And she knows so much about everything, too. We could learn stuff from her."

I took a long, even breath.

"Yeah, but we hardly know her, Gem," I said slowly. "I mean, she seems really nice. But supposing she starts to get on our nerves?"

"But it's only for a few days. If that happens we can split."
She folded her arms defensively over her tummy which—I
couldn't stop myself from unkindly noting—bulged over the top
of the sari.

"The thing is . . ." I stared into Gemma's shiny face, trying to
choose the right words. The truth was that something about
Coral made me uneasy. She pushed me out, that was what it
was. For some reason she wanted to be friends with Gemma but
not with me.

"The thing is," I said decisively, "I only managed to get the
two tickets. I wanted to get one for Coral, too, but they were the
last ones. And, anyway, I didn't think she'd want to come."

"Why not?" Gemma stared at me stubbornly.

I looked back at her, my face reddening. I'd told a blatant lie,
and Gemma knew. "I don't know."

Gemma stepped back in irritation, frowning and shaking her
head. "Well, that's great, isn't it, Esther? Once again, you get to
make all the decisions."

"It wasn't like that, I promise, I . . ."

I stopped. From somewhere above I had heard a click. I
turned slowly round. On the floor above Coral was standing in
the doorway of the flat gazing down at us. When she saw me
turn she smiled brightly and said: "Hi, guys. What's up?"

Gemma turned away from me, grinning up at her like a three-
year-old with a new toy. "Coral! Look at my sari!" she called
with a laugh.

Before I could say more, she'd pushed past me and was
climbing the stairs.

I stayed on the floor below. I felt nauseous: that heavy, dragging sensation that over the last few weeks had become almost a
part of me. I suppose it was partly because of Coral and the
train tickets. I *should* have asked Gemma first, I told myself; it
was arrogant to assume that like me, she would want to leave

tomorrow. And perhaps I should have asked Coral if she wanted to come; after all, what harm could she do? But mostly what I felt was guilt, my constant companion. I'd been trying desperately to ignore it, to tell myself that I'd done nothing wrong. But I had, you see, I'd done something terrible.

It was brutally simple. Steve was the love of Gemma's life and although she didn't know it yet, I'd stolen him from her.

Gemma gazed up at the soft, pink-blushed sky. She'd been awake for a long time, thinking about the things Coral had told her. Now, a million miles away, the silver moon was slipping imperceptibly into blue. In an hour, it would be gone; in another, her sleeping bag would be pinioned to the balcony by hot spears of sun. Beyond the railings the city was still coming into focus, the early morning mist slowly melting away. Somewhere above her head a bird chirped; from the lane below she could hear the rumble of a rickshaw's wheels. A few minutes earlier the azan had crackled into life with its strange, melodic cry, but now it was over, the minaret of the small mosque in the market silent. In the sleepy-faced buildings that surrounded them, people were praying.

If she wanted, she kept thinking, this could be it, all those things she'd been waiting for. She breathed in and then out, listening for her heartbeat, checking that she was still alive.

—

"WHAT a bloody racket!"

I opened my eyes and looked around. The azan had woken me from a deep, dreamless sleep. A few yards away from my head Gemma was sitting up and gazing gormlessly through the railings of the balcony.

"It's so loud," I said, stretching and clicking my fingers. "No wonder the Hindus get fed up."

"I quite like it," Gemma said. She didn't look round.

Sitting up, I started groping around the floor for my watch. "What's the time?"

"About five."

"Christ! We really need to get going."

I leaped up and started to stuff the various possessions that lay strewn around the balcony into my backpack.

Esther whistled as she worked, a rough rendition of "Careless Whisper." She was wearing a crumpled cotton dress, her eyes were puffy with sleep, and her long brown hair fell over her face in a tangled mat, yet still she was beautiful. Looking up suddenly from her packing she glanced at Gemma and winked. People always forgave her, that was the thing; everything she wanted fell straight into her lap.

"COME on, then," I whispered. "Let's go."

We decided to leave Coral sleeping. We'd sat up late with her the night before, drinking sticky Indian rum and smoking bidis, and I didn't see any point in waking her now. She said she'd probably stay in Calcutta a while longer, then head back up north. I was determined not to feel guilty about departing so suddenly. Backpacking was like that; we were free spirits, everything was spontaneous and unplanned. So Gemma wrote a note thanking her for giving us a bed for the night, propped it by the door, and we crept out of the flat. By the time we reached Howrah Station, the sun had risen high and bright in the sky.

*   *   *

THIS time we found our seats without trouble. We bought two clay cups of chai, a bunch of bananas, and a couple of chapatis and settled down to eat our breakfast in the waiting train. At exactly seven A.M. the steam engine began to pull out of the station. As we passed through the bustees surrounding the tracks, I felt the dull weight that had been pressing on me since our arrival in Calcutta finally lift. The train rattled through miles of suburbs, eventually reaching open countryside. It was being in the city that had made me so tense, I decided as the horizon stretched and unfolded into endless shades of green; thank God we'd managed to get away. Picking up the *Lonely Planet* I started to thumb through its pages.

"Apparently there are fantastic beaches in Puri," I said after a while. "After we've visited the shrine we can hang out there for a bit."

"Okay."

"Then I thought maybe we could go south, to Goa . . ."

I glanced at Gemma, who was perching on the bench next to me, her arms clasped tightly around her knees. With her mauve bangs and tasseled skirt she looked like an exotic hen. She seemed pensive; I suspected she had not heard what I'd said.

"Or should we ask the book to decide?"

She shrugged, then said absentmindedly: "Don't you think Goa might be a bit too hot?"

I paused. Her preoccupation with the climate was getting really irritating.

"The monsoons are different in the South," I finally said. "We'll have to look it up. It might even be raining."

She sighed and leaned her head against the back of her seat. Now that the train had finally picked up speed the carriage was filling with a warm breeze. She closed her eyes, then suddenly opened them wide and started to scratch violently at her wrists and arms, her nails leaving raw, red marks on her skin.

"Chamomile lotion?"

"It just makes it worse."

I eyed her wearily. It was unfair, but I couldn't stop myself from thinking she was making an unnecessary fuss.

"What's happened to *Middlemarch*?"

"Heroine happily married off, lessons learned, story complete."

"Now what?"

"The Tin Drum."

The train passed over a particularly clackety section of rail, making further conversation impossible. When finally it slowed, she added:

"Steve lent it to me."

The unexpected sound of his name sent the blood rushing to my cheeks. I turned my head toward the window, hoping she wouldn't notice.

"I didn't know he was into reading," I said.

"There's lots of things you don't know."

I glanced around sharply, but she was looking at me without any apparent malice.

"Maybe I'll read it after you've finished."

She shrugged. "What about Paul what's-his-name?" she suddenly said. "You've gone very quiet about him lately. Does he get honored with a postcard?"

"No *way*. I told you, he was a mistake."

She raised her eyebrows meaningfully.

"Poor sod, you're such a femme fatale."

"Gem! I am *not* a femme fatale!"

I laughed, probably too loudly, shaking my head and prodding her in the arm. We were sitting directly in the sun now, the light falling through the window in barred patches onto our arms and legs. She was just teasing me of course, but the label stung. I knew that over the years I'd inadvertently hurt a lot of men, but it was never something I enjoyed. They always seemed to get so intense about me, in a way that I couldn't fathom and found impossible to reciprocate. Yet it wasn't that I wanted to be alone either; rather, the reverse. I wanted very much to find the right person, but until I met Steve it had never felt right. Before that, even after the first date my mind would crowd with objections and misgivings. Sometimes I'd go out with someone for a couple of months, but it invariably ended in an awkward conversation or a row and I'd walk away with very little sadness and a great deal of relief. Paul, for example, who talked too much about himself and didn't believe in foreplay, had only lasted two weeks. The truth was that I was twenty-three and the longest relationship of my life—with Luke—had only lasted four months, ending disastrously in a crumbling, cat-infested hotel in Cairo when, no longer able to pretend I wanted to be with him, I'd shamed myself by having sex with a Dutch guy while he slept in the next room, then caught the next flight home in disgrace. No, I thought dismally. I was not a femme fatale; I was a coward and a bitch. And now there was this thing with Steve.

"Phew, I'm sweltering!" Gemma suddenly said. Standing up, she pulled the shutters down.

I closed my eyes and tried to relax. I could smell the hot wood and metal of the train, the spicy aroma of the kedgeree the family opposite were eating from their tiffin tins, and the earthy, sweet smell of sweat. Gemma was humming to herself, apparently unfazed.

The sun rose higher and higher in the sky and the train chugged on. Sometimes it would slow and stop for no apparent reason and for five or ten minutes we'd be marooned in the East Indian countryside, the grass buzzing with insects, the undercarriage of the train ticking in the fierce light. Then we'd jolt forward, the engine straining with the weight. In the heat-deadened center of the day, we slept, our heads lolling against each other's shoulders, our arms thrown back.

9

IT was dark by the time we reached Bhubaneshwar. In the *Lonely Planet* I'd been reading about dormitories for twenty rupees a night, but Gemma had other ideas and nothing I said could dissuade her. She wanted air-conditioning and a shower, she declared, and not a grimy trail into the center of town for a flea-bitten bunk. I didn't have the energy to argue. On her insistence we checked in to a small hotel opposite the station which smelled of damp but had wall-to-wall carpeting, "en-suite bathrooms," and even a telephone. The tariff of two hundred rupees was far beyond my planned budget, but it was now late and the expression on Gemma's face too determined for me to demur.

The hotel had already closed for the evening. We were let in by a dozing night guard and found the proprietor asleep at the desk. Only when I bashed the bell hard with the palm of my hand did he rouse, blinking in momentary confusion and wiping his face with a large red handkerchief. He was a small, rotund young man with a brightly flowered shirt and a mustache so thin it could have been drawn on his lip with a pencil.

"Welcome!" he cried, sitting up straight and stretching. "From what country do you hail? Please, come in, come in, you are most welcome."

I glanced at Gemma. A deep, irrepressible well of laughter was bubbling in my chest.

"The U.K.," I said simply. "Do you have rooms?"

"Rooms aplenty! Yes, madam. You are here for how long?"

He was scrabbling around for registration forms, glancing at the row of keys that hung behind him.

"Just one night."

"And then you will travel onward to Puri, for our beautiful beaches? Or do you intend to visit the temple at Konarak?"

He peered at us expectantly, his pen hovering above the paper.

"Does it matter?"

"Actually we're going to this place, Agun Mazir," Gemma put in. "It's in the Simili National Park, I think. Do you know anything about it?"

The man looked up at us perplexed. "You are hoping to catch some tigers in our great forest?" A small ridge of concern had appeared between his eyebrows.

"No," I said in my poshest Memsahib voice. "We're going to visit a shrine."

Out of the corner of my eye I noticed Gemma frown. The man looked down.

"Madam," he said. "There are so many beautiful attractions here in Orissa . . . why do you wish to go to Agun Mazir? This is a religious place, not a place for tourists . . ."

"We've heard it's got special powers. We're on a spiritual quest."

I smiled at him in a way that indicated I would not welcome further questions.

"But this is a Muslim shrine," he continued, taking no notice. "You are not Muslims, I think? And as you know, some of our people are very hurt at the moment about this book?"

"You mean Salman Rushdie?"

"Some of our people are very angry," he continued quietly.

He was gazing down at his fingers, which he was twisting together in an agony of embarrassment. "There have been . . . incidents. Stones thrown at some tourists in Jaipur, such like things. Our people get very emotional in such times. And this is the month of Pir Nirulla's mela. The town will be very full, I believe. I would implore you to change your minds and visit instead our world-famous historical temple at Rajrani, in this beautiful city. After that you can rest here for a night and then travel to Puri for your own relaxation . . ."

I looked away from the desk to the wilting pot plants and dusty, plastic covered settee of the lounge. What he was saying only heightened my desire to go to Agun Mazir. If it was going to be difficult then I'd embrace the challenge. Out of the corner of my eye I could see Gemma frowning at me, but I ignored her.

"Do you do food here?" I said, cutting into his words with one of my brightest smiles.

How could I have been so arrogant? Remembering these scenes today makes me squirm with embarrassment and regret. The poor young man was only trying to help, but I was young and pretty and British and I suppose I thought I could behave exactly as I pleased. I would do anything to change that now, but it's too late. I keep trying to claw it back, but the past has slipped unstoppably through my fingers.

WE were shown to our rooms and brought rice, vegetable bhaji, and fried eggs by a fey young waiter who hovered vapidly at the door until we realized why he was waiting and Gemma pressed a five-rupee note into his hand. After demolishing the food we collapsed onto our beds. Gemma had turned the air-conditioning onto full, and lay stretched out on the cotton sheet, her arms upturned. The rash had spread down their entire length, breaking off at her shoulders and appearing again in angry blotches at her neck. She scratched in sudden flurries of frenzied activity, her teeth clenched as she grunted in pained relief.

"Ahh, Christ, this itches!"

"You're just making it worse. What about that prickly heat powder?"

"I tried that yesterday. It doesn't work. Aghh . . . bollocks to this!"

"If you do that you're going to break all the skin and it'll get infected."

She stopped scratching and looked across the room. "I just need to get out of this heat. It was being on the train all day that did it."

Picking up the *Lonely Planet* I began to leaf languidly through it.

"Perhaps we *should* go to Puri," I said vaguely.

"I mean, what really worries me about this Agun Mazir place is the guest house. It says in that book the rooms don't have air-conditioning or anything. And it's right in the middle of the jungle . . ."

"It'll be fine . . ." I turned a page, not looking at her. "We'll only stay there for a night or so, then we'll head back."

"But I mean, like, suppose what that guy was saying is true?"

"What guy?"

I finally put the book down, looking across the bed at her strained face.

"The guy at reception. He said it was this mela . . . whatsit, and . . ."

"You mean the festival? I read about that in the book. It's every year, on the day of his death. It should be really wild."

"Yeah, but what if they stone us because they think we're agents of the devil, like old Salman?"

"Poly . . ." I took a deep breath and sat up. "Don't you want to do this? I thought the whole point was to do something unplanned and spontaneous. I thought we'd agreed?"

The sullen line appeared between her eyes. She looked away from me, chewing at her lip. "Yes," she said. "I do want to do it."

"Good. That's settled then."

Sighing, I stood up.

"I'm going downstairs to get some fags," I said, glancing across the room. Despite her closed eyes she was clearly still awake. "Any orders?"

There was no reply. I hesitated, my hand clutching the door handle. I wanted to say something else but felt unaccustomedly awkward. I was just about to finally turn the handle when suddenly, with a bleep which made Gemma sit up and open her eyes wide, the telephone on her bedside table gave a shrill ring. For a moment she stared at it, her hand hovering uncertainly above the receiver.

"Go on then," I said. "Pick it up."

It rang again, this time more accusingly. Reaching across the bed, Gemma gingerly lifted the receiver from the greasy telephone.

"Hello?"

She was listening closely, her face troubled.

"Hello? This is room 322. Yes?"

There was another long pause. She stared at the floor, still listening, still uncertain.

"Hello?"

Her face had darkened now, two spots of crimson appearing on either cheek.

"Yes," she said slowly, then: "Yes, that's right . . ."

She paused, then suddenly blurted: "Good-bye!" and slammed the receiver down. It landed on the telephone set with a wounded ping.

"What was that all about?"

"I don't know . . ."

"Who was it?"

"No one . . . it was just like . . ." She coughed, her eyes fixed to the dusty beige curtains hanging over the bolted windows. ". . . Um, like . . ."

"Like a heavy breather?"

"Yeah. I suppose so."

"So why did you say, 'Yes, that's right'?"

"Did I say that?"

I stared at her.

"Why didn't you just tell him to piss off?"

"I felt sorry for him."

"You *what?* God, Gem, sometimes you really are a complete fruitcake!"

"Am I?"

She raised her eyebrows at me. Something in her seemed to have lightened, the gauze of tension which had fallen between us a few minutes earlier inexplicably vanishing.

"Hang on, how did anyone know we were staying here?" I suddenly said. "Did they mention your name?"

She flushed, her eyes flicking away from my face and back to the curtains. Before she could answer I clapped my hand to my forehead. I'd just had a horrible thought.

"Oh my God, I've just realized. The only person who knows we're staying here is Mr. Friendly at reception . . . Jesus, that's so creepy! Yuck. I knew you were too friendly to that guy, Gem! You've got to be really snooty, otherwise they start to make assumptions. Did it sound like the receptionist's voice?"

"Dunno. It didn't really sound like anyone."

I paused, considering the possibilities.

"Ah well," I eventually said. "Perhaps it was that waiter."

"Yeah," she said, her eyes apparently brightening. "It probably was."

THE years flip back, like pages caught in the wind. A word innocently spoken, a stranger's face passed unexpectedly on the street and suddenly I'm there again: the months and weeks and days I've endured since I lost Gemma hurtling past like so many paragraphs of unread text.

As far as I am concerned they contain nothing of interest. Only those few brief weeks five years ago matter. I thumb through my dog-eared memories again, studying them for clues, but they are too faded and fraying to uncover anything new. The call was connected, that's obvious now. I want to reach back into the past and shake my twenty-three-year-old self, rough her up a little. Why didn't I watch Gemma's face? Why didn't I listen?

Later, after Esther had tucked her perfect, naked body under the thin hotel sheet on her bed and fallen into one of her perfect, undisturbed sleeps, Gemma put down her book and crept quietly across the room. When she reached the door she opened it as silently as she could and stepped into the corridor. In the lobby downstairs she could hear the telephone ringing, the beep of scooters and cars from the road outside. She skipped quickly down the stairs, not acknowledging the receptionist, willing herself into invisibility as she passed through the hotel doors onto the street outside.

It was after ten, but the city was still awake. She crossed the road and passed a large sparkling temple, glancing in amazement at the strings of flashing lights draped around its golden walls, the giant, gaudily painted Vishnu sitting on a pedestal outside. From the brightly lit interior she could hear singing and the melodic wheeze of an accordion. After that there was a row of shops and tea stalls, still busy with customers. She stepped around a small brown cow chewing contentedly on some straw, jumped over the open drain, and crossed the road.

She was bang on time, just like she had promised.

10

WE had planned to travel to Agun Mazir early the next day, but instead slept for the whole morning, rousing only to order tea and toast and then collapsing again for the afternoon. Lethargy covered the day like a thick blanket. In the evening, befuddled by a surplus of sleep, we staggered from the hotel to buy sweet-meats and chapatis from a nearby bazaar, then scurried back to our room like nocturnal foragers, pasty faced and blinking from the lights.

The next day was the same. We slept late, managed with what felt like vast willpower to visit some Buddhist ruins on the edge of the city, then returned to our beds. Perhaps it was jet lag, perhaps the heat. Whatever it was, it didn't matter, for something had shifted between Gemma and me, the uneasiness of recent days giving way to an all-embracing warmth which reminded me of how things used to be. It was like being at school again. We were in league, woven tightly together by the seamless chat that we spun around the day. Under the cool blast of the air-conditioner, Gemma stopped scratching. In the heart of the city, with its temples and markets and lolloping cows, the guilt which had been gripping at me relaxed its relentless clutch. What had happened with Steve was history, I told myself.

Gemma would never know; by the time we returned to Britain she might not even care.

The ruins turned out to be perfectly preserved temples of an intricacy and beauty which reduced us to silent awe. During the rickshaw drive back we sat quietly together, our knees touching as we gazed out from under the canopy at the fading sky. Later, we shared a thali in a food hall near the railway station and returned to the hotel arm in arm.

On the third day we strolled aimlessly through the backstreets of the town, gazing at the crumbling, miraculous architecture and giggling at each other's jokes. In the city museum we were pursued by a fat, desperate-looking German, his large torso strapped with cameras and travelers' contraptions. He offered us ganja, and when we seemed mildly interested, extended the invitation to include his bed. We eventually escaped, pleading Delhi-belly and slipping through a door in the bathroom to the heat-hazed streets outside. It was perfect, I thought as we jogged away, screaming with laughter; all my misgivings about traveling with Gemma were unfounded; it was everything I'd hoped it would be.

On the fourth day we finally caught our bus. At the ticket office we had been promised a "deluxe, extra luxury, air-conditioned touring coach." What eventually pulled up was a silver-tinseled charabanc, festooned with pictures of tigers and birds and London-bound planes and nothing remotely luxurious inside. The seats we had been allocated were stuck in the "recline" position, the "air-conditioning" broken.

The vehicle was crammed full, too. I searched the crowd for other travelers, but we were clearly off the tourist route, for the bus was filled with country folk returning to their homes. Behind us two old women gossiped and shared their paan; in front sat a stony-faced man and his inexplicably sobbing wife. Our backpacks went on the roof joined by sacks of rice, a pile of jackfruit, and several baskets of chickens; to my utter delight the old man in the seat opposite had two ducks nestling contentedly in his lap.

We set off, bumping over the pockmarked roads which skirted the city. After a few minutes the driver turned the sound system on, and the bus reverberated with the beat of Bollywood's latest hits. I yawned and stretched and tried to close my eyes. The window was jammed shut and the sun streamed through, making my head throb and my palms sticky. We had two hundred kilometers to go, and even I had to admit it was too hot.

The journey was interminable. We passed endless padi fields, the landscape flat and unpromising. Whichever direction the road turned, the sun chased us through the glinting windows. I was feeling increasingly sick, drifting in and out of irritable sleep as the wheels bumped beneath. We should have done as the proprietor had said I began to think: gone to look at temples and then the beach, not pursued this silly game.

After a short stop for lunch, the road started to climb. Suddenly we were surrounded by trees, the bus shifting into first gear as it negotiated the endless bends. From the window we could see the fringes of the forest: a mossy, damp interior of streams and clinging, creeping vegetation. Then the road swerved into another stretch of flatter scrubland, the bus honking its horn and accelerating as if possessed by demons. From time to time we passed a roadside shrine surrounded by flapping flags and candles and the passengers would mutter to themselves in prayer and toss coins from the doors.

Soon, I prayed, soon we would arrive. With each lurch and bump, my nausea swelled. The sad woman in front was already retching, her husband leaning over her with a cloth as she flopped against the smeared window. The acrid smell of vomit brought me close to the same fate. I twisted and turned interminably in my narrow seat, pulling my T-shirt over my nose. We had been on the bus for nearly nine hours.

Then finally it was over. The bus roared around a series of jagged bends, we passed an area of scooter workshops spread messily along the road and screeched to a halt opposite a ramshackle row of shops.

"Agun Mazir!" someone shouted, and we found ourselves propelled out of our seats by the helpful hands of the bus boys, who steered us along the aisle and down the steps to the road below.

Our backpacks were unfastened and thrown from the roof and the bus accelerated away. I stood by the side of the road, my hands on my knees as I breathed in the marginally fresher air. Already I felt less sick, but after nine hours of bone-shaking discomfort every muscle in my body quivered. Yet while I was physically relieved the journey was over, as I straightened up to see the silvery backside of the bus disappearing in a cloud of red dust I felt inexplicably abandoned. What were we doing here? I thought with a surge of regret. We could have been lying on a beach or drinking lassis with other travelers in the mountains but instead we were in the back of beyond. Why did I have to turn everything into such an uncomfortable challenge?

I looked around slowly, my spirits sagging. I'd imagined a vibrant little town, spilling over with color and eccentricity. But as I gazed down the road I realized that this was quite different; it was Nowheresville; a place where no backpacker in their right mind would get off the bus. We were standing in what appeared to be the town's only street, a long strip of wooden shops and tea stalls with a bus stand at one end, and a post office, medical center, and National Bank of India at the other.

The place was virtually deserted. On the other side of the road a couple of rickshaw drivers cruised aimlessly for trade; others slept inside their stationary vehicles, their legs flopped over the handlebars. Pye-dogs dozed in the dust, their scuffed scraggy bodies stretched out under the late afternoon sun. Opposite the bus stand a family of pigs rooted contentedly. This was a terrible mistake, I decided as I watched the pigs. We should have listened to the man at the hotel; this was not a place for tourists.

"Well," I said, turning brightly to Gemma. "Here we are. It's a lot smaller than I'd imagined."

She gazed up and down the road, her face gloomy.

"You can say that again."

There was another long pause, as we both considered our options. Personally, I was wondering when the next bus back to Bhubaneshwar was due.

"What do we do now?" said Gemma flatly.

"Find the tourist bungalow?"

"I guess."

We set off in the direction of the rickshaws. In the few minutes since the bus had departed we had accumulated a small gaggle of children who followed us down the road, giggling and whispering gleefully. When I jumped round, pulling a mock monster face and making as if to chase them they screamed with delight, scattering in all directions like a flock of unruly birds.

We continued walking down the street.

"Where is everyone, anyway?" Gemma muttered.

It was true that the place seemed unnaturally quiet. We shouldn't be here, I was thinking; it was like stealing through an empty house, waiting at any moment for the owners to return and demand an explanation. I shook my head, expiating the image from my mind.

"Do you think it's that road there?" I nodded at the crossroads. "All these bloody signs are in Hindi."

We turned left off the main street onto the smaller road. Behind us we could still hear the scuffles and whispers of the children. We passed a couple of stone houses, surrounded by walls, and then another row of shut-up stalls.

"I'm sure it'll be somewhere along here, let's just . . ."

I broke off and looked down. A clod of earth had landed at my feet. As I turned sharply around, another missile hit my forehead. For a moment I stood confused in the middle of the road. Then suddenly a small stone ricocheted off Gemma's bag.

"They're throwing stones at us!" I cried, spinning around and glaring at the children in amazement.

"Piss off!"

The impact of the earth made my forehead smart. Picking up a banana skin, I hurled it in their direction, but they had scattered again. I started walking faster, wiping my face as I strode ahead. For a moment or two I saw nothing, just a blur of green trees and the stony path. I dabbed at my forehead, cursing, and finally stopped to rest on a hummock of grass. I felt irrationally upset. Down the hill I could see Gemma straggling painfully behind, her face puce. As I gazed around I suddenly realized that I was standing opposite a large, hand-painted sign.

"Look!" I shouted down the path at her. "This must be it! 'The Tourist Corporation of Orissa welcomes you to the National Park of Simili. Be gentle on our natural wonders. Take only what you bring! Agun Mazir Tourist Rest House, one kilometer.' Hurray!"

"But supposing it's full?"

"Pol, for God's sake! It won't be."

We started to walk up the path. It was nearly sunset now, and the forest reverberated with the songs of the oncoming night. Toads croaked and geckos chattered; further away, we heard strange whoops and cries. Clouds of insects hung in the air, only dispersing as we pushed our way through the undergrowth; at one point we were surrounded by tiny butterflies which flickered around our faces then suddenly were gone.

Just as I was about to suggest a rest, the dense vegetation gave way to an area of rubbery grass and we were standing in front of a dilapidated wooden bungalow.

"Thank *Christ* for that!" sighed Gemma. "I'm totally, one hundred percent knackered."

We progressed up the overgrown path, only now noticing that an old man dressed in khaki shorts and a string vest was squatting on the veranda peeling potatoes. He was completely bald and very thin, and his skin was brown and puckered. As we approached he looked up and grinned, displaying a single front tooth.

"Namaste!" he cried, putting his hands together and nodding at us enthusiastically.

"Namaste. Do you speak English? . . . Do . . . you . . . have . . . a room?"

For a moment he looked at me quizzically, then he jumped to his feet, nodding vigorously and attempting to take our bags.

"Welcome, welcome! You coming a long time! We wait for you!"

"I don't think you can have . . ."

He ignored this, grabbing us by our elbows and, with an energy almost unseemly for such an apparently frail old man, pulling us inside the bungalow.

"This is your room!" he proclaimed, stepping aside to reveal three beds covered by mosquito nets, a bare stone floor, and, adjoining the room, a small bathroom with a shower and squat toilet.

"How much?"

He shook his head.

"No, madam. It is already paid."

"It can't be. By who?"

I'd already pulled a hundred rupee note from my money belt. I pressed it determinedly into his hand.

"If the room is prebooked, then just say there's been a mistake. We got here first."

For a moment the old man stared at the money. Then he shrugged and closed his fingers around the note. Pointing to himself he said: "Cookie wallah. Mr. P. J. Srinivan."

Gemma pulled off her rucksack and sat down heavily on the bed. The mattress looked lumpy and scratchy, as if filled with straw. As I'd suspected all along, the room did not have an air-conditioner, just a fan which stirred the air lazily above us.

"Does the fan go any faster?" she asked morosely.

Mr. P. J. Srinivan pointed to a box of electric switches next to the door. Worryingly, this was held to the wall by a single, fraying cord.

"Fan, light. On, off," he said unhelpfully.

"So," I said, mouthing the words slowly. "We've come to visit this shrine? Agun Mazir, yes?"

He grinned at me and nodded, his face creasing.

"Yes, yes, madam!"

"Where is it?"

Grabbing my elbow again, he led me out of the bungalow and pointed into the forest. "That way!"

"But how do we find the path? Do we have to go back to the main street?"

"That way!" he shouted, pinching my arm more tightly. "You, memsahib . . ." He nodded in Gemma's direction. "That memsahib, you go to see our Pir Nirulla shrine, yes? That way!"

For a moment, we just looked at him, then suddenly, at exactly the same time, we both laughed out loud.

*   *   *

WE spent the evening washing out our undies and reading under the sallow light of the electric bulb. By now Gemma was halfway through *The Tin Drum,* while I was conscientiously embarking upon a history of postpartition India which had seemed a good idea in the book shop but was now making my eyes swim with boredom. Outside, a determined army of insects buzzed and butted at the wire-netted windows. Occasionally a mosquito would break through the barricades and then we would listen for its whining song and swat it with our hands. Gemma had covered herself with almost an entire tube of insect repellent, yowling as she rubbed it into the rash, and now the whole room smelled of kerosene. Yet still they hovered; all down my arms were the splattered remains of those too drunk on my blood to get away. From time to time a giant brown cockroach scuttled across the floor. I pulled my legs up beneath me, and turning to page five of my book repressed a face-splitting yawn. I didn't wish to imagine what lurked under my bed.

I sat up with a start. Something had woken me—the sound of footsteps on the veranda perhaps, or the creak of an opening door—but now that I was fully conscious the noise had suddenly stopped. I peered around the room in confusion. It must have been nearly dawn, for a diffuse pale light filtered through the bolted shutters and from under my mosquito net I could make out the dim shapes of chairs and tables and Gemma's rucksack, lying upended by the bathroom door.

Slowly the bungalow came into focus. On the floor were the emptied plates of the dinner Mr. P. J. had cooked for us; strung up over the window was a row of underwear and bras. On the table were two empty bottles of Campa Cola and a packet of fags. I sighed, pulling the sheet around my shoulders. Whatever had woken me was gone.

Hearing a grunt from the other bed I peered through the mosquito netting and saw Gemma lying on her back, her arms thrown backward over her head. Very quietly, I pushed aside the netting and swinging my feet onto the wooden floor, leaned over the bed. Gemma was frowning and muttering, her eyes still closed.

"Tell them to wait," Gemma suddenly said. "I've had enough of it."

She seemed to almost sit up, her eyes opening and glaring at me, then shutting again as she collapsed backward, her head tossing from side to side.

"Gemma, sweetie." I put out a hand and touched her arm. "You're having a bad dream . . ."

She turned away from me, rolling onto her side. From the rise and fall of her back, I could see that she was crying.

"Gemma, honey, please . . ."

I reached out again and very gently shook her shoulder. I wanted to help her, to make it all better but I felt so useless. It was the same as always: I knew she was upset but didn't have a clue what to do. She always made it so hard, slipping away from my gauche questions like a silverfish, her responses indecipherable. Ever since that dismal summer of our A-levels there had been something going on, something blocked and swollen beneath the surface of our friendship. She became unreachable that year; skiving off school and walking out of her exams, even though she could have sailed through them with the minimum of revision. I guessed it was connected to her parents' increasingly bitter divorce, yet despite my desire to help I didn't know what to say. I would look into her resentful, closed face and the words which usually flowed so easily suddenly dried. On the rare occasion I tried to broach the subject, my hesitant questions were answered by monosyllables, my awkward comments greeted by grunts. After a while I'd had a bellyful of her sulks, her black, brooding silences. If only I'd acted differently, I keep thinking now; if only I'd been a different kind of friend. Yet I never asked and Gemma never told.

She opened her eyes. Her cheeks were covered by a wet trail of tears and her nose bubbled with snot.

"Hi," she said, looking up at me.

"Are you okay?"

"Never better. Got a hankie?"

"Sure."

I straightened up, still looking into her face. I wanted to say something else, but I didn't know what. All the easy platitudes I could think of—about wonderful changes, just around the corner—were so dishonest. It was obviously Steve who was on her mind. Yet I was too cowardly for the conversation I knew we should have. I started to walk across the room and suddenly, from somewhere outside, heard a crash.

"What was that?"

Very quietly, as if a vehicle was rolling down the hill with its engine turned off, I could hear the trundle of wheels.

"It's a car, or something . . ."

From the veranda there was another bang and then, very distinctly, a loud rap at the door.

As I strode across the room my heart thumped so hard I feared it might leap out of my mouth. When I reached the door I hesitated for a second. My legs felt unaccountably wobbly. Taking a deep breath, I threw open the door.

"I've found you at last!"

Standing on the veranda with the sun rising over the trees behind her was Coral.

11

I stood aside to let Coral in. She was dressed the same as on the train, her bag slung over her shoulders, her long skirt scraping the floor, but something about her had changed. Her body seemed more angular, her eyes, which darted quickly away from mine, more restless.

Walking into the center of the room, she plonked her bag on the floor and sat down heavily on one of the chairs. I remained standing by the door, staring at her in amazement.

"Whew! What a journey!"

"Christ almighty," I heard myself say hoarsely. "How did you know where we were?"

I glanced at Gemma, who was sitting on the edge of her bed grinning with what seemed to be relief. Why did she seem so un-surprised?

"The word for it is serendipity," Coral said, smiling to herself as she rummaged in her bag. "I was hitching a lift with a mate and hey presto, suddenly we saw the signs to Agun Mazir."

"Which we'd told you about in Calcutta," Gemma put in quietly. I stared at her. It was almost as if she was prompting her.

"So where was your friend going?" I said as evenly as I could.

"Jeez, girl, what's with all the questions? Aren't you pleased to see me?"

"Of course." I tried to smile, but not very successfully, I suspect. To be honest I felt as if I'd been punched in the face. Gemma must have secretly invited her, I realized with a pain that seemed to start in my stomach and work its way up to my chest. *That* was why she'd insisted on leaving her that note in Calcutta.

"What's the matter, Esther?" Coral cocked her head at me quizzically. "Still letting India get you down?"

Turning and winking at Gemma she pulled a couple of oranges, a jar of Vegemite, a tub of peanut butter, and a loaf of bread from her bag, all of which she set triumphantly on the table.

"There you go," she said. "My offerings. I have proper, Western-style food, smokes . . ." She threw a packet of Marlboros on the table.

". . . and extremely good dope."

She produced a small brown lump, wrapped in plastic.

"Not bad, eh?"

We gazed greedily at her supplies. Since we had been living off dhal, eggs, and chapatis for the last few days the prospect of something different made my stomach gurgle expectantly. I was also craving a proper cigarette. I picked up the packet, glancing down at it as I turned it over in my hands. "Duty Free Goods: not for resale" read the label on the bottom; the rest of the writing was in Arabic. Scrumpling the wrapper eagerly, I pulled out a fag. Coral picked up an orange.

"Do you want one, Gem? They're real beauts."

I winced. It was silly, but no one, other than me, called Gemma "Gem."

Gemma took the orange, tearing at it with her teeth. I watched her in disgruntled silence. Why had she arranged this behind my back rather than simply telling me that Coral would make her own way here? Was I *that* difficult to talk to?

"So," said Coral, looking at me. "Are you back on track?"

I stared at her, unable to think of an appropriate reply.

"Yeah," I eventually said. "We've been having a fantastic time."

"Doing all the temple-gazing sightseeing scene?"

"Pretty much."

"It's so easy here, doing all that stuff. It's like, set up for tourists? Jeez, you shoulda been in Cambodia. Like, you had to kinda get across these landmines before you could see the temples? It's *really* heavy. But when you get there, they're mind-blowing . . ."

I folded my arms. Despite my own quest for authenticity, I hated macho travelers who took pride in visiting places which on some undeclared scale had been judged "difficult," or "heavy." In Egypt I'd met several: a hefty American in khaki shorts who claimed to have hitchhiked through Iran and insisted on speaking what was clearly appalling Arabic with waiters whose English was in comparison quite fluent, and later in Luxor a stroppy Londoner who had been in Gaza and lectured me for several hours on the Palestinian cause. The company of both men bored and threatened me in varying degrees. Neither seemed to have enjoyed or been inspired by their experiences in a way that I could understand. Their stories were instead a claim for status, a way of pulling rank.

"Maybe I'll move further east after India," I said.

Coral nodded. "You'd like Thailand," she said. "That's kinda a softer option, you know?"

I swallowed. "So," I said, trying to sound casual, "how did you know where we'd be staying?"

Pulling a match from Gemma's box, Coral struck it with one sure swipe, then leaned over to light my cigarette.

"Wow!" laughed Gemma. "You must have the knack."

"Well, there's only one place you coulda been," Coral was saying. "That's what I figured."

I couldn't force myself to return her easy smile.

"For God's sake," Gemma suddenly said. "What's with the Spanish Inquisition? It's just great that Coral's made it!"

Jumping off the bed, she hopped across the uneven floorboards to where Coral was sitting and kissed her on the cheek. Then, still not looking at me, she sat down on the other chair.

"This looks great," she said, reaching out for the bread and tearing off a chunk. "I was getting really sick of chapatis."

"What about you, Esther?" said Coral. "Aren't you going to have any?"

I shook my head. "Nah, I'm not hungry," I said, pulling my dress over my head. "I'm going for a walk."

As soon as I was outside I stood with my back against the wooden walls of the bungalow, sniffing at the warm morning air as I struggled to regain my composure. From the veranda I could see trees, the sweep of forested hills opposite, and, about half a mile below, the tops of village buildings. Frail lines of smoke rose up above the roofs: beneath me, the chulas were being lit for breakfast.

I took a deep breath and started to walk down the hill. It was ridiculous, but I was inexplicably upset by Coral's reappearance. Perhaps it was just jealousy, I told myself, for she was disquietingly close to how, in my secret fantasies of India, I'd imagined myself becoming. And it was hardly her fault that she was the more seasoned traveler. Yet there was more to it than that: I recounted the previous conversation, trying to discover the source of my irritation, and realized with a rush of angry recognition that it had involved an almost endless series of putdowns. What was it that she'd said about Thailand? That it would be a *softer* option, the cow.

And then there was the little matter of Gemma not telling me she was coming. I kicked at a stone lying in my path and it flew up into the air, hitting an overhanging branch with a ping. She must have revealed our plans after our row in Calcutta, I thought darkly. She'd done it deliberately.

But why would Gemma keep Coral's intentions secret? I picked up another stone, this time lobbing it into the trees. The missile smashed into a tree trunk with a crack, causing its branches to shudder and a flock of brightly colored birds to rise squawking into the air. Somewhere, not far away, I could hear the whoop and chatter of monkeys. I took a deep breath, forcing my mind to shift gear.

"Calm down, Esther," I whispered to myself. "It's not important."

I looked out over the trees. It didn't really matter if Gemma had invited Coral, I told myself; it was pathetic to feel so betrayed, for she was a friend, not a lover. At this word, my stomach gave a sudden, sickening jolt. It was me who was guilty of dishonesty, I thought disgustedly, not her; so why was I behaving so enviously? Did I have to be the top dog the entire time? I turned back up the path, no longer able to bear my own company. Coral's unexpected appearance was probably just a miscommunication rather than a deliberate secret, certainly not worth another fight. After all, I should be pleased that Gemma was becoming more outgoing. And so what if Coral got on my nerves? I'd only have to put up with her for another few days. Taking another breath and brushing my hair out of my face, I turned and walked back toward the bungalow.

By the time I reached the guest house, the table was covered in orange peel and the room fuggy with the heavy herbal aroma of marijuana.

"Esther! Where've you been? We've got the munchies. Come and eat some of this before we finish it all!"

Shuffling up, Gemma made room for my bottom on her

chair. We sat clumsily together, our thighs touching, our arms around each other's shoulders: a vision of intimacy. I glanced at her uneasily. How had things got so complicated between us? We'd been best friends since the age of five: our blood pricked and mixed, the oath of loyalty taken. Back in those days we lived in each other's gardens, spent whole summers together: swing ball, messing around with bikes, make-believe ponies leaping over jumps constructed out of crates, that kind of stuff. Inseparable, that's what our mothers said we were: the terrible twins. But somehow it'd all got snarled up in these concealed jealousies and insecurities and necessary truths that neither of us dared voice.

Sharing the seat was agonizingly uncomfortable. After a minute or so I stood up again.

"We were just talking, like, about Pir Nirulla?" Gemma said, rolling another joint.

Coral leaned back in her chair, her eyes fixed to my face.

"I didn't know how famous he was. Coral's been telling me all this stuff?"

I raised my eyebrows enquiringly. Was it just me, or was Gemma beginning to acquire an Australian accent?

"Like, the shrine has these really strong powers?"

Coral took the joint from Gemma's lips and dragged at it.

"Give us a puff," I said. They didn't seem to hear.

Coral inhaled deeply. "You know that people come to the mela from all over India?" she was saying. "And further, too. He's, like, one of the top guys."

She looked at me knowledgeably: the Wise One, lecturing her disciples. How come she was suddenly so well informed? Okay, so she'd been in India for "five years" and had experienced "heavy stuff" in Cambodia, but this was *my* adventure, not hers, I thought with a fresh blast of exasperation. *I* was the one who had originally found out about Pir Nirulla and planned to visit his shrine, yet now she was suddenly some kind of world authority on the subject.

I sucked at my teeth, trying to appear indifferent.

"So why's this place so small?" I said quietly.

Coral shrugged. "Outward appearances aren't everything. Things aren't on the surface here, like in the West. They're deeper, more hidden. You know?"

"No." I stared into her inscrutable eyes, overtaken with hot dislike. Of course I *knew*. It was the whole reason I'd wanted to come to India: to push myself to the boundaries, to discover an alternative way of being alive. But I was damned if I was going to be patronized by her.

"Don't you believe in transformation?"

I looked at her grudgingly. Why did she think I'd traveled all this way? For a sun tan? And why was Gemma staring at her so reverentially?

"Well, yeah, I suppose so . . ." I said at last.

"Like, take me. The deeper I go, the more I leave my old self behind. You can start out being Esther, or Gemma, from England, and end up being someone completely different. That's why we journey, isn't it? To change things?"

"But only if you know how," Gemma suddenly put in. "It's too easy, isn't it, to just make it into a game?"

"Too right."

Taking a last drag, Coral finally passed the joint to me. I put it between my lips and inhaled, relieved that the lecture was finally over. The dope was even stronger than the stuff in Calcutta. As I took the smoke down the top of my skull felt as if it was about to detach itself from the rest of my head.

"Jesus!" I said, trying not to cough. "That is *so* strong."

"I got it in Puri. In this government shop. Like, it's legal there?"

"You're kidding!" Gemma looked at Coral animatedly, her eyes gleaming with admiration.

"Sure, straight up. It's for the fakirs and temple wallahs. But they'll sell it to anyone."

"Well, it certainly does the biz."

I took another long drag. Now my whole head felt as if it was about to explode. Around me, the room was starting to blur. I focused resolutely on the table.

"Transformation," Coral suddenly said. "That's what it's all about. It's also why I've got a new name. Because the journey is only just beginning."

I sucked at the spliff. I'd nearly reached the roach now, and the smoldering paper was burning my lips. I squinted at her, feeling my face grow hot and cross once more.

"What are you talking about?"

Smiling serenely, she looked into my face. "Well, sister, it's like this. Up in the mountains, where I've been living, I'm not known as Coral. I'm Santi. That's my spiritual name. It's, like, I'm at peace. And that's the name they've given me—you know, as a disciple?"

I stared at her uncomprehendingly. For a moment her words made complete sense, and then—like a pile of balls being juggled in the air—they suddenly collapsed.

"You mean, you've got two names?" I said slowly. My voice was beginning to sound strange now: too slurred and then suddenly too quick. Next to me, Coral had started to roll another joint.

"Sure. My guru gave the new one to me."

She gazed at me for a moment, then started to laugh. Next to her, Gemma was chuckling, too. They knew something I didn't, I thought wildly; they were in league. That was it. The whole thing was a plot against me. I stared wildly at Coral and then at Gemma, my palms sweating. It was definitely a trap. Then Coral lit the joint, put it to her lips, and suddenly I understood. It was all perfectly fine. They were as stoned as me.

We smoked in silence. My thoughts kept tumbling into strange images and sequences, then I'd remember where I was, and rein them in again. I imagined we were on a train, then jerked back into reality. Staring at the top of the table, I was suddenly engrossed by the pattern in the grainy wood. There were faces there, I thought, and they were watching me. I dragged my eyes away and suddenly saw Gemma and Coral exchange glances and collapse into another bout of giggling. They seemed a very long way away.

Then suddenly everything was normal and Coral was saying something completely mundane about the heat and passing the joint onto me. I took it from her, puffed at it for what felt like about an hour but was probably only thirty seconds, and passed it onto Gemma. My mind kept slithering into nonsense. I could feel my mouth hanging open, my hands lying like lumps of stone in my lap. I stared at Gemma and then at Coral and suddenly realized that their faces had changed. In fact, they were no longer human. They had turned into lizards.

"Arrrrghh!"

"What?"

I jumped up, caught my feet in the bottom of the chair, and half fell across the table.

"You . . ." I looked up at Gemma. She had turned back into a person again; her hair flopping over her face, her eyes small and bloodshot. Everything was perfectly, one-hundred-percent fine; I was just stoned.

"Gem . . ."

The words clogged in my mouth, like sodden balls of cotton wool. And now Gemma and Coral were looking at each other in slow motion and laughing hysterically, their faces contorted, the veins on their necks standing out.

"You're off your head," said Gemma eventually.

"I'm fine."

I blinked at her in confusion. Was that really all this was about?

"So why did you scream like that?"

"I don't know . . ."

"Perhaps the dope is, like, too powerful for you?" Coral was saying. She glanced at Gemma, and once again something seemed to pass between them.

"What are you saying?"

"*Nothing.* Jesus, Esther. You've really got the paranoias. You need to lie down."

"Like I said, I'm fine."

I picked up the water bottle, held it unsteadily to my mouth, and took a long drink. This was horrible: how had I allowed myself to get in such a state? In fact, I now remembered with fleeting lucidity, I'd never enjoyed getting stoned. Ever since my twenty-first birthday—when I'd got so off my head that I could only crawl around my room mewing—I'd vowed to never touch the stuff again. Speed and coke were more my things: I liked to be able to dance and talk all night, to feel alive, not as if my mind was mired in thick, gloopy glue.

"I'm going down to the village," said Coral, standing up. "There's someone I gotta call."

"Then after that, we'll go for an explore, yeah?"

She looked back at Gemma and winked. "Sure thing. Catch you later!"

Picking up her bag, she walked out of the bungalow. I could hear her footsteps on the veranda and then, a few moments later, crunching down the path. She must be used to the Orissan dope, I thought, for she seemed completely sober.

Gemma and I sat opposite each other at the table, staring into space. There was a prolonged silence which seemed to become increasingly laden with meaning, then I leaned over and picked up a slice of bread, and everything shifted again. Gemma's eyes were closed, I realized. The silence meant nothing for she was as out of it as me. I stuffed the bread into my mouth. It was claggy and tasteless, like cardboard.

Now was the time to clear the air, I thought. I'd tell Gemma I didn't mind about Coral joining us and perhaps she would explain why she hadn't informed me of her plans. We would reassert our bond. If only I wasn't so stoned.

"So," I said after some more time. "It's nice that Coral's here, isn't it?"

"Uh-huh."

She gazed at me noncommittally. I paused, looking at her through the blue smoke. She was scratching at her arms and looking vacantly across the room, her eyes red and heavy lidded.

"Did you tell her where we were going to be?" I suddenly said. I knew it wasn't the way I should have phrased it, but the words just popped out of my mouth. Gemma looked up, her face defensive.

"No."

She was staring at me now, her expression suddenly sharp and focused. Why had I thought she was stoned?

"So how did she find us?" I muttered.

"What's the big deal?"

It was too late. Everything was slowing down again.

"I just . . . thought . . ."

"Uh-huh . . ."

". . . that we'd agreed . . ."

There was a long, unbearable silence.

". . . not to."

Gemma smiled. Or was it a grimace? I no longer had a clue.

"Gem . . ." I said slowly.

She looked up. I was struggling for words, aware that it would be better to say nothing, yet unable to stop myself.

"Is everything . . ."

Another long silence.

"You know . . ."

"What?"

". . . Okay?"

"Okay?"

"I mean . . . Like, you know . . "

She was gazing at me, her pupils so small they had virtually disappeared. Suddenly I felt inspired. This was the wrong way to proceed. I should stop going on about Coral, it just riled her. What I should do was just give her a big hug and tell her how much I loved her. Perhaps she thought I was still upset about the money belt. I gazed at her, fleetingly convinced that this was all it would take.

"I, like, do love you," I announced. But even as I said it my heart sank.

Gemma blinked. Then her hands flew up over her face, she rocked back in her chair and she howled with laughter again.

12

AFTER about an hour of fumbling around the bungalow we eventually set off for the village. The outside air made me feel better. I took a deep breath, trying to focus on the sky and the trees. We'd only smoked two or three joints, I kept telling myself. It surely wouldn't take long for the effects to wear off. And the scene with Gemma—that was just because I was stoned, nothing more.

We found Coral sitting on the sidewalk outside the post office, pretending to sort through her bag as a large group of young men ogled at the strange spectacle of a bare-armed, blond-haired Western woman.

"Jesus," she said, standing up with relief as we approached. "Anyone would think I'd come from Mars."

"Well, I guess that in some ways you have." I smiled at her. To be honest I was pleased to see her looking so flustered. And I really was beginning to feel more normal. The only remaining effects of the spliffs were slightly blurred vision and the impression that everything around me had slowed down.

"Did you make your call okay?"

"Nah. It was hopeless. Apparently all the connections from here are really dodgy."

We started walking down the high street, the onlookers following close behind. Their gaze made my back tighten self-consciously. I was wearing a long dress that I'd assumed would be appropriate for visiting a religious site, but it was so hot that the thin material was clinging to my body. Wherever I looked men were watching. One spotty youth was walking so close that I could feel the soft brush of his fingers on my thighs. I glared back at him.

"Fuck off," I muttered, only half expecting him to hear or understand. He blinked at me in surprise, then his eyes dipped away from my face and he was gone.

"What shall we do now?" said Gemma, looking at Coral. "Shall we try and find this famous, world-transforming shrine?"

Her face shone with excitement, I noticed resentfully, as if now that Coral was involved, she thought it was the best idea ever.

"I asked about it at the post office," Coral replied. "There was this sweet old guy, who said it was on his family's land, or something? You go down that path there, into the forest, and it's a kilometer or so down the track."

"Come on then, let's do it."

I followed somewhat unsteadily as Coral and Gemma strode across the street, stepping over the open drains which gurgled at the edge of the jagged pavement. The crowd of onlookers had dispersed now, the place settling back into its normal routine like water smoothing after the rippling disturbance of a skidding stone. Rickshaws creaked past, their drivers whistling; children spilled shrieking from the gates of the school; a bus roared through, honking its horn at the stray dogs which lay nonchalantly in the road. Everything was one-hundred-percent hunky-dory, I kept telling myself; we were going to look for the shrine, stay the night in the bungalow, then head off. It was true that everything was oddly muffled, but it was just the residues of the dope; soon it would wear off.

When we reached the junction we stopped, shielding our eyes from the sun and looking around. The path led down the hill into dense forest. Beside a small, red-splattered effigy of Ganesh at its opening, there was no sign that it was anything more than a track for cattle or goats.

"It doesn't look right to me. It's too small."

"Ah well, let's take a look and see."

Coral edged past, smiling at me and squeezing my arm.

"At least those guys aren't following us anymore," she whispered. "Your stare-out tactic seems to have worked."

I glanced at her in surprise. As I gazed into her large blue eyes, the animosity which had enveloped me like a rank shroud all morning fell away. Why had I felt so hostile? As we stood together in swift and unexpected solidarity, I could no longer remember.

We set off down the path, which wound through the tangled trees. For a few final moments we remained under the bright sun, then the canopy closed above us and the world turned green, the few rays of light which penetrated the thick roof falling to the dank ground in dusty, insect-buzzing spirals. For a second or so I was disoriented; I rubbed at my eyes, trying to concentrate on keeping my feet moving. I was beginning to feel strange again.

We walked further into the forest. In some places the track was crossed by a stream; in others it disintegrated into a bog and we had to pick our way through the mud, holding our skirts up with our fingers. Despite the shade it was greenhouse hot, the humidity rising up over the path in steamy clouds.

After about five minutes Gemma suddenly stopped. Sighing heavily, she tucked the hem of her dress into her underwear.

"Bollocks, it's *suffocating*."

She turned to Coral, assuming her to be the leader. "Are you positive this is right?"

"Sure it is. We just have to trust."

"And these little sods, like, keep biting my face?"

I looked at her. Her T-shirt was sticking sweatily to her back and shoulders, her cheeks shiny.

"But thank the Gods for the insect repellent, Gem?" Coral was saying.

"Yeah, but it itches like buggery."

I opened my mouth. I wanted to say something affectionate, something to reassert my place as Gemma's closest friend, but all I could think of was that she'd used so much of the stuff that she smelled like a petrol bomb. The moment seemed to last forever and then we were trudging on and my opportunity to speak had gone.

We reached a small glade and stopped, panting and peering around in search of the track. Above us a small colony of monkeys perched in the branches, apparently oblivious to our intrusion. They were eating some kind of exotic fruit which they stuffed greedily into their mouths, spitting the chewed peel onto the ground like delinquent children. They were remarkably beautiful, I thought as I stared up at them: their eyes as expressive and meaningful as any human's. Why had I never noticed that before? In fact I was so transfixed by the incredible and profound spirituality of the one nearest to me that I was unable to move another step.

"I mean, like, how could this be the path to a major shrine?" Gemma suddenly said. I was *right,* I thought with a flash of lucidity. She *was* talking like Coral. I started and the monkey was gone, leaping across the tree in a single elegant bound. Next to me Gemma was wiping her forehead with the back of her hand.

"It's too small!" She looked at me petulantly, her face glistening.

"It's just a monkey," I whispered.

"Just stay with it," Coral was cooing at her now. "It, like, *has* to be right."

Uncharacteristically, Gemma simply smiled at her and shrugged. "You're the boss."

There was a long pause which seemed to last another hour. Then I was staring at a leaf, watching a tiny red spider crawl across it. It must seem such a vast terrain to a creature so small, I thought in amazement, my little finger a towering mountain.

"Let's just go around one more bend," I heard Coral say. "And if we can't see it we'll head back, right?"

Gemma nodded.

"Okay."

"Look," I said thickly, "there's a spider! And it's so small! Isn't it incredible?"

Gemma hunched her back, not looking at me.

"All I think is that it's too hot."

We continued to batter our way through the vegetation. This time I went first in the mistaken belief that if I kept walking I would sober up. The path seemed to be growing progressively narrow, the overhanging creepers so thick in places that I had to bash them back with a stick. I wished I was wearing heavier shoes; a few meters earlier I'd noticed a large leech clinging to a buttress root; I didn't like to think what might be happening to my ankles. I stumbled on, whistling loudly to try to make myself feel better. The path turned another bend.

"Just one more, and then we'll go back," I muttered, even though Coral and Gemma were lagging far behind, walking so slowly that they seemed on the verge of giving up. I glanced back at them and started to trudge toward the final bend which curled out of sight down the hill, all the time taking deep inhalations of air in order to get more oxygen to my brain. Over the last few minutes my thoughts had started to become jumbled again. I kept imagining I was at home: the long roots which hung from the canopy of trees the curtains of my childhood bedroom, the leafy ground the thick, shag-pile carpet. It should have been easy: we were in the forest, looking for the shrine, but I kept forgetting where I was. I could feel the brush of leaves against my face, and very distantly, the mutter of Gemma's and Coral's voices, but everything else had grown silent, as if I was walking through a tunnel. I took another gulp of air, turned the final corner, and suddenly I was standing at the opening of a large clearing.

Bright sunlight streamed relentlessly through the broken canopy. I blinked, trying to steady myself as I gazed around. It was the shrine, I saw with a jolt. That was what I was meant to be looking for and that was what I had found.

And there it was, directly ahead of me: a huge stone edifice, rising from the undergrowth like the battered hull of a wrecked ship. The forest was on the verge of claiming it, for creepers and ivy had spread across its crumbling stone walls, in places pulling it down so successfully that all that remained of the original construction was a pile of mossy rubble. On the other side of the walls, I realized as I took a few hesitant steps toward it, was the actual tomb. When I reached them I pushed the thick foliage back with my fingers and saw the faded outlines of stars, a crescent moon, and Arabic lettering inscribed into the soft, lichen-covered stone. Beyond this lay a slab of what seemed to be deep red granite, on top of which someone had placed a large garland, its once white flowers now brown and rotting. Surrounding the shrine, long poles festooned with ragged silk flags were stuck into the ground; although there was no discernible breeze, they rustled as they moved gently to and fro. On the other side of the clearing was a small pool of water encircled by coconut trees. Opposite this, a track led into the undergrowth to a small whitewashed mosque.

The clearing was strangely still. I stepped into the pool of light, sniffing the hot air. For a moment I couldn't place the heavy scent, then I noticed a stick of incense smoldering in a small brass pot on the ground. Someone must have been here very recently, but now the place was deserted, so quiet that all I could hear was my own soft breath and the rustle of leaves. On the path I had been feeling slurred and dreamy but now I was wide awake, my skin prickling with unease. Something was wrong, I thought; this was not a good place to be.

Suddenly, behind me, a coconut plopped into the pool. I started and spun round. It must have been the shape of branches against the light, or my own befuddled eyes, but for a moment, as I glanced at the trees on the other side of the tomb, I thought I saw a figure dart between the trunks. I peered into the dappled light, my pulse quickening. Perhaps it was just an animal in the undergrowth, but there had been a strange cry, too, a shout of anger or of pain.

From the path I could hear footsteps and, as they rounded the corner, Coral's and Gemma's voices.

"Jeez, we've finally found it!" Coral said loudly, striding past me to the side of the tomb where she laid her hands on the stone wall and took a deep, exaggerated breath.

"Oh yeah," she said softly. "Yeah, I can really feel the energy."

Closing her eyes, she took another breath and sank slowly to her knees, her head bowed as if in prayer. I stared at her, dimly registering how pretentious she was being; I must have imagined the man, I was thinking. It was an illusion, brought on by the heat and the dope.

Next to me, Gemma sat down heavily on the grass.

"I'm knackered and thirsty and I've had enough."

"Let's just go back," I said in a strange, slurred voice. "This place gives me the creeps."

She ignored me.

"Look, there's a pool of water!"

Hauling herself up, she hurried over to the pool. Before I could formulate the words to stop her, she had placed her cupped hands into the water and was drinking from it.

"Gemma, you're mad!"

She looked around at me crossly. She was pouring the water over her head now, her purple hair plastered over her forehead as the moisture trickled down her face. Perhaps she and Coral had planned the whole thing, I thought wildly, just to frighten me. Perhaps it was all some kind of weird joke.

"I'm going back," I eventually managed to say.

"And I'm going to have a rest and a little snooze."

With a loud sigh she closed her eyes and collapsed onto her back. As I stared at her I was suddenly overcome by a crawling sense of dread. The place was evil, I thought; there was something or somebody who did not want us here. Unable to speak another word, I turned and ran back up the path.

The forest closed around me. I kept glancing over my shoulder, irrationally convinced that I was being followed. When I reached the first hairpin bend I stopped and looked back. I could just about make out the stone hulk of the shrine, the coconut trees, and even the tops of Gemma's and Coral's heads. They seemed to be kneeling on the ground, as if in prayer. From the canopy above there was a sudden commotion and a flock of rainbow birds lifted into the air. It meant nothing, but in my paranoid confusion I gasped, lurching forward at the bushes to steady myself, then ran as fast as I could back up the hill. From inside the dark interior of the trees, other unknowable beasts chattered.

I stumbled on, my fear only beginning to subside when I reached the glade where I'd seen the monkeys. I had been running for five or ten minutes now, and with the humidity and heat I was exhausted. Finally I stopped, putting my hands on my knees and panting as the sweat dripped from my face onto the grass below. The figure in the trees was a hallucination, I kept telling myself; I was still stoned, it was as simple as that. At last I dropped onto the floor, relaxing as the heat caressed me, coaxing me away from reality, toward the promise of sleep. After a moment I closed my eyes, but just as the image of trees and the tomb started to blur into something else I sat up with a start. I'd heard another scream, this time coming from the direction of the clearing.

Jumping to my feet in alarm, I peered down the hill. There seemed to be a flurry of movement in the trees, the branches rustling and shaking as if something was trapped inside. Perhaps there was human habitation hidden from the track or perhaps I was confused again but for a few brief moments I smelled the smoldering, acrid smell of burning.

I held my breath, my heart hammering. There it was once more: the cry I'd heard at the shrine.

"Gemma?"

Turning back to the path I began to jog back down it, my voice rising in panic. This time I was sure something was there.

"Gemma? Are you there?"

There was no reply, just the whispering of trees and distant cry of birds.

"Gemma! Coral!"

I was almost at the first hairpin bend now. Through the trees, I could still glimpse the tomb. Beside it, I noticed now, Gemma and Coral were standing up and walking across the clearing. They seemed to be moving very slowly.

And then it happened. There was a roar, like the sound of gas rushing into a hot-air balloon, and a terrible, animal scream. For a second there was silence, as if the whole forest was holding its breath, then suddenly a ball of flames came bursting through the trees. I stared at it numbly for a moment, then sucked at the air in shock, my legs almost giving way. What I could see in the clearing beneath me was a human figure, its arms flailing, its torso and head surrounded by leaping flames.

I must have screamed. I lurched forward, my feet slipping.

"Coral! *Gemma!*"

They were nowhere to be seen. I was running back to the shrine now, screaming hysterically.

"For God's sake, where are you?"

And then, as if nothing had happened, Gemma and Coral appeared around the corner. They were walking up the path, their arms linked.

"Wow," Coral was saying as they reached me. "That sure is an amazing place. What a vibe."

I gazed at them, dumbfounded.

"What's the matter?" Gemma said. She was regarding me unsympathetically, blinking and shielding her eyes as she stepped into a stream of light pouring through the tree tops.

"What's the *matter*? Did you see that guy?"

She looked up at me blankly. "What guy?"

"Didn't you see? There was man . . . in the clearing . . ."

She folded her arms, unimpressed. "We didn't see anyone."

"But there was a man! I just saw this man, on fire . . . !"

"There wasn't anyone," Gemma said quietly. Behind her, Coral was staring at me. She had scratches on her arms, I noticed, and the bottom of her sarong was torn. Unlike Gemma, who was frowning censoriously, her mouth was hanging slightly open, her eyes wide.

"What do you mean, on fire?" she whispered almost reverentially.

"He was burning . . . he came out of the trees . . ."

Gemma stared at me silently. *She doesn't believe me,* I realized. She thinks it's because I'm stoned.

"There's nothing there," she said firmly.

I followed her gaze. The figure had disappeared. There was no lingering smoke and no sign of a fire; from what I could see, the grass wasn't even singed.

"Shit, there's a stone in my shoe."

She crouched down, presumably to pick it out, and as she bent over, I saw that the wispy hair at the nape of her head was singed black. I must have shrieked again because she and Coral both jumped back a fraction, like horses shying at a sudden noise.

"What's happened to your hair? Look! Oh, Christ, Gem, it's *black*!"

She put her hand to her neck.

"What are you going on about?"

"It's all burned."

"What do you mean, it's all burned?"

Her fingers came back with a clump of charred hair.

"How did that happen?"

"I told you I *saw* something . . ."

She paused, looking at the hair in her hand and then up at Coral's face.

"It must have been that match I lit," Gemma said slowly. Coral was still staring at the charred hair. "When we had that fag."

"I don't remember," Coral whispered.

"Of course you do. The bugger flew off. Remember?"

"It must have got caught in your hair . . ."

I stared at them. Gemma seemed irritated, her eyes screwed up against the light, her cheeks hot; Coral, for some reason, was smiling. Then, very slowly, Gemma leaned over and put her hand on my shoulder. For perhaps a second she looked into my face. Possibly it was longer. I couldn't tell, for time suddenly slowed and as our eyes met something passed across her face

which I'd never seen there before. Was it an assumption of supe-
riority, or something closer to triumph? Whatever it was, I did
not like it. I flicked my eyes away.

"The thing is," she said gently, "you really are very stoned."

"I mean, like, it's a powerful place?" Coral was saying now.
"I could tell from the moment I walked into the glade it was really, really heavy."

"You don't believe me," I whispered to Gemma.

"I just think you need to go back to the bungalow and sleep
it off," Gemma said slowly, as patiently as if she was talking to
an errant child. "Look, think about it rationally. All that's happened is that I set my hair alight with a match. You've just
smoked too much dope. It never agrees with you, does it?"

I shook my head. I felt empty, drained of every emotion, utterly alone. "Okay," I said eventually. "I guess you're right."

13

CORAL and Gemma linked arms and strode up the track as I trailed slowly behind. From time to time the breeze carried snatches of their conversation down the hill. I heard Coral say, "Focus your energies," missed Gemma's quieter reply, and then caught the word "Esther" and the muffled sound of laughter.

I felt overwhelmingly anxious. Perhaps Gemma was right and in my stoned state I had hallucinated the burning figure, but I was *sure* I'd seen it. I took one careful step after another. Now that I was moving away from the clearing I felt completely sober. My head was clear, my reactions normal. Could I really have imagined it? If there had been a fire, there would have been smoke, yet when I had looked back at the shrine the air was clear. And Coral and Gemma said they'd seen nothing. It *must* have been a mirage, I decided, a trick of the light.

Yet it wasn't just the illusion of the burning man that was making me feel so desolate. As Coral and Gemma disappeared up the track, I brooded over my increasing sense of isolation. It was as if *I* was the stranger, and Gemma and Coral the old friends; they'd been giggling at me in the bungalow, and even now, when I was clearly shaken and upset, seemed intent on ignoring me. Gemma, in particular, had been completely dismissive. I picked my way miserably over the stony path, no longer attempting to catch up. It was almost as if she didn't want me around.

Finally the path came out on the main road. There was no sign of the others. I turned dejectedly onto the sidewalk. Gemma was obviously angry with me, I thought miserably, yet as usual she refused to express it directly. It was the same old pattern. When she flunked her A-levels and I did better than expected, she didn't ring me for weeks; when I took up my place at Sussex she withdrew from our friendship for almost a year, leaving my letters unanswered and only visiting once. Even then she was in such a sulk that she caught the train back to Stevenage early rather than party with my new friends. And now there was this thing with Steve. But how could she know about that? It was my terrible, shameful secret.

I sniffed, trying not to cry. Since I'd kissed him that rainy evening three weeks ago, I felt as if I was dragging a great sack of guilt behind me. I pictured my betrayal as a dismembered body: the bulk of flesh massing at the bottom of the sack, the hessian stained a sticky, reddy brown. I wanted to dispose of it quietly, forget the whole thing, but every day it grew heavier, the stench from its contents more overwhelming. What I had to do was confess, I knew; but I didn't have the courage. And what could I say to absolve my guilt? That I hadn't meant it to happen? That I wanted her to be happy, for it to all work out? The truth was that even though Gemma had been giving me blow-by-blow accounts of her every encounter with Steve for the last six months, I'd flirted with him from the first moment we met.

I couldn't bear to think about it. I stared at the battered post office, the dusty window of the pharmacy next door, but still couldn't prevent the image of Gemma sitting in the pub that night from forcing its way back into my thoughts. She'd been squeezed up next to him, her thighs touching his, and they were laughing. When she saw me she waved eagerly, beckoning me over. She thought of him as hers, I suppose, and she wanted to show him off. She'd lost weight, and was wearing pink lipstick and, under her battered suede jacket, a pair of tight jeans.

"This," she said proudly, "is Steve."

And there he was. I'd been expecting a slightly improved version of the other boyfriends she'd produced over the last few years: no-hoper slobs, to the last man, all of whom had managed to hurt her in ways I found impossible to comprehend. She was so manifestly their superior, and yet she always let them take the upper hand. Like Gary, the so-called "thrash guitarist" who had acne and a runny nose and who got off with someone else in front of her at an R.E.M. gig for which she'd supplied the tickets. Or Neil, the creepy manager of the pub where she sometimes worked, who'd sacked her the day after he'd bizarrely told her that making love to her was like sleeping with his granny.

But from the moment I glimpsed him from the other side of the pub, I knew Steve was different: not a spotty creep, but jaw-droppingly good-looking, with a mass of dark hair, amused brown eyes I could have gazed into all evening, and beautiful, strong hands I wanted to reach out and grasp. And what was my first, shameful thought as I saw them sitting and laughing together? Not that Gemma had chosen well, or that I should be sisterly and try to help her in her quest for his affections. No, what I thought—even as I pushed the disloyal words hastily from my mind—was that she was aiming far too high, that she'd never be able to get a guy like this.

"Hi."

I smiled at him, glancing guiltily away from his eyes. But just by the way he took my hand and moved over for me, I knew that he fancied me, too.

And now I was in this terrible mess. I walked more quickly, resolutely ignoring the men who milled around me. Why had it had to happen? Despite his good looks he was, after all, just an ordinary Stevenage bloke with a penchant for motorbikes and the Smiths, who'd flunked his A-levels and now wanted to work with the mentally ill. And yet I couldn't stop myself from being drawn to him, for he had another quality which I'd never yet encountered in a man his age, a grounded certainty about life, some kind of internal calm which made all the others seem like little boys.

And yet Gemma thought of him as hers. Even if, so far, he'd done no more than kiss her goodnight—an event she had related in detail to me several times—she was convinced that their relationship was a fait accompli. She was obsessed with him, talked about him all the time, told me this was really "it."

And what had I done to avert the inevitable? Absolutely nothing. I carried on meeting them in the pub, night after night. Of course I knew what was about to happen; I'd had enough experience of men to recognize the signs. But unlike all those other dalliances, when I'd been unable to let myself go, with Steve I was unable to stop the feelings which sprang up so suddenly between us. All those rapidly appearing shoots, the spreading, fertile green which pushed my qualms aside, taking root. I just stood and watched them grow. And one evening, when Gemma had conveniently left the pub early, I gave him my number. He called the very next day, just as I knew he would. I should have taken the situation in hand there and then, feigned disinterest or an absent boyfriend but instead I pretended to myself that it was all part of Gemma's campaign, that Steve and I would meet and what we'd discuss was her. And even after he'd spent all day walking with me in the woods and not mentioned Gemma once, still I didn't come clean. And then finally, when Mum and Dad were out, I let him come around and kiss me and tell me how he'd never even remotely fancied Gemma.

And what had I done to help my best friend? I'd kissed him

back. I'd betrayed her, I thought bitterly. I'd taken the only man she'd ever really wanted and didn't even have the decency to tell her. Instead, I'd carried on as if nothing had happened.

WHEN I reached the bungalow I found Gemma lying on top of her bed, her arms outstretched under the fan's halfhearted flutter, her eyes closed. I stared at her for a moment, listening to her snuffly snoring. I could put it off no longer, I decided. We *had* to talk about Steve. That was the cause of all this hostility; like a throbbing abscess, it had to be removed. When she woke up I'd tell her the truth. I glanced away from her, trying to think of what I'd say, and suddenly jumped back with a gasp.

Crouching in the other, darker corner of the room, was a figure.

"Christ almighty!"

It was Coral. As my eyes readjusted to the light I saw that she was sitting in the lotus position, her clothes strewn untidily around the room. She looked better with them on; in her angular pose the bones jutted uncomfortably from her thin brown skin and her hard, rubbery tits seemed even flatter.

"What are you doing?"

She opened her eyes and jumped up. "It's you!"

"Who else did you expect?"

I stared into her face. Her pupils were dilated and her eyes kept darting across the room to the door, as if she was expecting it to open. She looked back at me and suddenly smiled, her eyes creasing up, her white teeth small and sharp.

"No one. I was just meditating."

"Why have you taken off all your clothes?"

"My skin needed to breathe."

Behind her, she groped for her dress. When she found it she pulled it on over her head.

"It doesn't, like, offend you? I thought you guys would be cool."

"No, it's fine."

She took a step toward me. Instinctively, I took a step back.

"Sister," she said softly. "Let me touch you."

Before I could stop her, she'd reached out and placed the tip of her finger on my cheek. I swallowed uncomfortably. I wanted to jerk my face away, but then she'd see how embarrassed I was. She was gazing into my face.

"So you felt it, too?" she whispered.

"What?"

She looked enigmatically at me, then cupped her hands and placed them around my face. Her fingers were warm and moist. I couldn't stop myself from wincing.

"The power of the Pir. It hit me like a wave the moment we walked into the glade."

"I was just stoned."

"Oh no. No way. It wasn't that."

I moved back a step. She had bad breath, and was standing too close.

"I didn't see anything," I said decisively. "Gemma was right. I just imagined it."

Coral laughed. "You don't want to listen to Gemma, hon. She's just struggling with all the things that are going to happen. It's, like, a lot to take onboard?"

I didn't know what she meant. She was still gazing meaningfully at me.

"You guys have just got to open up," she said. "I mean, can't you sense it? All around us?"

"What?"

"The power of transformation!"

"I'm sorry, I don't have a clue what you're talking about."

I turned away from her, edging across the room toward the table and chairs. She walked unsteadily toward the door, then changed her mind, diving back toward the table to her bag, which she rummaged through manically, pulling clothes and books onto the floor in a heap. Finally she flung it down.

"What are you looking for?"

"Nothing."

"Are you all right?"

"Sister, I'm *fantastic*."

She muttered something else unintelligible under her breath then lurched toward the door. Taking a deep, meditative breath, she threw it open and stepped onto the veranda. The door slammed behind her.

I sat down at the table, panting with relief. From outside I could hear the monotonous dirge of chanting. It was enough to put anyone off meditation for life, I thought tartly; I should have followed my instincts at the outset: she was a weirdo. Determined to ignore the noise I pushed aside the orange peel, dog ends, and shredded tobacco, and pulled a large notebook from my bag. Placing it on the table, I frowned and started to write.

Dear Steve
Well, here we are in this amazing place in the forest . . .

I stopped, read what I had written, and scrubbed it out.

Dear Steve
How's it going? I bet you thought you'd never hear from us so quickly!

Too jaunty. Why not get straight to the point?

Dear Steve
I thought I should write to clear up this "thing" between
us. It's been on my mind since we left the other week and I
really want to communicate (wrong!) . . . to convey . . .
(wrong) . . . to share (Yeuch!)

Cursing, I tore the page out of the book and twisting it violently with my hands threw the letter across the room. What did
it matter what I wrote? There was nothing I could honestly say
to make the situation better. I hadn't wanted it to turn out like
this, but the fact was that even running away to India couldn't
change what had happened.

Outside, the chanting had abruptly stopped. Coral's head
passed the window, there was a pause, and then it reappeared
again; she was pacing up and down. I hated this place, I suddenly thought. In fact, I didn't want to spend another moment
here. I glanced at my watch. It was half-past twelve. If Gem and
I moved quickly we could probably catch a bus later that afternoon. Coral could come with us as far as Bhubaneshwar, but after that, I would insist that we leave her behind. Once we were
alone again, perhaps in Goa, things would improve. I would sit
Gem down over a warm beer and tell her about Steve. Perhaps
she wouldn't be as upset as I'd anticipated.

I stood up, pushing my chair aside and stepping across the
debris of Coral's bag. From the veranda I could hear the clump
of feet down the steps, then sudden silence. Peering through the
wooden slats of the window I saw that she'd disappeared.

"Gemma!" I called gently. "Wake up!"

Darting across to the bed, I picked up Gemma's arm and
shook it. "Gem, let's get packed up and go!"

She grunted and turned over.

"Come on, I can't stand this place any longer!"

She sat up. For a few seconds she stared down at the bed,

frowning and swallowing. Then slowly she turned round. Something was very wrong: her cheeks were ashen, her eyes glazed; sweat laced her forehead like dew.

"I'm going to be sick."

She swallowed again, muttered something, and then suddenly clapped her hand over her mouth.

It was too late. Vomit spurted through her outstretched fingers, splashing my hands and splattering into a lumpy yellow puddle on the floor.

"Oh God!"

Leaning over the bed she groaned, then retched again. When she'd finished, she looked up. Her face was gray.

"I've got to get to the loo!"

Swinging her legs off the side of the bed, she stood hunched on the floor for a moment, took a few steps forward, and then suddenly clutched at her belly. "Oh no, oh shit, no!"

There was no mistaking the smell. I stared at Gemma in horrified pity as once again she doubled over and a thick glob of diarrhea slid down her legs.

AFTER I'd cleaned Gemma up, I helped her climb back into bed. The vomiting had temporarily abated, but her hands and cheeks were hot and sticky, her forehead clammy. She was delirious, too. She kept muttering incoherent sentences which I only half heard or understood. At one stage she struggled to sit up, saying loudly: "Not this!" then collapsed back onto the stained sheets, her arms clenched tightly around her stomach. Every fifteen minutes or so she groaned in pain, doubled up, and dragged herself back across the floor to the hole in the bathroom.

I hovered by the side of the bed, unsure what to do. At first I'd dabbed at her forehead with a wet flannel, but now even this was warm. There was no hope of replenishment: in the midday sun, the water trickling from the shower was steaming. I stood biting my knuckles and frowning as she squatted over the rancid hole in the bathroom for the umpteenth time. She was in serious danger of becoming dehydrated but we'd run out of bottled water. I thought I should give her some of the salts we'd brought with us, but I'd have to go back to the village and I didn't want to leave her alone.

Gemma climbed unsteadily back into her bed, her eyes dull.

"Poor old poppet," I whispered as she tried to straighten the sheets around her. "It's just the shits. You're going to be fine."

She rolled over, her fingers reaching out at the wall.

"He'll come back soon," she said, her fingers tracing shapes over the cool stone. "It'll be the end of it then."

For a moment she seemed about to say something else. I leaned over the bed, struggling to understand. Then she closed her eyes and fell back. Finally, she was asleep.

She slept for hours, her face twitching and her lips forming incommunicable sentences as she moved through the impenetrable terrain of her dreams. I pulled a chair over to the side of her bed and sat watching her. Now that she was sleeping I should hurry down to the village but something—which, even now, I can't fully explain—stopped me. I would wait until Coral returned, I decided, and send her out instead. I was Gemma's true friend, not Coral, so I should be the one to stay by her side.

As the afternoon light dimmed, my eyes grew heavy and my thoughts began to blur. I'd opened the windows as wide as I could, but there was little breeze and the heat enveloped the bungalow in an oppressive fug. In the surrounding forest the insects heralded the approaching night. Unable to fight it any longer I closed my eyes. A few hours earlier I'd been determined not to spend another night here, but that was clearly what was going to happen.

However hard I tried to stop them, my thoughts slipped back

to Steve. Over the last weeks I had been fobbing them off with constant movement and activity, but now that I was forced to be still they crowded unstoppably into my mind. I shouldn't feel so guilty, I started to tell myself now. So, Gemma had a crush on him. And once, when he was drunk at a party, he'd pecked her on the lips. Did that mean he had to live like a monk? He'd never been her boyfriend, it was all in her head. She wore that stupid eternity ring like a trophy, but he'd only bought it for her because she'd run out of cash at Camden Market and he was too embarrassed to ask her to pay it back. It was me he was in love with, he'd told me so. And that evening, when I opened the door and saw him standing in the drizzle with his nervous, hopeful eyes, I knew there was no going back. I wanted to slam the door, to turn and run back up the stairs, but all I could do was stare.

Gemma, suddenly roused, sat up and looked around.

"Is Coral here?" she whispered.

My face stiffened. "No," I said. "Not yet."

Closing her eyes, she collapsed back onto the bed again.

I fell back into my thoughts. Steve had stepped into the hall-way, his body so close that I could smell the cigarettes and rain in his hair. He'd placed a single, drooping snowdrop in the buttonhole of his jacket and was smiling. It wasn't what I wanted to happen, I swear it wasn't. But when he leaned across and gently pressed his lips against mine, I didn't move.

14

Gemma saw him through the haze, his hands outstretched. For a moment there was calm, her mind peaceful as she remembered what they had agreed. Then the memory was obliterated and she was back at home, standing in the oppressive, dirty lounge.

She looked around carefully. It was the same as always, the place crowded with the furniture from the old house, the dust that no one had the energy to wipe away lying thick and furry over every surface. And there, she suddenly noticed, standing in the corner with her back to the room, was her mother. She stared at her sloped back, the baggy Marks & Spencer's trousers, the long gray hair tied back with a rubber band, and suddenly understood. All this was her *fault. She hated her, and always had.*

Then the image fragmented and her body was shot through with burning pain. She opened her mouth to shout and felt herself being pulled roughly from the dream. There was something that she urgently had to do. Diving from the bed, she pushed aside Esther's outstretched hands and stumbled toward the bathroom.

~

When the door finally clicked open I jumped and turned round. I had been drifting in and out of sleep and for a moment didn't recognize the person standing in the doorway.

"Coral? Is that you?"

"Sure is."

She stepped into the flickering electric light. She had changed from her red sarong into a long orange kaftan and was smiling at me glazedly. For a moment I thought she was stoned, but her eyes were clear, her face radiant.

"What's up?"

"Gemma's really, really ill. She's been shitting and puking nonstop since we got back."

"My sweet child."

Whispering something to herself, she stepped lightly across the room and laid her hand on Gemma's forehead. She looked up at me, smiling serenely.

"Poor Gem. Poor you."

I swallowed down the self-pity I'd been repressing all afternoon.

"We have to get some water for her," I said quietly. "We've finished all the bottles and she must be getting really dehydrated. I've got some saline, too . . ."

"There's water in that bag." Coral nodded at a plastic carrier bag she had placed by the door. "And bananas and chapatis? We've got to make her drink."

Leaning over the bed she gently put her arms around Gemma's shoulders and pulled her up.

"Come on, my honey," she said softly. "You've got to have something to drink."

Gemma murmured something, her arm flopping over the side of the bed. Opening the bottle Coral held it to her mouth. She struggled for a moment, water dribbling down her chin, then, like a baby taking a bottle, was suddenly quiet. By the movement in her throat and the glug of the water in the bottle I could tell that she was drinking. I hovered behind Coral, biting my lip. I'm ashamed to admit it, but combined with my relief lurked something close to jealousy at how tenderly Coral held her. I'd been hopeless, I thought despondently; I'd just sat at her bed brooding about my problems when she was clearly desperately dehydrated.

When the bottle was almost empty and Gemma had finally turned her head away, Coral lowered her gently back onto the bed.

"You should drink, too," she said over her shoulder to me. "It's real hot in here."

I took the bottle and gulped some water down. She was right, I'd been thirsty. When I'd finished I wiped my mouth and handed it back. Coral was staring at me intently.

"There's a reason this is happening," she said.

"You said it. And the reason is right there back at the shrine."

She suddenly grabbed my hands, her eyes glinting. "That's what I think, too! I've been meditating on this all day, willing you to believe . . ."

Her grasp was so tight that her fingernails dug into my skin. Glancing down, I noticed that they were encrusted with grime.

"You can be part of this, too," she was saying. "You don't need to be alone!"

I glanced quickly away from her eager, searching face.

"I don't know what you mean. I'm not alone. I'm here with Gemma. All I want at the moment is for her to get well again."

Coral smiled condescendingly and shook her head. "This is all happening because it was supposed to, Esther," she said. "Don't you see? We were like, led here, to this place? That fire you saw, the one you don't want to admit? That's just the first step."

She smirked, her perfect, heart-shaped face with its pert nose and large, dilated eyes filled with conviction. I gazed at her, trying to think of a way of changing the subject. She'd been such a laugh earlier: who would have thought she was so utterly bonkers?

"That's not what I meant," I muttered.

She peered at me intently. "So what did you mean?"

"What I meant was that the reason Gemma is sick is because she was stupid enough to drink that frigging water. It's typical of her. She never looks after herself properly . . ." I stopped, clenching inwardly with shame. How, when Gemma was so ill, could I even think about blaming her? What kind of a friend was I?

Coral's face dropped. Shaking her head, she stepped back from me.

"You have to look deeper," she said. "There's a reason for everything."

"Is there?"

"Sure there is. Now let's try and get some saline down her."

I walked across the room to my rucksack, rummaging through my gear until I found the Boots bag where I kept my malaria pills and aspirin and packets of bandages. Coral's New Agey nonsense was *really* getting to me, but she was the only support I had; I'd have to try to be tolerant. At the bottom of the bag were some sachets of oral rehydration salts. Pulling them out I handed one to Coral, who took it with a nod. Squatting down, she poured the salts into the remains of the water, her face serious. I watched her give the bottle a vigorous shake. So what if she was slightly strange, I told myself. She'd been kind to us in Calcutta and now was helping us again. It was all going to be absolutely fine; Gemma would be better in a few days' time; then we'd get away from this horrible place and enjoy ourselves again.

Coral walked back across the room and perched on the edge

of Gemma's bed. "I'll give it to her in a moment," she said. "Let all that water settle?"

There was a long silence. She sat holding Gemma's hand as she murmured something vaguely melodic under her breath. Perhaps it was a song, perhaps a prayer. I couldn't tell.

"So," I said, trying to retain a semblance of normality. "Where've you been all day?"

There was such a long pause that I thought she hadn't heard me. Then she suddenly said, "At the shrine, watching the burning."

I looked at her in surprise. "What do you mean? What burning?"

She ignored me, leaning over and gently putting her hand on Gemma's inert shoulder. "Come on, little sister. Drink this up, too."

Gemma sighed, opening her eyes momentarily as Coral put the bottle back to her mouth. Coral was whispering something to her now, her head bent close to Gemma's pillow. Finally she straightened up.

"It's all, like, part of the transformation . . ." she said. "We purify and purify until there's nothing left."

I stared dumbly across the room at her. Perhaps it was irrational, for—as I kept telling myself—she'd brought water and food and was now doing her best to help, but I was starting to feel nervous again.

"That's what the fire was for?" she went on. "Don't you see? The only way she's going to recover is by going back to the shrine and finding the heat again? The whole thing is connected."

"What do you mean?"

She gazed at me, her face suddenly bright.

"When she's better, we'll take her there," she said. "It's always the answer."

I couldn't think how to respond. In the end I said, "I think I'll go and get some more water."

Striding across the room I threw the door open and stepped onto the veranda. The evening air was warm and balmy. Breathing it in with relief, I started to jog down the hill.

Heat and pain in waves. With a huge effort Gemma pulled her eyes away from her mother's back. Whatever happened, she thought, she must not see her. She turned, trying to force her feet to move herself back toward the door, but they must have got stuck on the floorboards. For some reason they wouldn't move.

Suddenly she stopped. She looked around the room, her heart thumping. She always knew this is what would happen but when her eyes came to rest on the window, she still felt shocked. It was open, she realized now, and a breeze was blowing in. She shivered at the sudden cold, the fear dropping away from her like a shroud. Outside the window, looking in at her, stood her man.

At first he said nothing. His eyes were the blue of mountain skies, his hands outstretched. She stepped out of the pain and forward, toward him. Very gently he whispered her name.

~

I gasped and sat up. It must have been the stifling heat or the hike into the forest, but after my trip to the village I'd been overtaken by a lethargy so irresistible that I had fallen asleep on my bed without even removing my clothes. Now, in the deep core of the night, I'd been abruptly woken. There had been movement: the sound of voices and the creak of the door. Peering into the darkness I could make out the lumpy shape of Gemma's sleeping body; on the other side of the room, Coral's bed was empty.

Holding my breath I swung my feet onto the floor. Somebody else was in the room.

"Coral? Is that you?"

There it was again: the soft shuffle of feet across wood. I thought I heard a sigh, or perhaps it was simply the whisper of the wind that rattled the windows.

"Who's there?"

This time I was sure: from outside I heard the click of a car door, and the grumble of an engine starting up. Running to the door, I flung it open, but the veranda was empty; the only movement, a small animal scuttling across the path. Turning back to the room I saw with a jolt that Gemma was sitting up in bed, staring at me.

"Where's he gone?" she said.

"Who?"

I started to walk toward Gemma's bed, adrenaline pumping through my veins. Gemma was gazing unblinkingly ahead.

"There was an angel. I saw an angel . . ." Her voice was slow and slurred, almost drugged.

"You've got a fever, poppet. There wasn't anyone . . ."

"He's come for me. I've been waiting all this time and now he's come."

"Gem, listen . . ."

But as I reached the bed I stopped, for I suddenly realized that she couldn't see or hear me, for she was still asleep.

15

I was woken the next day by the scrape and fizz of matches and the smell of burning sulfur. I lay without moving for a few moments, not really taking it in, then slowly opened my eyes. The morning was already well advanced, for outside the chant of insects had been replaced by the whoop and squawk of birds and rays of brilliant yellow filtered through the cracked shutters.

But it wasn't this that filled the room with dancing light. Looking around I saw I was surrounded by small white flames that hissed and flickered at me like snakes. I sat up, staring around in surprise. A circle of candles formed a halo around my bed; they covered the table, too, and were arranged in an arc around the door. On the far side of the room Coral was leaning over yet another, her eyes closed as if in prayer, her lips forming a liturgy of broken words and phrases which floated unintelligibly on the dusty air.

"What are you doing?"

She swirled round, her eyes gleaming. "Puja. The day of transformation has arrived."

I stared at her in shock. Her thin body was draped in a red and gold sari tied in an unwieldy knot around her thin waist and pulled loosely across her chest. She clearly wasn't experienced in sari management for despite a rough effort to tuck the ends in, the material kept falling away, revealing her skinny ribs. Placed on her head was a sparkly rhinestone tiara; around this she had roughly wound one of the sticky jungle creepers that hung from the buttress-rooted trees on the path; its tendrils dangled down her neck and over her face like false hair. Attached to the back of the tiara with a large red bow was what looked like a hair extension, its synthetic black fibers swinging unnaturally down her back. She was sitting cross-legged, staring solemnly through the candles at me.

But it wasn't just her strange clothes. Something over the last seven or eight hours had hollowed out her face, making her eyes appear larger and her cheekbones more sharp. She seemed feverish, too, her pupils glinting darkly, her forehead beaded with sweat. She smiled bountifully at me and held out her hands, palms up, as if making an offering.

"We meet again."

"Why are you dressed like that?"

"It's almost time. All the signs are here."

"All what signs? Are you okay?"

She shrugged and almost laughed, her eyes flicking distractedly away from my face and around the room.

"We all have to change, don't we? It's all part of the process. Like, I'm not Coral anymore? I'm Sarti."

She nodded in the direction of Gemma's bed and suddenly laughed. "And she's not Gemma! That's the miracle!"

I took a deep breath. Her wild appearance was frightening me.

"Where've you been all night?" I said as calmly as I could. She looked at me coyly.

"With my master?"

"Your master . . ."

She shook her head knowingly. "Can't you guess? Look at me. I've been joined to another."

Standing slowly she stepped over the candles toward me. Peering at her more closely I saw that her hands and arms were painted with what looked like henna; she was dressed in a botched imitation of an Indian bride.

"Be calm and still and everything will be revealed."

I stood up, folding my arms defensively. She must have been doing an awful lot of drugs.

"How's Gemma?"

"Sleeping."

"Has she still got a fever?"

"She's calm. She knows it's nearly over."

The way she said this made my stomach turn. Her face was unreadable, her eyes fixed to the candles.

"What do you mean?"

"Just that. She's, like, been through the worst and now she's stepping toward the true answer. It's all connected, don't you see?"

I shook my head. I was so tense that my shoulders were virtually touching my ears.

"Not really."

"Then you need to open up and listen."

She laughed again, spinning around coquettishly, like a flirty whirling dervish.

Turning my back on her I leaned over Gemma's bed. She was clearly still very sick. Her eyes were surrounded by dark bruises, her cheeks speckled with the rash which had spread onto her face in angry red blotches. She was soaked with sweat, too: her short hair stuck up from her head in wet clumps and behind her head her pillow was damp. Very gently, I placed my hand on her forehead.

"Christ, she's burning up!"

I started to tug at her T-shirt, pulling it up and away from her skin.

"Calm down, sister," Coral intoned from the other side of the room. "Heat is good. It's cathartic."

"We have to get her cooler . . . it's like an oven in here . . ." I glanced up at the ceiling. "Have you turned off the fan?"

"The electricity's gone. It's another sign."

"Fucking great."

Biting my lip, I looked around the room. I was trying to remain calm, but I was beginning to panic. Why of all the people who could have rescued Gemma's money belt did it have to be Coral?

"Is there anything left to drink?" I said. "What about that P J Wallah bloke? Can't we get him to bring us some tea or something? We need to get some liquids down her . . ."

"He's not here. It's like, a festival? Relax, sister. Today is going to be a great day."

I breathed in the stuffy air, my chest tight. From the corner of my eye I saw Coral bend unsteadily, her hands pressed together in prayer. I suddenly desperately wanted to get away from her. It had been a disastrous mistake to come here, I thought. We should never have got off the bus.

Coral was now attempting a complicated yogic position, standing on one foot with her hands held aloft. I glanced across the room at her and wanted to scream. However outrageously she behaved, we would have to stay in this stifling place until Gemma was better and I didn't think I could stand it. Striding toward the door, I kicked the candles out of the way with my foot and threw it open.

Sunlight flooded the room. Coral suddenly sat down, her hands folded in her lap and her head bent in apparent supplication. Her eyes were tightly closed.

"At least that should get a breeze through the place," I said brightly. "Now let's put these stupid things out. They're just making it even hotter."

Walking toward the bed I pushed past Coral, who had started her interminable chanting once more. When I reached the candles around Gemma's bed I bent down and, one by one, started to blow them out.

"No!"

I jumped and turned around. Sitting up in bed, her hands clasping the covers, her eyes dark with anger, was Gemma.

"Gem! You're awake!"

"Stop it! I want them here!"

"But they're making the place so hot . . ."

"I don't care . . ." She glowered at me for a second longer, then dropped back onto the bed.

My forehead flooded with pain. I felt unexpectedly sick, too, as if I had the deadliest of hangovers, the sort that creep up surreptitiously as the morning progresses. It was the heat, I thought with growing desperation; if only I could cool down. I swallowed unhappily, unable to prevent myself from picturing my parents' garden as it would be now, the cold dawn dew spread like jewels across the grass, the spiders' webs sparkling translucently in the hedge. From the other side of the room I could sense Coral watching me. I took another step toward Gemma's bed.

"How are you feeling?" I said gently.

"It's all because of you . . ." She started to shake her head vigorously, hitting it hard against the stiff pillow, then she sat up again, her eyes wide. "He's gone! You made him go!"

My gut clenched.

"Who?" I whispered.

Gemma snorted, her hands flailing weakly in the air.

"You know who," she said, and fell back onto the bed.

I blanched, feeling my cheeks grow scarlet, then reached out and picked up Gemma's hand. If now was the time that she wanted to talk about Steve, I thought grimly, then that was what I'd have to do.

"I know you must be feeling pissed off, Gem," I said slowly. "But I didn't mean it to work out the way it did, I promise you . . ."

But she didn't want to hear.

"Why can't you just stop meddling?" she muttered as she turned her head back to the wall. "All I want is for you to leave me alone."

I turned slowly round. It was just the fever talking, but the exchange had winded me. For a moment I stared at Coral, who was now sitting cross-legged in a circle of candles, mumbling. Then, as evenly as I could, I said, "Coral, I'm going down to the village to find a doctor or get some medicines or something. Can you please make sure Gemma keeps drinking that water?"

She ignored me.

ONCE outside, I strode quickly down the hill. I should have carried an umbrella or even a giant tropical leaf to cover my head from the sun for only the most desperate would consider walking without protection in the middle of the day, but nothing would induce me now to return to the bungalow. I tried hard to keep to the edge of the path where the trees cast their deep green shadows, but kept being forced into the angry glare. Even when the sun drifted behind the watery tropical clouds I had to shield my eyes against the light.

But it was good to be outside; at least I was no longer cooped up in the oppressive heat of the bungalow. I trudged down the hill, trying to calm down. It was bad enough that Gemma was so ill. What was really frightening me, though, was Coral. In Calcutta she'd seemed just like any other backpacker but now she seemed to be spiraling out of control in a way I'd never experienced before and couldn't hope to understand. I swung my arms high in the air, clicking my fingers at the insects which flew blindly into my face. How did we get so involved with her? Despite my bluff we were innocents who knew virtually nothing about how the world worked, and we had somehow picked up this woman who had God knows what demons to deal with. We were sharing a room with her, taking her food and her drugs, and trusting her like little children taking sweeties from strangers in the park.

I started to jog down the hill. I'd wanted to be open to new experiences and people, but not like this. I couldn't handle it, I suddenly realized, my eyes smarting with tears; I was too young and too inexperienced. This wasn't the India I'd wanted to discover and now I yearned for Gemma and me to be out of Agun Mazir and as far away from Coral as possible. In fact, I wanted to be at home, to be back in my old bedroom, opening the curtains onto another cool, calm English day. I blinked back the tears. What I wanted, more than anything, was my mum.

Turning the final corner in the track I saw the roofs of the village houses, the low ridge of domestic smoke drifting above the trees. I should try to be practical, I resolved: get medical help for Gemma, then, as soon as she was able to crawl onto a bus, return to Bhubaneshwar. I would tell Coral politely that we didn't want her around; perhaps I could make up some story about meeting other friends. After all, just because we'd hooked up with her for a few days it didn't mean we had to stay with her for the rest of the trip. She would understand, she knew the score. I shouldn't get in such a panic. *It was all going to be fine.*

16

Gemma lay on the bed staring at the wall. She could hear the others discussing her, but was no longer interested in what they said. Her head was too heavy to lift, her skin on fire. She tried to scratch at it, her fingers tearing at the burning rash, but she was too weak and her hands kept flopping back onto the bed. She needed water and medicine, she knew, but could no longer be bothered to ask.

He was with her for much of the time now, but only when Esther was away. In the fractured shards of her dreams she could hear his words; when she opened her eyes he was there. There was calm in his voice and as they lightly touched her head, his palms were cool.

But it was his face which pulled her back, his smooth, quiet face. The more she stared into it the more she understood; she wanted him to never leave, for his eyes gave her hope and with his mouth he promised endings and beginnings and so much more.

WHEN I reached the main road at the bottom of the hill, I stopped, staring at the scene ahead of me in amazement. A day earlier the place had been just another sleepy hamlet, apparently existing only to service the interstate buses that sporadically roared around the bend. Now it was transformed into a sprawling mass of vehicles and people. Crowds spilled over the sidewalk and into the road; spreading down the hill was a temporary shanty of canvas tents and hastily erected stalls. Where previously a couple of listless vendors had sold onions and shriveled potatoes to the intermittent traffic, now a veritable marketplace had sprung up, the incoming traders squatting behind piles of oranges and pineapples, prickly pears and giant, succulent jackfruit. Other stalls were selling robes and prayer caps, rugs illustrated by scenes of haj, religious books and tapes. Immediately opposite me was the source of Coral's candles: sitting meditatively on the pavement, an old man in pebble glasses was selling them for a paisa each. Next to him a turbaned, thick-bearded mullah was preaching into a makeshift sound system, his pious, wavering voice crackling tremulously with religious ecstasy and electric static. It sounded like Arabic. I dodged past, not wanting to be caught in his accusatory stare.

I wandered down the sidewalk, gazing around as I tried to take it all in. At the farthest end, where only the day before rickshaws had aimlessly cruised and pigs rooted in the dirt, a line of brightly painted buses was disgorging yet more pilgrims. There were beggars, too: a long line of emaciated and broken bodies squatting by the side of the road with their sticks and bowls and dreadlocked hair. Some were moaning and calling out for Allah and alms, their reedy voices rising and falling in an orchestrated wail. I could smell incense and frying oil and the thick scented stench of human urine.

I must have been standing and staring gormlessly around for at least five minutes. Shaking myself into action I stepped tentatively into the road. I would have felt better had there been more women, or even children in the place, but, with the exception of the beggar-women whose pleading eyes I didn't wish to meet, I could see only men. Crossing my arms and turning my face away from the gazes I was attracting, I hurried across the road. I passed the beggars, shocked at how strongly they repulsed me, and, focusing on the medical dispensary opposite the buses, pushed my way along the sidewalk, my head down. I'd buy some stomach medicine for Gemma, I thought, and inquire about doctors. Then, as soon as possible we would leave.

"Where are you going, young lady?"

I stopped abruptly, almost colliding with the old man who had stepped into my path. He was a bulky, kindly looking person, dressed in a safari suit and sandals, a few oily hairs scraped hopefully over his balding head. He'd been wearing dark glasses, but now took these off and peered at me thoughtfully.

"Mr. Sanjiv Chakrabarty, M.A. in archaeology, University of Calcutta, at your service." He held out his hand. "And yourself?"

I shook my head, my arms still crossed. "I'm in a hurry."

"You have come to see our mela? Perhaps you are a student of Indian culture?"

"I just want to get to the chemist's," I said tensely. "My friend is sick . . ."

"But all our shops are closed today. It is a holiday . . ."

He smiled expansively. I stared at him. The tangle of tension which all morning had been knotting in my chest was pulling tighter.

"The dispensary is closed?"

"Of course. Today is the celebration of our great Pir Nirulla."

"But how am I meant to get medicines for my friend? She's really ill!"

"For that, you must visit another village. Where are you and your friend staying? May I offer you my personal services?"

I glanced at him, noticing his fleshy lips and the hair sprouting from his ears. I didn't have the time to be exchanging niceties with an old buffer, I thought impatiently; I wanted to be doing something, taking some sort of positive action.

"No, no, it doesn't matter . . ."

"But this is not a good time to be a young lady alone . . ."

Given what was to happen later, I am ashamed to say that I ignored him. Turning on my heels, I jogged across the road into the crowd. For a moment I was disoriented. I glanced in the direction of the buses, yet couldn't see the junction for the turning that led up the hill. From the other side of the road, and with so many people, the place looked completely different. I could still hear Mr. Chakrabarty calling something at me, but not wishing to listen, walked quickly back in the direction of the preacher. His lecture had reached a pitch of emotion now, and as he ranted spittle sprayed the crowd like the first drops of an oncoming storm.

I was sure the turning was opposite the National Bank. Skirting the edge of the preacher's generator I came out by the bolted post office and found I was standing directly next to it. I started to cross the road again, planning to buy some bananas and bottles of water, and then noticed a silver four-wheel-drive Suzuki, parked in front of the bank at the bottom of the track.

I stared at the vehicle, my eyes screwed up against the light. On the other side, facing the track, the driver's door was open. As I peered across the road, I could just about make out the tall figure of a man standing with his back against the jeep. He was dressed in the maroon robes of a Buddhist and his head was shaved. At first I assumed he must be one of the pilgrims, but as he moved to one side I saw he had the pale complexion of a European. He was also not alone.

I instinctively didn't want to be seen. Dodging behind a large, tiger-painted truck, I gazed across the road. They'd moved slightly, the man's companion stepping out from the side of the vehicle into the sun so that she was directly opposite me. At first it took me a moment to refocus my eyes; I blinked in the bright light, then suddenly stepped back. The man's companion was Coral, I realized with a start. She was still draped in the sari but had taken the headgear off and was standing almost subserviently in front of him. As they talked, she kept glancing anxiously around, her fingers flicking restlessly by her sides.

They were in the middle of what appeared to be a passionate discussion or even an argument. Coral nodded then stepped back, as if on the verge of leaving. The man seemed to be imploring her to do something. He gripped her arm, his face serious, but she shook her head, said something more, and then he placed what looked like a small packet into her hands. It was hard to tell, for at that moment she turned away, but I thought I saw her tuck the parcel into the folds of her sari. Then, with a movement so swift and unexpected that it took me a second or so to work out what she was doing, she bent down and touched his feet, her eyes lowered in supplication. Suddenly she leaped up again, and was gone.

The man stepped from the sidewalk into the crowd. Shielding my eyes from the sun with my hands, I tried to follow his movements but a large bus piled high with people and luggage lurched across my view. Something was flickering at the edges of my mind, a faint memory or image I could not grasp. I pushed into the road, swearing at the rickshaws and pedestrians who milled in my way. Although in retrospect nothing had really happened, my hands were trembling and my mouth was dry. It wasn't just a matter of Coral behaving oddly, I was thinking with growing panic; there were other people involved. I really *had* heard a vehicle in the night; it wasn't my imagination, something odd was definitely going on. I glanced desperately at the traffic, willing for a lull so that I could cross the road, yet every time I stepped into the road another motorbike or car chugged past and I was forced back on the pavement. My skull was throbbing so violently that I thought I might throw up.

When I finally reached the other side of the road I hurried toward the jeep, which was parked haphazardly over the sidewalk, its front wheels bridging a broken gap in the drain. Unlike the other mud-splattered cars and rusty buses clogging the street, it had clearly been acquired at some expense from abroad; it was new, too, the bull bars gleaming, the silver paintwork unblemished. Standing on the tips of my toes I peeped through the front window. I was not searching for anything in particular; I just wanted to find out more.

There was not much to see: spread over the passenger's seat was a regional map of Orissa; on the back seat a leather holdall, and scattered on the floor in the passenger's footwell were a couple of empty water bottles and a scattering of orange peel.

"Hi."

I gasped, my heart jolting, and leaped around. Standing behind me, his arms folded belligerently across his chest, was Coral's man. I gulped, my face swamping red with embarrassment. My legs felt weak; my chest was pounding so hard I could hardly speak. I think I must have breathed "Hello" and tried to smile. He held out his hand and took mine for a few limp moments before dropping it.

"I'm Zak," he said, staring at me closely.

My initial impression had been correct. He was European; under its freshly shaven stubble, the top of his head was pink, his thick eyebrows blond. His skin was unlined, but it was impossible to guess his age: he could have been anything from thirty to fifty. He had small, regular features which crowded into the center of his face, giving him the appearance of an intelligent dog, sniffing out a scent. Most strikingly, however, were his bright blue eyes, which were now focused closely upon my face as if trying to memorize it.

"Be at peace, and let me help you," he said. His accent was hard to place: American with a touch of German or Dutch, perhaps. He cocked his head at me, the tips of his mouth curving in a slight smile.

"Possibly you are looking for something?"

I girned at him inanely, my mind stalling. My memory is that he was towering over me, but I know now that he was only a few inches taller. I remember noticing that thick blond hair grew on the backs of his hands and that his feet overhung his worn flip-flops.

"No," I blurted, still trying to hold my ridiculous smile. "No, I'm fine. I'm sorry. I was just being nosy . . ."

"Good. Yes, it's good to meet you."

The way he said this implied that he knew exactly who I was. His face arranged itself into a smile. Still those cold blue eyes held me in their gaze. As far as I can remember, I muttered something like "I've got to go," gave a high-pitched giggle, and turned on my heels.

But what do I know? I've recalled the scene so many times that my memory has grown frayed; sometimes I fear I no longer know the difference between what actually happened and the pensive stitches I've sewn to keep the memory from falling apart. I'm doing my best to tell it as truthfully as I can, but like all our histories it's just a story, and at times I'm no longer sure where it ends and I begin.

A while later I reached the path which led into the trees. By the time the bungalow was in sight I was slippy with sweat and my heart was battering violently against my ribs. It had started to spot with rain, a jungle shower which sprinkled my forehead and splashed my cheeks, but I hardly noticed. I rushed across the rubber lawn, leaped up the veranda steps, and burst through the door. I'd made up my mind, you see. I was determined that Gemma and I should leave Agun Mazir on the very next bus.

The first thing I heard as I opened the door was laughter. Taken aback, I peered across the room and saw that Coral was perched on the side of Gemma's bed, a tropical bird of prey with ragged red and gold wings and thin dusty feet. They were giggling, their heads close together, their hands touching. Laid out on the bed was a large bottle of water, a bunch of bananas, and a couple of chapatis. As she heard me approach, Coral glanced over her shoulder and said in a voice I was convinced was filled with derision: "And here she comes!"

For perhaps a second or two I observed them laughing together in silence. Coral was pretending to be our friend, I suddenly thought, but although only I could see it, she was our enemy. Perhaps it was the heat, or perhaps the unavoidable result of the nervous energy that had been contracting in my gut all morning, but for one crazy second I was overtaken by an image of her pushing Gemma into the pillows: not holding her hand but gripping it so tightly that she couldn't move; not laughing, but grimacing as she held her down.

I could no longer control myself. Flying across the room I grabbed her arm and jerked her off the bed, pushing her aside with such force that she stumbled and slipped, landing hard on her bottom, the tinsely hem of her sari rising up to reveal thin mosquito-bitten legs and bony knees.

"Who's that man you were with? What's going on?"

She rolled over in the dust, then sprang to her feet, gazing at me in amazement. "You're mad, girl!"

"No, I'm not! You're up to something, I know you are!"

Still she stared at me, her eyes goggling. I swallowed, my mouth dry. I hadn't meant to say anything so direct, and certainly not to knock her to the floor.

"Jesus Christ, Esther! What the *fuck* are you doing?"

From her bed Gemma was sitting up and glaring at me angrily. I bit my lip, already wishing bitterly that I could go back to the door and start again. Beside me Coral had closed her eyes and was taking deep, meditative breaths.

"I'm sorry," I said slowly. "I didn't mean to do that."

"Well, what the bollocksy hell *did* you mean to do?" Gemma said curtly. "What's the matter with you?"

I stared at her. It was amazing how much she had improved since the morning. The fever had obviously gone, for despite the patches of inflamed skin where she had been scratching, her face was pallid and tired looking rather than puce. Her eyes were still hazy but her hair had been brushed from her face and damp flannels placed across her bare arms and belly.

"There's nothing the matter with me. I'm sorry. I'm just feeling tense, that's all. Hey, Coral . . ." I swiveled round, trying to smile at her, but she was staring at the floor, her face rigid. "Look, what can I say? I don't know what got into me . . ."

Gemma's face puckered with what I could only read as distaste. Sitting on the edge of her bed, where Coral had been, I reached out and tried to take her hand.

"Look," I said slowly. "I know you've been ill, but this place is seriously creeping me out and I really, really, *really* want to leave."

She looked at me blankly. Her hand hung lifelessly between my fingers.

"Go on then," she said.

"What, are you up for it?"

So slowly that it must have been deliberate, she shook her head. "I'm not coming."

I leaned closer to her. I didn't want Coral to hear. "Gem, I know you like Coral, but she's been behaving really strangely. She keeps going on about burning and fires and all this bridal shit and there's this bloke hanging around in the village . . ." I trailed off. "I just think something weird's going on, that's all . . ."

Gemma looked down at her hands, her forehead furrowed with irritation. "You can think what you like, but I want to stay here."

I plowed on. I was becoming obsessed by my desire to leave. ". . . and because of this festival thing all the chemists are closed, too. I mean, why don't we just get to the nearest town where we can get you some medicine? Please, Gem. This place is bad news . . ."

"Tough," she said quietly. "You'll have to leave alone."

"But, Gem, I can't leave you here with *her*."

I glanced at Coral, who had now dropped cross-legged to the floor, her eyes closed.

"Why not?"

"She's a nutcase."

Gemma snorted and jerked her hand away.

"Listen, Esther," she said quietly. "It's quite simple. If you don't like it, then go somewhere else. It's you that's behaving strangely, not Coral. To be honest we'd be relieved if you went."

I stared at her, feeling myself turn hot and then cold.

"What do you mean?"

"It's *you* who's behaving weirdly, not Coral. You're sending out bad vibes."

"That's Coral talking, not you!"

"Bollocks." She sat up now, staring hard into my face. "The truth is, *Little Miss Perfect,* that you're projecting all your crap onto her. We all know what's really going on."

My heart was now thumping so hard she must surely hear it. I tried to take a deep breath.

"What do you mean?" I whispered.

"Well, since you fuck up every relationship I have, I suppose even you must be feeling guilty."

I felt as if she had poured freezing cold water over me. I gasped, shuddering with shock.

"I don't understand," I stammered.

"Of course you understand. You're the one with the wonderful degree in social fucking anthropology, aren't you? It's just a little thing about human relationships. When one girl steals the other's boyfriend then it's the custom for the first girl to feel guilty and the second to want her to fuck off. What do you expect?"

From her corner, Coral was silent. Gemma gazed across the bed at me, her mouth a small pink pout. I gazed back at her. I knew her face so well, had grown up with it, seen her whole history pass over it, but never had I seen her eyes so cold and so filled with dislike. I swallowed again. I felt sick.

"I don't know what you're talking about . . ." My voice was small and faltering, like a little girl about to be punished.

"Yes, you do. I'm talking about Steve."

She spoke his name with such vehemence, it was as if she had speared my chest with a seared knife. I was shaking my head in foolish denial, my face scarlet, but the same stinging row of words kept repeating in my mind, over and over: *she has known all along.*

"I didn't steal him from you, Gemma," I whispered. "It wasn't like that."

"Oh no? What was it like, then? It seems exactly like that to me."

"We're just friends . . ."

"Which is why you were snogging him."

I stared at her, too stupefied with shock to speak. There was nothing I could do and nothing I could say. I was trapped in the irrefutable truth of it. *All this time she had said nothing, and yet she had known all along.* For the briefest moment I remembered the way Steve and I had been kissing, just before the doorbell rang and she came in. The memory made me want to puke. Still shaking my head I reached out and tried once more to take her hand, but she pulled it violently away.

"I couldn't help it, Gem . . ." I muttered weakly.

She snorted, her voice heavy with sarcasm. "Yeah, *right.*"

"I promise you, I . . ."

"Oh, come on, you were after him the moment I mentioned his name." She was spitting the words at me now, her eyes dark with hatred, her cheeks flushed. "You couldn't just leave it, could you? You have to take everything I want, just so you can prove how much better than me you are."

This was suddenly too much. I jumped up.

"That isn't true! You know it isn't!"

But her face was set, the mixture of stubbornness and defiance she always assumed when she was sure that she was right.

"You do it all the time."

"How can you say that?"

"You like to keep me in my place, you always have. You have to be the best and the prettiest and the one with the most boyfriends and be one hundred percent in control of everything, and when you're not you can't stand it so you trample over what someone else has got."

"That's not true!"

But she was no longer listening, for she'd turned her face to the wall, her role as the victim assured. And now, as I gazed at the martyred slope of her shoulders, a new emotion rose up and broke inside me like a wave. It was anger, my only defense.

"That's just the version you want to believe!" I cried. "But it isn't true! Jesus, you weren't even going out with Steve! Nothing bloody happened between you!"

I took a deep breath. I knew what I was saying was deadly, but now that I'd started I couldn't stop. *Fuck it,* a voice inside me was hissing, *why don't you just tell her the truth?* I took a deep breath.

"Nothing ever bloody happens for you," I heard myself say. "And you know why not? Because you never let it. Because deep down you think you're too bloody perfect. That's why you always choose men who are completely impossible. It's you that's the control freak, not me . . ."

I stopped. There was so much more I could say, things I had kept inside for years about how she never let people get close, or how she pretended to be superior when really she was just afraid, but I didn't want to hurt her anymore than I already had. She was my best friend, you see. In spite of the tangle we were in, I still loved her.

There was a long, lethal silence, the room filling once more with the sound of birds and the click of the geckos which darted up and down the walls. I could hear the thudding of my chest, and from down the hill the distant ranting of the preacher. I turned away from Gemma's bed, stunned at the enormity of what I'd just said, and found myself caught in Coral's gaze.

"It's time for you to go, sister," she said softly. "Can't you see? You're messing everything up."

I sniffed, dabbing at my eyes with my knuckles and stumbling around the bed. A part of me still couldn't believe what was happening. I leaned over Gemma, desperate to take the whole thing back, to wipe the slate clean and start again.

"Is that what you want?" I said. I was pleading, I knew, but by now I was completely out of control.

"Please, Gem. I didn't mean to hurt you. Please . . ."

Very slowly, she rolled over. For the very last time, our eyes met. Then, so quietly that it was almost a whisper, she said: "I don't want you around anymore."

"Gem, please, I can't leave you here. Don't make me."

"Just fuck off."

I gasped. I wanted to be sick, to expiate the terrible feelings inside me with one violent retch. Digging my nails into my palms I limped slowly toward my own bed and picked up my rucksack. My clothes were heaped in a pile on the floor. Bending down I stuffed them into my bag. My cash, passport, and locker key were tucked inside my wallet. The pressure in my chest was almost unbearable. I shouldn't have said those things, but the situation had escalated out of my control and now she would never forgive me. If I tried to speak I knew I'd burst into tears. Pulling the pack over my shoulders I walked toward the door.

When I reached it I stopped. I wanted to turn round, but could only stand rigidly facing the handle, my shoulders stiff. There was so much more I needed to say, but the words wouldn't form in my mind and my mouth refused to open. I tasted salt, the tears running down my cheeks and over my lips.

"I'll leave a note for you in the locker," I mumbled. "Telling you where I am."

Then not turning to look back I opened the door and stumbled into the hot breath of the forest.

17

To my surprise I only had to wait a few minutes before a coach en route for Bhubaneshwar roared around the corner. Waving frantically at it to stop, I grabbed the outstretched arms of the bus boys and jumped aboard, thanking God that at least one thing had gone right that day. I didn't think I could spend another second standing by the side of the road; as I waited I'd attracted a small, jostling crowd, who stared at my red eyes and disheveled appearance with pitiless curiosity. A day earlier I'd have shouted at them to piss off, but now all I could do was sniff and gaze sorrowfully at my feet.

I couldn't believe what had happened. I knew Gemma would be upset by what had happened between Steve and me, but each time I recalled the hatred in her eyes I was overcome by a fresh surge of shock and pain. It was as if she was a different person, I kept thinking; a stranger. And now, here I was, leaving Agun Mazir without her. It didn't make sense.

I swayed down the aisle, searching for a place to sit. Unlike the bus we had ridden into Agun Mazir three days earlier this one was only half full so I soon found a seat. Propping my rucksack beside me I leaned into the sticky plastic cover and stared unseeingly from the window as, gathering speed, the bus clattered through the village. We passed the track leading up the hill to the bungalow and the National Bank, and finally were among the rickshaw workshops on the edge of the village. Pulling the rickety window down, I leaned forward, the breeze blowing on my face and through my hair. Finally, I was beginning to cool down.

A few minutes later, the road plunged down the hill, leaving the village far behind. I gazed blankly at the passing landscape. I didn't know where I was headed or what I was going to do. One moment I felt completely numb and the next I'd be overcome by a blast of drenching shock. I kept replaying the argument over and over in my mind, my thoughts leaping wildly from Coral to Steve and then back again to Gemma and my terrible guilt.

The road meandered in endless loops up and down the sides of the forested hills, across rivers and through tiny deserted hamlets. We passed goats grazing at the side of the road, laborers laden with vast bundles of firewood, and in a clearing next to a sign marked "Sri Krishan Estate: Keep Out," a group of thin, dark women hacking at the trees, their faded saris pulled up over their shins. A few miles further the bus came to the roadside shrines which the passengers had thrown coins at on their way to Agun Mazir. This time it didn't slow down.

I closed my eyes, uninterested in the view. All I could think was that because of my selfishness, I'd messed everything up. I knew I could be careless, could become fixated on my own goals and not notice when people got in the way, and I knew I was a liability around men. But until now I'd always been a good friend to Gemma. Whatever happened in her life, and God there had been enough dramas over the last few years, I'd been there for her. I was loyal, that's how I saw myself, a loyal old Labrador, lying lovingly at her feet. And she needed me to be like that. Her parents were a disaster: her dad unavailable and Up North, her mum distant and depressed; her older brother long gone. She'd always been so shy at school, so she stuck to me like ivy to a tree.

And this was how I'd repaid her trust. I started to cry again, my nose filling with snot, hot tears splattering messily down my cheeks. How could I have done something so terrible and even begin to think of myself as her friend? She'd been down for so long, stuck in her grotty flat above the Alliance and Leicester, working at the Kodak factory while I lorded it over her at university, sleeping with a string of Stevenage losers who never stayed for long, while her mother fell apart. And all I did was complacently repeat the same tired clichés: it was just a phase, soon she would meet someone to rescue her: all those fairy stories for grown-ups.

It hurt so much it winded me all over again, but what she said was true. All the time I'd been reassuring her, I was also smug in the knowledge that my life was different. And perhaps, I thought with a jab of self-hatred, that was the way I wanted it to be. It was easy like that: I was the pretty, successful one, while she was the troubled failure.

And then, one day last summer, everything changed.

"I've met someone," she had told me triumphantly. "And this time, it's going to work."

At first she wouldn't let me meet him. But she told me about him in detail, describing conversations and dates in phone calls between us which would last for hours. Did he feel the same way as her? What had it meant when he kissed her good night? Which finger should she put his ring on? I counseled her at every stage, relieved that she was happy and we were close again. I told her he was a slow mover, that she should drop a few hints, take the initiative. Christ, I think I even told her that I would sort him out!

I squeezed my eyes shut, dabbing at the tears angrily with the side of my hand. She had accused me of stealing him deliberately, of always coveting and destroying what she had. But it wasn't like that at all. I had no intention of taking him from her, but he had worked his way into my life in a way I couldn't fully explain. He was so determined, so sure that we should be together that he made my fears sound like weak excuses, my reticence, stupidity. And he was right, deep down I knew he was. When he finally came to my door that evening I'd run to answer it like a schoolgirl, my heart bumping against my ribs. I didn't want to hurt her, but as he leaned over and brushed his lips against mine, I realized how much I wanted him.

"What about Gemma?" I'd whispered, but he just shook his head. "Gemma, Gemma, Gemma. What's it got to do with her?" And then, before I had time to step back, his arms were around my waist and he was pulling me toward him and kissing me properly, and suddenly Gemma no longer seemed to matter.

After that first kiss, we stepped apart. I could hardly bear to let him move away from me. I wanted to merge and melt into his body; I wanted to never ever let him go. My parents were out. It felt like everything was just beginning.

"Hello," he said. "I've been looking for you."

I looked into his face, a little bit nervous, a little bit ashamed. I had never examined him so closely before: his chin was sprinkled with stubble and he had a small scar above his eyebrow. I reached up and touched it lightly with my finger.

"You know I'm going to India?" I said, but he just laughed and shrugged. I kissed him back, running my hand down the back of his shirt and over his smooth warm back and pulling him closer. And then, of course, the doorbell rang.

Oh, Christ, how *could* I have? I was meant to be a feminist, for God's sake, someone who put womankind first, not some flaky femme fatale. I sat up, peering through the grimy window at the potholed road. That was what Gemma had called me on the train, wasn't it? She must have made that comment deliberately, knowing how guilty it would make me feel; in retrospect, her comments about writing to him had been barbed with poison, too. We passed the rusty carcass of a broken bus, a group of people milling around it unpurposefully. All that time when I thought Gemma suspected nothing, she had *known*. And now that I remembered the scene with Steve I could see that my guilt must have been completely transparent. I sniffed, wiping my nose in despair.

The doorbell had rung and Steve and I had jumped apart. I remembered that Gemma said she would come around after work. I think I wiped my hand across my lips, as if his kiss—my betrayal—was plastered there in paint. I knew my face was scarlet and clothes askew, wanted more than anything to creep away from the hall and hide. But it was too late: through the frosted glass I could see the slope of her shoulders, the lumpy profile of her face. I squared my shoulders and opened the door.

She stared at us for a moment, then pushed past, stumbling along the corridor and into the sitting room.

"Hi," I said in as casual a voice as I could manage. "What's up?"

But she just shook her head. Guilt-tripping without accusation, it was her tour de force.

And of course it worked. I spent the whole night awake, horrified at what I had done. The next day I rang Steve and told him I wouldn't be able to see him again. He sounded stunned, but I put the phone down on him before he could say more. Then, to further pacify my raging guilt, I asked Gemma if she wanted to come with me on my great trip to India. And to my surprise she'd agreed. I'd been so stupidly, naively relieved, convinced now that she suspected nothing, praying that she never would.

Yet now it was clear that she'd always known, and as I recalled the things she'd just said I realized that her jealousy fractured our entire relationship. And now something new started to trickle into my thoughts, a drip-drop of resentment which, as I repeated her accusations, began to flow with increasing speed. How could she say that I wanted to destroy the things she had, that I was competitive? Ever since we were children I'd shared what I had: friends, invitations to parties, clothes, everything. It was hardly my fault that I'd done what was expected, worked hard and achieved the required grades for Sussex. What did she expect? For me to mess up my life, too, so that she'd have someone to keep her company? Oxford had offered her a scholarship, for God's sake; all she'd had to do was pass. But then, for some reason that she had never explained, she'd chucked the whole thing away, skipping almost a whole term of lessons and turning up stoned for her exams. It was nothing to do with her parents' divorce, I thought angrily, that was just her excuse. No, it was that she couldn't bear to put herself on the line. That was why she had deliberately messed up her A-levels and why she always chose hopeless men. And *I* was the one who was supposed to feel guilty?

That summed it up, I thought. Through a clever mixture of passivity and covert aggression she always managed to put me in the wrong. Sure, getting off with Steve wasn't the best thing I could have done. But she should try to get it into perspective. He was a *friend* who she had a crush on, not her lover. Just because she had met him first did not mean that she owned him.

The bus had nearly broken free of the hills now; we turned a corner and were speeding through padi fields, the horizon flat and uneventful. For a brief moment I'd been starting to feel better but now my spirits suddenly plummeted again. So, Gemma might be jealous and destructive, but it didn't absolve me. No matter how hard I tried to justify my actions, there was no escaping the fact that I had not acted like a true friend to her. She'd been desperately infatuated with Steve, and I'd got off with him. I'd lied and deceived her, and there was nothing to be gained in being defensive. I could rehearse any number of excuses, tell myself that the things she had just said were unfair, yet the bitter fact remained: her heart was broken, and it was my fault. I had seen what she wanted and made sure that I was the one who got it. No wonder she didn't want me around.

I turned away from the window, no longer able to bear my own reflection. All I could think now was that I had to somehow make it up to her; that I'd do anything to make it better. As well as saying where I would be I'd leave an apologetic letter for her in the locker in Delhi. She'd have to come back to it to get her gear; thank God they had supplied us with two keys. Then, after she'd had a few days to cool down, I'd try to talk to her again.

I stayed overnight in a youth hostel in Bhubaneshwar, using up most of my cash on a plane ticket back to Delhi. I planned to spend the night in the Connaught Circus hotel, then go to the railway station to retrieve my things. After that, I decided, I would travel south.

18

THE Delhi morning dawned with the roar of traffic and the sound of slamming doors. In the corridor outside my room I could hear loud British voices. As they passed my door I heard a man say: "It was like, fucking cool, I mean . . ." I didn't catch the end of the sentence.

I lay on my back for a while, staring up at the dirty, flaking ceiling. I'd been dreaming muddled, fearful scenes, the details of which had wholly disintegrated as soon as I'd woken. In their wake a thick residue of anxiety remained, something to do with Gemma and Coral. Without warning, I pictured Gemma staring at me with such hatred and pain from her bed and felt suddenly nauseous. Although two days had passed since our row, still I couldn't purge it from my mind; no matter how I tried to distract myself the details of what was said kept replaying themselves over and over. I'd given up trying to justify my actions now; all I was left with was the overwhelming desire to somehow make Gemma forgive me. And yet what real hope was there of that? She had told me to get lost, said she would be pleased when I was gone.

I shuddered, sitting up and pushing the memory from my mind. What I had to do, I told myself for the umpteenth time, was to forget about what had happened in the past and concentrate on being here. I had spent almost a year planning this trip and I should try to enjoy it. This thing with Gemma was just a silly fight. As the days passed, her attitude would soften; she would forgive me in time. Then she would come back to Delhi, find my note, and we would be reconciled. After all, it wasn't as if I was still seeing Steve. The relationship was over.

But in spite of my efforts to cheer up, an unformed anxiety gnawed at my insides. It was partly that it felt so strange to be alone. I'd always seen myself as an adventurer, but as I sat up and pulled my dress over my head I realized that I was horribly afraid. Nobody knew where I was, I thought; and here, in this vast, unknown country, anything could happen. I wandered over to the grimy window and peered out. Outside was a small balcony, but the window was painted shut. Traffic fumes rose chokingly from the road, my view obscured by hazy pollution. I didn't want to stay in Delhi a moment longer.

Pushing the few possessions I'd strewn about the room back into my rucksack, I pulled the drawstrings tight and hauled it onto my back. I told myself I should treat the next few days as a challenge, but recently my famous spirit of adventure had become increasingly flimsy. As I put my hand out to open the door I was suddenly overcome by what faced me outside. I didn't want to struggle with it all alone, I thought with a wave of self-pity. Compared with the huge continent that lay before me I was so small and vulnerable. For a moment I was unable to move. Then, bracing myself, I opened the door and walked out of the room.

Once outside I hailed a scooter rickshaw and asked the driver to take me to the station. I told myself everything was going to work out. In a day or so, I'd be in Goa; in under a week Gemma might even be with me. The scooter puttered contentedly past the cyclists and rickshaws that creaked by the side of the road. In spite of all my rationalizations, just thinking of Gemma made my stomach heave with guilt. Who was I kidding? After what had happened how could I seriously think we would spend the rest of the trip together?

I clutched the rusty rail above my head, my jaw tight. Yesterday I'd been convinced that I was right in coming to Delhi, but all morning I'd been feeling increasingly uneasy, a lumpen, unfocused fear swelling in the pit of my belly. I swallowed, closing my eyes in distaste at the view of a beggar defecating in the drains. It was being in the city, I told myself. I just needed to get away.

Forty minutes later the rickshaw puttered to a halt outside the station. Unfolding my numbed legs I climbed with relief out of the cramped canvas cabin. I stretched my arms above my head and took a deep breath in a futile effort to calm down. For some reason it seemed imperative that I get to the locker as quickly as possible.

I gave the driver sixty rupees, walking quickly away so he wouldn't have time to object. A train had just come in and all around me people were shouting and pushing, running across the platform in an effort to get onboard. I stepped back, almost treading on a small, half-naked girl who immediately started pulling at the hem of my dress, holding out her hand for money. I turned sharply away, jogging toward the bridge which led to the lockers.

As I descended the steps, the row of lockers finally came into view. Now that I had them in sight my heart started to pound again. There could surely be no rational reason why I felt so jumpy. All I had to do was open up the locker and take out my ticket, and my traveler's checks. I had the key right there in my hand; Gemma's was tucked into the money belt in Agun Mazir. Yet as I approached the metaled bank of doors a distant memory kept running through my mind, a vague thought or connection that I couldn't force into focus.

It was something about the money belt. Turning onto the platform, I searched the row of lockers for our number. There it was: written in English under the Hindi numeral: 54. I clutched the key in my sweaty hands. Placing my rucksack on the concrete floor, I knelt down and pushed the key into the lock. Behind me I could hear the incomprehensible fuzz of a train announcement, the slam of carriage doors. I was twenty-three. Despite this blip with Gemma nothing had ever really gone wrong in my life. I still thought nothing really would. Whistling under my breath, I turned the key.

The locker door swung open.

I peered inside, the pit of my stomach plunging in horror. For a moment my brain simply refused to register what I saw. I stared at the key and then back at the door, but the number was the same. Swallowing back my mounting panic, I groped inside until my hand found the wall.

There could be no mistake. The locker was empty.

Someone pushed past, making for a locker a few rows down. I moved to one side, dimly aware of large amounts of baggage being unloaded next to me. For a few moments I struggled to make the connections. If our stuff had gone then someone—a thief presumably—must have removed the locker key from Gemma's belt either before or after it dropped from the pack onto the station platform. Yet when Coral had handed it back to us the key had been there—or at least they were there in Agun Mazir; on the train all I remembered seeing when I'd hastily unzipped the belt and glanced inside was a wad of rupees. Yet if the thief had taken a key and nothing else, how had he returned it to the belt before Coral saw it drop to the floor? And why hadn't he taken the money? I stared into the dark space of the locker, its door hanging jeeringly open, then suddenly gasped. Of course! How could I have been so stupid?

It was Coral who had taken one of the keys. She must have

removed it from the belt before going to the lockers then handing it back on the train or gone back to the lockers after Calcutta then returned the key in Agun Mazir. Her story about
seeing the belt fall to the ground was fiction; *she* had stolen it. I
closed my eyes, forcing myself to concentrate. A dim image was
starting to appear.

"Oh my God!"

I clamped my hands over my mouth, my guts dissolving with
horror. With her false braid attached—the one she had been
wearing with her fake bridal gear—Coral became the woman
I'd seen at the airport. And without the braid it was she who
had bumped into me on our first evening in Delhi. Whatever, or
whoever, she'd been running away from, we must have been noticed there, too. And the silver jeep at the mela was also the
same: I'd seen it in the airport car park when I'd gone to look
for buses; that was what I'd been struggling to remember in
Agun Mazir. In fact, I realized with cold, drenching dread, the
man in the robes—Zak, he'd called himself—was the same person as Gemma's tall yellow-haired hippie; the only difference
was that he had shaved his head.

"Please, excuse me. I have many bags."

"Sure."

Not bothering to look up, I shuffled a few feet further down
the row. Ever since they spotted us at the airport Coral and the
man must have been following us. It had all been part of a plan
to rob us. But why go to such lengths to give the belt back? If
she wanted to steal our gear, fine—I'd read about the drop-out
druggies that preyed on other travelers—but why follow us onto
the train? I shook my head violently, as if trying to dislodge
some vital clue. Whatever Coral's motivations, the fact was that
we now had no traveler's checks and no tickets home. The only
money I had left was three hundred or so rupees, folded into my
wallet.

"Fuck, fuck, *fuck* . . ."

Sobbing quietly to myself I stood up. I knew I should try to calm down and focus rationally on the situation, but all I could think of was Gemma. I'd clearly made an appalling mistake. The row was irrelevant; all that mattered was that I'd abandoned my best friend to the clutches of two people who were clearly working together and wanted God knows what. I should contact the British High Commission, I suddenly thought. No, it was Sunday and the place would be closed. By the time I got to talk to someone anything could have happened. I had to get back to Agun Mazir and Gemma as soon as I possibly could. Pushing my fingers inside my wallet I slowly counted my cash. I had exactly three hundred and eighty rupees left, just enough to pay my fare.

19

THE Bengal Express was fully booked, so I bought the cheapest ticket on a slower train that left in under an hour. Wedged between countless other passengers I clutched my rucksack on my lap, willing the train to move faster as it slowly progressed through the city's rail-side bustees. At least I had a seat; all around me people were standing, their collective bodies swaying like corn in the wind each time the train clattered over a rough section of track. People were hanging out of the doorways, too, and, judging by the thumps above my head, sitting on the roof.

I was faint and wobbly with hunger, and so hot that all I could think of was ice and snow and the cold north wind. When the woman sitting opposite pulled a folded chapati and a couple of chilis from the tied ends of her sari I must have been gazing at it so longingly that she took pity on me and tore it in half. I accepted the offering eagerly, noticing for the first time the tiny baby clamped to her breast. She must have been on the edge of destitution, for her feet were bare and besides the infant and the food, she was carrying no luggage. We nodded and smiled at each other in fleeting comradeship as we chewed, our knees almost touching.

The journey seemed to have no shape or form, nothing to distinguish the endless hours that dragged slowly by. The carriage was so crowded that I could only glimpse the window, but I was dimly aware of vast expanses of land chugging past, the villages and fields I'd watched so avidly a week earlier blurring into an endless shimmering vista of green and brown and yellow. Just as the train seemed to be finally gathering speed I'd invariably feel the drag of brakes and for no obvious reason it would slow and stop, sometimes for many hushed minutes. All I could do then was tap my foot and click my fingers impatiently as I willed the train to start moving again. I felt literally as if I was melting, my body sticky with the sweat dripping down my back and between my breasts. I'd begun to smell, and my hair was a crazed mass of curls, but it no longer seemed to matter. I had only one goal: to reach Calcutta and then travel onto Orissa as quickly as possible. I was panicking, you see, unable to think straight.

I wished I could calm down, but it was impossible. Now that my worst fears had been realized—the money and tickets stolen, my only friend hundreds of miles away—my imagination was running wild. What in God's name was going on? If it was our money that Coral wanted, why didn't she simply steal Gemma's money belt in Delhi and be done with it? I kept remembering the sense of being watched in the moonlit bungalow and the distant sound of the jeep and shuddered. I'd assumed that Coral was simply deranged, but clearly there was more to it than that. She had deliberately followed us, planning where we would stay in Calcutta and prebooking our room in Agun Mazir. Over and over again, I replayed the events of the past few weeks. In Agun Mazir the situation had seemed so clear, but now I could no longer remember why I'd left Gemma behind. Why did I always act so impetuously? I'd already betrayed Gemma with Steve, but now I'd done something even worse: I'd left her alone with someone who may be highly dangerous. I never stopped to think things through, I told myself bitterly; despite my gestures at caring, I always put myself first. It was I—the would-be traveler with my stupid degree and interestingly stamped passport—who insisted that the gods decide my destination, I who steamrollered Gemma's hesitations; I who had really got us into this mess. The whole trip was solely about me: my needs, my ego, and my adventure. No wonder Gemma was upset.

I closed my eyes, drifting into a nervous, semiconscious sleep. I saw the shuttered doors and windows of the bungalow, gray smoke gently spiraling upward from them, and suddenly pictured Gemma lying in her bed as Coral walked slowly across the room toward her. With a screech of metal, the train jolted to a stop again. I sat up with a start, my eyes open and my heartbeating wildly. Whatever happened, I had to get back to her.

THE train reached Calcutta in the early hours of the morning. I found myself an unoccupied patch of platform and huddled up with my rucksack among the other shadowy sleeping bodies. I was so tired that my eyes kept closing, my grip on the scene loosening until it almost slipped away, but I dared not let myself sleep. I had to keep my wits about me, I thought, otherwise God knows what might happen. I tried to pretend that it was all just an amusing adventure, a traveler's tale to be embellished and narrated back home, but felt only a bottomless, swamping anxiety. I was alone and without money in a vast, unknown land and if I didn't keep clamping it down, the formless fear which had been gnawing at me since Delhi would finally spring free.

Gradually the light began to change, a diffuse pink hue spreading slowly across the quietened station. After a while the people around me began to stir; the crows that during the day pecked at the empty tracks cawing in the dawn. I sat up, gripping my knees and looking around. I was chilled and hungry. After paying my fare to Bhubaneshwar I had less than one hundred rupees left; just enough for a cheap meal and the country bus to Agun Mazir. My rapidly depleting funds terrified me. I was flying without wings: on the brink, at any moment, of tumbling catastrophically to the ground. Perhaps it was lack of food, perhaps lack of sleep, but I could no longer think straight; my thoughts kept leaping in different directions, my mind perpetually changing. I should have rung my parents in Delhi, I realized now, or contacted the police. Once again I'd made the wrong decision and now it was too late for I didn't even have my return fare to the capital. If Gemma and Coral had already gone—and with this horrendous thought my stomach plummeted again—I'd be truly lost. Standing shakily I dragged my rucksack across the platform to the first chai wallah to set up shop, his urn of tea steaming over a newly lit fire.

Finally the Orissa train arrived. Climbing wearily aboard I collapsed into the nearest seat. The other passengers pushed past. A week ago I'd been perpetually stared at, my presence shining bright and strong as heads turned in my direction. Yet this morning few people even glanced at the crumpled foreign girl huddled by the window. It was as if I was becoming a non-person, my bearings and identity lost as I faded into the distance.

The train chugged on, the sun reaching up and through the barred carriage windows until it fell in slatted patches across my face. Pushing my rucksack against the window in an attempt to block out the light, I closed my eyes.

THE train reached Bhubaneshwar just after sunset. I couldn't afford a hotel, so spent five rupees on a rickshaw ride to the bus station where I had distant memories of a ladies' waiting room. It was late evening now, and the town increasingly deserted, the food stalls where Gemma and I had dined a week earlier closed down, the shops shuttered and dark. All I had to do was get through one more night and then I'd be on the bus to Agun Mazir and reunited with Gemma, I tried to convince myself as I paid the rickshaw driver and limped slowly across the road toward the bus station. If I found myself a dark corner no one would even notice me.

The ticket office was closed, but a couple of late night buses were about to depart, their running engines filling the yard with fumes as the passengers inside slumped wearily against the windows. I spent another few rupees on peanuts, bananas, and chai from the vendors by the side of the road, then slowly walked toward the waiting room. As I glanced through its glass doors I noticed with relief that a couple of European women were sitting inside. From their clumpy sandals, drawstring cotton trousers, and blond hair I guessed they were German or maybe Scandinavian. I pushed open the door, smiling at them eagerly. I was desperate for conversation, for any contact with normality; perhaps, I thought vaguely, I might ask them for some kind of help.

"Hi!"

Swinging my rucksack of my back, I placed my tea on the floor and sat down expectantly. Like me, they had probably not been in India for long: their rucksacks were pristine and their Teutonic skin pale.

"Hello."

The girl sitting closest to me smiled frigidly and looked away quickly.

"Where are you off to? I've just got in from Calcutta . . ."

Picking up my tea, I took a sip. The women glanced covertly at each other and shifted imperceptibly in their seats.

"Puri."

"Oh yeah? I've heard that's really nice . . ."

They nodded coldly, then looked pointedly away, signaling an end to the exchange. A few awkward moments passed, then they stood up, pulled their rucksacks onto their backs, and walked out of the room.

"Bye then."

They didn't reply. The door slammed behind them.

"Have a nice day."

I sipped at my chai, the strong, sweet liquid briefly reviving me. What did they think I was going to do to them, for God's sake? I sighed, letting my body finally relax, and suddenly caught sight of my reflection in the glassed-over door.

I looked like a junkie. My pale face was sunken and thin, my forehead covered in spots. Smeared across my cheeks and smudged in a black blob on the end of my nose, was what could only have been oil from the train. My hair, unmanageable at the best of times, sprang from my head in dusty dreadlocks. My eyes glinted back at me, the mad expression of a drug-crazed freak. Looking slowly down I noticed that my skirt was torn, my hands black with grime.

I tried to smile, but under the sallow electric bulb of the waiting room only looked more psychotic.

"Jesus Christ!"

No wonder the Germans had scarpered, I thought grimly; they must have been terrified.

I spent the next hour or so picking despondently at the peanuts. When a station official came to lock up the waiting room, he eyed me with distaste and pointed to the door. I didn't have the money for even an attempt at baksheesh, so passed the rest of the night sitting on the pavement. When daylight finally came and the first eastward-bound bus rattled into the station, I climbed aboard with relief.

Once more I gazed from the windows as the bus sped through the lowlands, the padi stretching endlessly toward the horizon, the sky wide and blue. After three or four hours it stopped at the eating house on the edge of the forest. I spent the last of my money on a plate of rice and dhal and tried to wash my face under an outside tap. The bus set off again and a few miles later the road started to climb and we plunged into the forest.

I started to doze, my eyes jolting open each time the bus bumped over a pothole. I thought of the bungalow at Agun Mazir, Gemma's dingy bedsit in Stevenage town center, and then, unaccountably, my mum sitting in the garden, a bowl of gooseberries balanced on her lap. I would never have thought it possible a week ago, but now I longed for home. Why had I thought that life in rural Hertfordshire was so boring? I'd have given anything to be there, topping and tailing gooseberries under the mild English sun. I blinked back the tears beginning to gather in the corners of my eyes. Without warning, I pictured Steve the last time I'd seen him, his collar turned up against the rain as he trudged down my parents' drive. It should have been him with me in India and not Gemma, I thought with sudden, searing regret. Why in some misplaced gesture of loyalty to Gemma had I pretended to myself that he didn't matter?

The bus swung around a hairpin bend, its brakes squealing and its horn blasting so loudly that I sat up straight and stared out of the window in alarm.

"Aiee!"

In the surrounding seats passengers were craning their necks and pushing their faces to the window in an attempt to see what had happened. I peered down at the road in shock. From my place at the back of the bus it was hard to make out the details, but clearly we had narrowly avoided an accident. Hurtling toward us in the opposite direction another vehicle had suddenly appeared around the bend. Now it was partly tipped down the hillside, its front wheels whirring madly as it attempted to pull itself back on the road. For a moment I gazed at it dumbly, then suddenly I jumped up.

"Let me out! I have to get out!"

It was the silver jeep. I could just about make out the face of the shaven-headed man in the driver's seat, his features narrowed in concentration as he stepped down hard on the accelerator. I stared at him in shock. My throat was constricting so tightly that I could barely breathe. And now I saw that in the back seat there was a passenger. Her head was leaning against the rear window, her face turned from the road, but as she shaded her eyes from the sun I could see the red and gold of Coral's sari.

"Coral! Wait!"

But it was too late. Before I could push myself out into the aisle the jeep suddenly lurched back onto the road, gravel spraying from its wheels. I turned desperately back to the window, but too many heads blocked my view and then it was gone.

AFTER that I couldn't bear to sit still for a moment longer, so spent the rest of the journey hanging onto the luggage rack at the front of the bus. The driver kept waving his hand at me to sit down but I was so terrified of missing Agun Mazir that I didn't dare take my eyes off the road. We passed through a large village which I recognized from before, came to the roadside shrines, and then climbed even further into the hills. Every time the bus rounded a bend I shouted "Agun Mazir?" but the driver just laughed and shook his head.

It was late afternoon now, the shadows of the trees extending across the road, the light slanting and copper red. Any moment, I kept telling myself, and I'd be there. Finally the petrol pump and workshops came into view. A minute later we were in the main street of Agun Mazir.

"This is it!" I screamed. "Stop the bus!"

The doors wheezed open. Grabbing my rucksack I clambered

down. From the sides of the bus I could sense the other passengers staring down at me. Some were grinning as if enjoying a good joke; others seemed to be shaking their heads in what I could only interpret as disapproval. They must have thought I was mad, or perhaps they believed all Western women behaved in such a demented way. Trying to ignore their curious faces, I waved at the driver.

"Thank you! Good-bye!"

Still laughing he revved the engine and the bus pulled away, its bald tires spraying mud across the road. Swallowing heavily I looked around.

The mela was over: the pilgrims departed, the street empty. The only evidence of the previous crowds were the abandoned remnants of the stalls and a thick layer of litter. It must have rained recently, for dirty pools of water lay across the sidewalks and the drains were bubbling. Stepping gingerly over the banana peel, bits of paper, and broken clay pots, I walked across the road. With the exception of a thin, dreadlocked fakir lying on his back under the awnings of a shop, there was no one around. By now only a few last glints of sun remained; the far side of the road already lay in darkness and in the trees opposite a flock of birds were roosting, their dark bodies weighing down the branches like overripe fruit. Further up the hill I could hear the rhythmic thud of drums.

I turned onto the track that led to the bungalow and started to hurry up the hill, my feet slipping on the muddy stones. Above me the sky was dipping from blazing orange into cooling blues and greens. The birds were quiet, too, the cacophony of voices I'd heard from the road fading into a single, plaintive song. I slapped away the mosquitoes which buzzed around my face. Above the trees the first star had appeared.

"Please, God, let it be all right."

As I approached the bungalow I began to run, my heart leaping wildly. I turned the last corner and finally saw the stretch of rubbery grass and straight ahead of me, the clapboard building, its outline silhouetted against the deep blue sky.

"Christ, I'll do anything. Just let her be there . . ."

Yet even as I ran up the path, I knew that I was too late. Ahead of me the windows of the bungalow were dark, its wooden doors bolted with a large metal bar.

"Oh, God, no, please . . ."

I leaped onto the veranda, throwing myself hopelessly against the door.

"Gemma? Are you there?"

But there was no reply, just the squawk and screech of the forest as it slipped into the night.

20

DUMPING my rucksack by the door I turned and ran back down the path. When I reached the first bend I stopped, gazing vacantly down the hill at the dark treetops and the scattered lights of the village. I must try to remain calm, I told myself; it could still be all right. Forcing myself to walk, I tried to focus my thoughts. I had to remain positive; there might still be a simple explanation. There was only one passenger in the jeep, so the likelihood was that Gemma was still in Agun Mazir; perhaps, like me, she had grown sick of Coral and found some other backpackers to hang out with. I should go back into the village and ask around. Even if no one had seen her, there might be a phone I could use. I glanced down at the jerry-built roofs and rickety television aerials below me, my heart sinking even as I tried to buoy myself up: even if there *was* a phone, who on earth would I call?

I took one restrained step after the other. So, I'd run out of money and lost my ticket home, I told myself slowly, but the fact was that I was *British*. When I explained what had happened people would help. The world wasn't bad—at least not for people like me—but basically benign. It was what I'd always believed, and now I repeated it over and over again like a mantra. By tomorrow—or at the very latest, the day after—this whole nightmare would be over. I swatted another mosquito away from my face and turned the final corner. I would go to the first respectable-looking house, I decided, and knock on the door.

When I reached the bottom of the hill, I stood by the road looking around. The electricity must have failed again for the shops and houses were in darkness and above me a sagging cable fizzed disquietingly. From the trees on the other side of the road I could hear the chant of crickets; somewhere further up the hill a dog was barking. Unable to decide what to do I stepped off the sidewalk. I was unable to think straight, my thoughts skidding in a thousand directions at once. What I needed was some kind of sign, something to point me in the right direction. I glanced up at the sky. For a second all I could see was darkness then suddenly the clouds parted to reveal the large yellow face of the rising moon.

The shrine. That was where Coral had said she was going to take Gemma. At the time I thought she was talking nonsense, but now, as I stared over the tops of the trees at the star-speckled sky, I suddenly remembered how she had said she would take her there for some kind of cure. "Transformation": that was the word she had used. What on earth had she meant?

Turning on my heels I began to run back down the road in the direction of the track leading to Pir Nirulla's tomb. I told myself even if Gemma wasn't physically there. I might discover some kind of clue. There was no need to be afraid; I'd been stoned before, that was why I'd found it so creepy. It was just a forest. And now, all I was going to do was run down the track and look for Gem. It would only take half an hour. What did I have to lose?

Now that the clouds had drifted away the moon shone down with unexpected brilliance, its calm silver light illuminating every stone on the path, the trees and creepers and bushes as vividly as day. I bounded quickly down the hill, my footsteps crunching on the track as the dank foliage buzzed with invisible life. I was surrounded by a croaking, amphibious chant which seemed to rise with intensity with each step I took. I reached the first bend, the path suddenly narrowing and darkening with the shapes of overhanging trees. I was beginning to feel very afraid again, but this seemed like the only alternative left. Swallowing down my growing sense of dread, I turned the corner, brushing foliage and insects from my face. From the surrounding forest came strange cries and barks, the creatures that made them unseen and unknown.

I hurried on, my breath coming in short, exhausted gasps, the wet mossy smell of the jungle rising up around me. Perhaps all this was happening for a reason, I thought wildly. The gods had led us here, after all, so now they would lead us back. I turned the last corner and finally saw the clearing, just as I'd remembered it, at the end of the path. I could hear the drumming again, coming from further into the forest.

Swallowing, I walked toward the shrine.

"Gemma?"

The question was blatantly ridiculous. There was no reply, just the flap and squeak of the huge fruit bats which lifted from the trees into the air above and the endless singing of cicadas. I stepped into the pooled light, the silver rays of the moon pouring over my face. In their luminous glare I could see every detail of the shrine: its lichen-green stone and painted walls, the stars and crescent moons decorating the sides of the vault. On the other side lay the lily-covered pond with its sweeping steps and arching, elegant ring of coconut trees. The only evidence of the mela was a row of candles melted on the crumbling balustrade and a tinsel garland, placed on top of the tomb. Piles of dead flowers were scattered over the scuffed grass. I could smell jasmine, and just as before, a lingering trace of incense. The drumming had inexplicably stopped.

I took another step toward the shrine. My heart was pounding so violently I could only take hasty, shallow breaths. I glanced quickly around.

"Hello?"

From the direction of the water tank there was a scuffle and the rustle of leaves, as if a person or animal were pushing their way through the bushes.

"Who's there?"

A small creature scuttled across my feet, its body crashing back into the undergrowth. I gasped, my feet tripping on the root of a tree. Using the overhanging branches to pull myself up I walked slowly past the shrine toward the pond, my chest hammering uncontrollably. Someone was in the trees, watching me, I was sure.

As I drew closer to the pond I could see that on the other side of the coconut trees another smaller track led further into the jungle. It was clearly little used, for thick creepers hung across it. Bashing a path through with my hands I started to progress up the track, calling Gemma's name over and over again in the vain hope that she was somewhere near. Even now I don't know why I thought she would be. There was certainly no rational reason; it was just something I could sense, a deep, swelling certainty. I'd been right, I kept thinking, Gemma *had* returned to the shrine.

"Gemma? Are you there?"

I took another few steps up the path. All around me, I could sense the shuffling, darting movements of animals, the secret cries of the trees. The drumming had started again, but the sound kept changing direction, as if carried on a faltering breeze. I was feeling increasingly panicked.

"Gemma!!"

I kicked down another branch and stopped. My skirt was entangled in thorns and from the cold sensation of water ebbing over my toes the track seemed to have disintegrated into a small stream. I leaned over, cursing as I pulled at the thin material. "Fuck it!"

I gave the material a final vindictive tug and as it came away in my fingers I fell backward into the stream. My bottom splashed in the mud, my knee bumped against a tree trunk, and, my hands going out to break my fall, my fingers touched something soft and unexpectedly crumbly. Perhaps it's a detail I've woven in over the years, but I'm sure I smelled burning, too, a sudden carbonic whiff of smoke, so sweet and strong it made my stomach turn. Even before I understood what it was I was touching, my bowels were turning to liquid. I remember it now in slow motion: me fingering the thing and then turning and groping through the leaves; it still not making sense, all those long seconds before my life was changed for good. Then finally me screaming and dropping what I'd been holding and leaping back.

It was the ring that made me realize what I was holding. The thing I had touched, the thing which was so soft and pliable that its powdery substance was coming away in my grasp, was a charred hand. Most of the fingers were unrecognizable, the blackened stubs clumped together in a tight fist, but the middle finger was still largely intact. And there, at its bony base, its once silvery gloss black, were the twisted remains of the ring that Steve had bought for Gemma at Camden Market, the interlinked hearts melted into a grotesque blob.

And of course the thing lying under the blanket of leaves, the twisted thing with its back to me, its one attached leg gently bent beneath the stumpy torso as if asleep, the other apparently melted into its flank, was Gemma's body. Her head was turned away from me, as if in sleep. For those first few brief moments I was too numb to think or feel anything. Bending over, I peered at the corpse. There was nothing much to see: the skull was as empty as a Hallowe'en pumpkin, the flaky features burned away. For perhaps two seconds I thought it was a joke, some kind of macabre prank, then the words flashed into my mind and I knew it was not a joke at all but the dreadful, unbearable truth: *Gemma is dead.*

I screamed, hurling the detached hand into the undergrowth and jumping backward. My legs were buckling beneath me, my stomach heaving with the odor of burned flesh. Then, doubling up, I vomited copiously onto the muddy ground. My vision kept tilting and tipping, the world around me spinning uncontrollably. I would collapse, I remember thinking, and never wake up again. It was the end of everything.

Eventually I managed to stand up, but my mind was still not functioning. All I could think was that I had to get help. The remains of two large candles were lying under a bush, close to where I'd been sick, I noticed blankly, the wax melted into a contorted gloop. I turned slowly around, trying not to look in the direction of the leafy mound where Gemma's remains lay. It seems ludicrous, but I had an image of ambulances and doctors, as if she might still be saved. It must have been the shock, because despite an uncontrollable shaking, which was making it hard for me to walk, I now felt strangely calm. All I needed to do, I told myself, was get back to the village. Once I was there, people would help me. Perhaps I'd find out, after all, that it *was* a joke, and Gemma was not dead after all.

I glanced up at the trees just as the moon drifted through a misty veil of darkness, appearing a few seconds later with a burst of light on the other side. For a moment, in the eerie brightness of the night, I saw what I assumed to be the track. I started to run down it. My arms and legs were moving but I felt nothing. Gemma was dead, I kept telling myself, but the words didn't make sense. Above me the trees stirred in the breeze, the moon finally disappearing into cloud.

Pushing aside the thick vegetation I ran faster, not noticing when my clothes ripped on the tangled, thorny thickets that sprang in my way. I hadn't remembered so much mud before, but now my feet kept sliding in deep, squelching ruts, the stuff splashing over my legs and face. When my foot plunged into a sticky pool and I pulled it out without the accompanying sandal I carried on running, kicking the other one off as I went.

The track was becoming increasingly impassable. I stopped, wiping my face with the back of my hand and looking around. *Gemma is dead*: I whispered the words over and over and over again until they stopped making sense. *Gemma is dead*. As I looked up I noticed vaguely that I was surrounded by tall trees which I didn't remember from before. I peered up through the outstretched branches of the trees in an effort to locate the moon, but the sky was darker than ever. From far away, I could hear the distant rumble of thunder.

The drums were louder now, and very faintly the sound of amplified singing or prayer was carried in fragments on the breeze. Turning in the opposite direction I began to bash my way back along the track I'd just come down. Suddenly, directly ahead, I saw the graceful shape of the coconut trees surrounding the water tank. I was back at the clearing. I stumbled toward the trees, the creepers and thorns gripping my bloodied arms. I must be approaching from a different angle than before, I thought, for now that I was almost upon them the trees seemed taller and more numerous. Gulping, I stepped through their shadows.

There was nothing on the other side: no pond, no shrine, and no track to safety, just thick impenetrable undergrowth, which stretched endlessly ahead.

"No, no, no!"

Spinning around, I tried to get my bearings, but it was impossible. The drumming had stopped again, or—I realized with mounting horror—it had simply moved further away. All this time I'd been using the sound as an anchor when in reality it had never been fixed to the same place.

I started to run again, the cold shock of the last five minutes giving way to molten terror. *Gemma is dead:* it was all I could think, and as I stumbled through the mud the dreadful image of her furnaced body was all I could see. She'd been set on fire, her head burned so savagely that her face had caved in like the beams of a blazing barn. And as for me, I was completely, utterly lost in a vast expanse of virgin woodland, the forest spreading across the hills for endless uninhabited miles. There were no roads, no villages, nothing; just me and whatever beasts hid in the darkness.

I started to cry hysterically, the tears pouring down my face. I never wanted to hear them again, but still the words in my head went on. *Gemma is dead and it's all my fault.* How could I have been so completely, utterly irresponsible? I'd left her in this hellish place with a stranger who wanted God knows what from her, and now she was lying under a pile of leaves, as burned and blackened as kindling wood.

I was sobbing so violently I could no longer see clearly where I was going. Sometimes I slipped into mud up to my knees or my feet gave way beneath me and I found myself skidding down steep, unexpected slopes. All I could hear now were the shrieks and cries of animals, the steady throb of insects, and the desperate pounding of my feet on the ground.

An hour passed, or maybe it was more. As I plunged deeper and deeper into the darkness, I began to lose track of time. From the stickiness of my legs, and the stuff smeared on my hands, I knew that I was bleeding; I was growing dizzy, too; my vision suddenly tilting, my head light. It was all over, I kept thinking. Gemma was dead and I would never escape. In the sky above, the moon did not reappear.

My memory grows blurred. I remember thinking it was all a dream; any moment now I'd awake to find myself at home, the weak English sun filtering through the curtains. I think I stopped then, slumping to the ground as I slowly ran my fingers over my face. "My name is Esther Waring"; I can remember saying it out loud, my voice echoing in my head. It sounded surprisingly normal, as if nothing had changed after all.

Perhaps I was feverish, for time was moving strangely; I kept thinking that only a few minutes had passed and then noticing that behind the clouds the sky had begun to lighten. The coconut trees were a distant memory and the long slope which I was battling against seemed to have gone on forever. If I climbed to the top, I might be able to see over the trees and find the path once more. Yet every time I progressed a short distance, my feet would slide on the loose earth and I slithered back to where I'd started. The sun was starting to rise now, the first weak rays pushing through the trees. More time passed. I remember feeling unbearably thirsty, and looking up as the sky glinted tantalizingly through the trees. If only I could reach it, I kept thinking, I'd be able to see where I was, but I was trapped: my past, my present, and my future slipping ever further away.

Slowly the sun rose further in the sky. I kept forgetting where I was—I was at home, my mother's fingers stroking my hair as if I was a small child in need of comfort. Then my eyes would jerk open and it would dawn on me that the sensation was caused by the overhanging tendrils of a creeper or the brush of leaves against my face. By now my feet were completely numb, my legs blazing red and raw.

I must have still been trying to reach the top of the trees, for I was climbing a hillside so steep that I could only progress on my hands and knees. I grabbed at the roots that clung to the loose earth and swung my body upward, but they kept giving way and I hardly had the strength to move. I had to keep going; for my parents, for everything I had believed myself to be, but I knew that I was almost finished. My vision kept fading at the edges, my legs wobbling treacherously. Above me I could see the woody roots of a large tree which was growing vertiginously out of the hill. If I could just reach it, I'd have a stable base where I could rest.

Clutching at the roots I made one last attempt to scramble upward, but my feet suddenly slipped and with a large crack the root snapped in half. I screamed and tumbled backward in a flurry of earth and leaves, landing first on my bottom, then rolling down so fast that all I could see was a kaleidoscope of leaves and earth and glinting, patchwork sky.

This was it then. This finally was the end. When I stopped falling I lay for many long minutes listening to the shriek of the birds and the drone of insects around my face. I could taste blood and knew my legs would no longer move.

"Forgive me, Gemma," I mumbled. "I didn't mean this to happen." But my voice was too faint to hear.

Perhaps it was justice, for if Gemma had died, so should I. I closed my eyes, reality dimming. I started to imagine Gemma was bashing her way through the jungle to reach me. I could hear the thwack of sticks against the bushes and then the sound of footsteps growing closer. Now I could sense Gemma's arms around me and felt myself being lifted and lain down on the soft earthy floor. I could feel the warmth of her body, the comfort of another heartbeat next to mine. What happened to us now no longer mattered, I thought as I drifted in and out of consciousness. Our fight was forgotten, I was forgiven, and here, under the endless outstretched trees, our bodies resting in the warm, dry leaves, we were together again.

"Gemma?" I muttered, turning my head and finally opening my eyes.

"Thank God, young lady, you're alive!"

I was lying on a makeshift stretcher and looking into the rounded face and shocked eyes of Mr. Sanjiv Chakrabarty, M.A. in archaeology, University of Calcutta.

21

Interlude

So there you have it: the story of my great disaster, the trip that changed my life. After Gemma died, I got lost and was found; it was as horribly simple as that. After that it's all just noises offstage. I was blank, a nothing person in a nothing place, the only element to distinguish me from the beds I lay on and the walls I dumbly traced my fingers down was the roaring that now filled my head. It must have been a refracted memory, a piece of imagined history wedged inside my thoughts, for it sounded just like fire and no matter how hard I tried, I could not put it out.

Of course stuff happened, how could it not? There were hospitals and inquests and funerals to attend. But what's odd is how jumbled up they've all become. I passed through them like a shadow, like someone who no longer deserved to be there. And then, as suddenly as if those final, terrible weeks had been fast-forwarded into a blur of faces and voices and shifting, insubstantial scenery, I was back in my Hertfordshire bedroom, staring up at the ceiling and the roaring had stopped and I wished that I was dead.

But there are gaps I should fill in, details to provide. My memories merge and blur into a confusion of faces and voices and sensations, with sudden lucid flashes. I can clearly picture myself being carried by Mr. Chakrabarty, his podgy face puce. I remember the way the canopy of trees kept breaking apart to reveal the cloudy sky, the reassuring smell of human sweat, and the labored sounds of his breath. From time to time he put me down, wiped his face with a large white handkerchief, and muttered to himself in Bengali, but most of the time he spoke gently in English, chattering endlessly as if to reassure me. It was lucky he had found me, he said, for he'd only decided to take a hike in the forest as a whim.

After what seemed like only ten or fifteen minutes, we came out on the track. The main thing was not to worry, he said. There were good doctors nearby; if necessary, he would take me personally to Bhubaneshwar. Was there anyone I would like him to contact? What about my friend who was sick? I think I passed out again after that for I remember nothing more. Even now it still upsets me that I never thanked him for what he did, or apologized for my rudeness the week before.

After various to-ings and fro-ings with doctors and the police, the British High Commission had me flown to Delhi, where I was made to stay in bed. I was still alive, still functioning; no real cause for concern. My injuries were minor, my treatment slight: I had a bandaged foot; a sliver of gauze across my face; and the temazepam the Delhi doctor gave me to help me sleep. Little yellow capsules of peace, I still hide and hoard them around my flat; adult Easter eggs, deliverers of release.

They found Gemma's body a few days later, lying a hundred meters or so from the main path. Despite my impression that I had wandered miles from the shrine, it seems that I'd actually been stumbling around in small circles. It was amazing that I'd got so lost, the British High Commission lawyer told me with an embarrassed laugh, for rather than being deep in some imagined wilderness I'd been only half a mile from a village in the east and even closer to another large track in the west.

But while I should never have been lost, Gemma's remains

had been more difficult to locate. By the time the police found them the jungle and jackals had both had their turn: much of her head was missing, her torso rotted into the mud. In the end, the only thing to identify her was Steve's ring. I don't know the exact details, but they arranged to fly what was left of the corpse back to Britain. She was buried in Stevenage, her mother had insisted; it was where she belonged.

From the outset the police said the death was an accident. There was no hard evidence of anything suspicious, you see, nothing to back my story up. Apart from me, there were no witnesses to Coral's strange behavior or her meeting with the man called Zak, just the old cook who swore that he'd rented the room to two girls, not three. The Calcutta flat was owned by a Bengali businessman who claimed no knowledge of foreigners; the jeep could not be traced. All they found inside the bolted bungalow was Gemma's rucksack, three empty water bottles, and a pile of orange peel, shoved behind the door.

What could have been the motive, the police inspector asked, for such a senseless death? The traveler's checks and air tickets had been taken in Delhi, not Agun Mazir, was it not so? There had been no theft from the bungalow, none of Miss Harding's possessions were missing. And why, if foul play were involved, were those candles found at the scene of her death? Was it not the case that she had been suffering from fever? Left alone in such a state, with no friend to care for her, might she not have wandered into the forest in a state of confusion and lit the candles herself? Surely I was aware accidents involving open flames were very common? Perhaps, in my state of grief and shock, I had imagined the sinister elements. And all I could do was nod, for the way everyone was talking, all my stories of a strange hippie with a silver jeep and his crazed Australian accomplice sounded increasingly outlandish: a fantasy, a delusion, a denial.

The British press had other theories. In the wake of the

Rushdie affair there had been local tensions, a Delhi-based hack reported; British tourists were advised to take care. There were a couple of news stories in the broadsheets, a longer commentary in one of the Sunday papers. During the heightened emotions of the mela a site such as the Pir Nirulla shrine would have been a dangerous place for a lone Western girl to be, the writer argued. It was true that there was no specific evidence of an attack, none of the locals would talk, and for obvious political reasons the Indian police did not want to know. Yet what was clear was that the young women should never have been there in the first place. Backpackers who treated the world as a vast global playground, laid on for their personal thrills and adventure, ran the risk of being violently disabused.

The author was right. Whatever had actually happened, I should never have taken Gemma to such a place, let alone abandoned her there. I'd behaved worse than foolishly, I realized now: I was reckless, arrogant, hopelessly selfish. I'd ignored the warnings of the receptionist in Bhubaneshwar, slighted Mr. Chakrabarty, treated the forest and its shrine like a theme park. However inadvertently, I had led Gemma to her death. Three weeks later the British coroner might record an open verdict, but as far as I was concerned the case against me was closed.

After a day or so in Delhi my parents arrived to take me home. I remember Mum sitting next to me in the British High Commission, her face pale, her forehead more lined than before. She told me I shouldn't blame myself, that whatever had happened to Gemma, it wasn't my fault. It was just a terrible tragedy, an act of God, she kept saying as she stroked my hand; I should try to forget all these odd theories for if there was really anything suspicious the police would surely be looking into it. It was time to come home.

The eyes of Gemma's mother said something else. She flew to Delhi as soon as she heard of her daughter's death and I met her a few days later at the High Commission, over biscuits and watery English tea. She had always looked a mess, but now her face seemed to have imploded, her red eyes sunken and bruised, her cheeks caved in around her sharp, pinched nose. I remember my shock at seeing her; the chain of events which I'd released when I left Gemma a week ago working its way across the world and into her body, turning her from a disheveled fortysomething housewife into a broken old woman. She held her tea on her lap, staring at my face—but never into my eyes—while I tried to explain what had happened. I told her about Coral and the man in the jeep, but she just looked past me to the wall, her face dead. She'd never liked me, I realized, but now she hated me. I could hear myself drone on, my pathetic, futile excuses falling around me like drizzle in a desert. When I'd finished she shook her head, her bony fingers still clutching her saucer. "But I still don't understand, Esther," she whispered. "It was such an out-of-the-way place and Gemma was so ill. Why did you abandon her like that?"

All those questions; all those blanks I found so hard to fill. What could I say? That I'd stolen the man Gemma was obsessed with, betrayed her in the worst way a girlfriend could? That I'd broken her heart, then dumped her in the jungle? That she'd never wanted to go to Agun Mazir but I'd insisted, that I'd known she was sick but had left her with a raving druggie all the same? I'd done all those things, there was no excuse, no self-justifying story to tell.

But if those unspeakable truths were embedded deep inside me, there were others I searched for, questions which over the years have become part of my surroundings, endless echoes in the place where I am trapped. The answers I wanted were of a different order from those asked by the Indian police and the British press and Gemma's mother. They were both more simple and more complicated and they are central to who I am today.

How does one gain absolution from an absence? the echoes cry. How is release ever possible when the only person who could set one free has gone?

Five years later, I lie in my London bed staring across the darkened room, and I still don't know. All I am sure of is that I'm surrounded by memories that hedge me in and block my every move. They come back to me in fragments: scenes from the crime, pieces that no longer fit.

Stubbed out spliffs and candles and Coral's manic face. The temples at Bhubaneshwar, the soft fall of morning light across the room. Omelettes and rice and sticky sweet, clay-cupped chai. The dank smell of foliage, brushing against my face; orange pith, bitter on my tongue. The camels outside Delhi; Orissan elephants on the road. A bus with painted tigers; rickshaws, bikes, and cars. And then, glinting through the jostling mela crowds, a silver, Suzuki jeep.

I was sure there had been something going on, everything pointed that way. But when I started to tell it, my story disintegrated, the fragments of fact hurtling from my grasp like shattering glass. Perhaps if there had been people willing to listen I could have *done* something, but there was nobody. Gemma's father had moved to America; her mother had suffered a breakdown and now spent her days drugged and blank. My parents suggested productive diversions and my small and rapidly diminishing group of friends said I should try to move on. So what if our gear was stolen from our locker and we were joined for a while by a kookie Australian hippie, they seemed to imply. What's new?

So many, too many thoughts to hold together; as I lie beneath my covers, it all comes pouring out. Sitting on the Bengal Express, chatting as the sun came up; that roof in Delhi, looking at the stars. The pub at home: Gem, fag in hand, vodka and lime in the other, taking the piss out of everyone except herself. Did we really spend every weekend and evening together, or am I re-membering it wrong? My bedroom was our lab, our secret lair, where we experimented and schemed before breaking out on the world. Our first secret ciggie, puffed from the window when my mum was at Sainsbury's; the afternoon we discovered *The Joy of Sex* hidden under my parents' bed; the night—some years later—we got so drunk we could only crawl across the room. Gossip, bitching, dreams. Later on there were boys, and some-times other girls: a shifting crowd of hazy faces whose names I've long forgotten. I know there were discos and drinking, other relationships and alliances which at the time seemed im-portant. But without Gemma it is meaningless, my adolescence a burned-out, abandoned set. She was my mirror and now she has gone I can't see myself anymore.

I miss her so much, you see, and part of me still can't accept that she's dead. One day she was there—my old mate Gemma, the girl I grew up with, the person who knew me better than anyone else. Then suddenly she was gone: frazzled to a cinder, all that was left, just ash and bone. I try to get it straight in my mind, but it still doesn't make sense. Is life really as fragile as that?

22

BUT life does not stop, however much one wants it to. Even in the most desolate of places, where it seems that all feelings have been bricked up and nothing more can ever grow, those bright green shoots still push their way through.

Steve came to visit the day after the funeral. I remember hearing the doorbell ring downstairs and his calm, polite, young man's voice in the hall, but I still couldn't force myself to get out of bed. I was afraid to face him, I think; convinced that like everyone else he would blame me for what had happened. Downstairs I could hear Mum telling him that I was too ill and too upset for visitors, then a few moments later the roar of his bike on the road.

After that he returned every day for a whole week. Each time I heard his bike I'd hide in my room, peering out from behind the curtains, desperate and yet dreading to see him. Sometimes he didn't even bother to ring the bell, just left his offering on the doorstep: sweet peas picked from his granddad's allotment, pink stocks, wildflowers from the high-banked village lanes, all the flowers that I loved.

Eventually Mum persuaded me to get out of bed. After she had left the room I stood in front of my long bedroom mirror, the place I'd posed so many times with Gemma. My body seemed different from before: thinner, certainly; no longer clearly mine. When I pulled on the jeans and jumper Mum had laid out on the chair for me, it was like getting dressed for the first time. The clothes didn't fit the same, for they belonged to a stranger, discarded from another life. After that I went downstairs and sat in the dining room window, waiting for Steve. When he arrived, I answered the door myself.

He was obviously not expecting me for he blinked in surprise, his face flushing. He looked different from how I'd pictured him in India: younger and less self-assured, his skin pale and slightly blemished. Perhaps, like me, he'd been unable to sleep over the last few weeks, for his eyes were surrounded by dark rings, his face drawn. He was just a boy, I remember thinking: a twenty-four-year-old lad with a rusty motorbike and a passion for Arsenal, whose main ambition in life was to be a psychiatric nurse. And yet as I stood on the doorstep and stared speechlessly into his face, I knew that my need for him was infinite, that although he wasn't the arty, globe-trotting anthropologist I'd once envisaged for myself, I couldn't imagine being apart from him. Given what had happened, perhaps it was paradoxical, but in a strange way he was my last link with Gemma. And although in India the mere mention of his name made my stomach rock with guilt, now that he was standing before me I realized what we'd started was quite different from anything I'd had before and despite the terrible thing that had happened, I had to see it through.

"Hello there," he said, and then he leaned across and kissed me on the cheek in a way that seemed to say: *Relax, don't worry, I love you: everything is going to be just fine.*

AFTER that, we went out walking every evening, like an old-fashioned courting couple. It was May now and the countryside was overtaken by the wild optimism of early summer, each day dawning as warm and bright as the next as if that was the way it would always be. It should have been pelting with rain, for what I deserved were gales or freezing fog, but for long weeks the skies remained blue, the breeze warm. We wandered endlessly up and down the village lanes: each hedgerow crammed with cow parsley and buttercups and forget-me-nots, the trees heavy with delicate blossom, bluebells spread across the cool, scented woods. I can't remember what we talked about, only the route we always took: across the fields, past the church, and down the lane, every summer evening. It was as if I was walking my way back to England, very slowly coming home. And each time Steve delivered me back to my front door, just as the light was finally fading and the sparrows were roosting in the trees, India was a little further away.

At some point during those warm, hazy months we became a couple. There must have been a moment when he kissed or touched me in a way that sealed our relationship, but I have no memory of it, only of a gradual drift toward intimacy, and the sense of inevitability that followed. Whatever it was, it was different from before, when we had laughed and fancied each other so much. My stomach wasn't gripped with excitement and nerves; I didn't spend the whole night imagining his hands on my body. In fact I was disarmingly able to put him from my thoughts. Did I desire or love him? Was he "the one"? All I know is that I reached a point where I could no longer imagine it any other way. He was so calm, you see, so rooted in his English male matter-of-factness that I came to rely on him, became dependent on his company as my crutch.

We never mentioned Gemma, yet her memory was the foundation of our relationship: something intrinsic that we shared; something which would forever drive us apart. Like everyone else, he believed that her death was an accident, some weird freak that we would never understand. He never asked me about it. Like most men his age he thought courage meant staying silent, believed we should move on and away from the past. He wanted to be a nurse, not a therapist; his faith was placed in medical science, not talking things through. And so Gemma's name became taboo: our black box, that we never dared to open up.

As for me, guilt lay like thick dust over everything, obscuring each color and texture of my life until before long I barely registered it was there. I was bad, and to blame, and there was no point trying to prove otherwise. Even as I uttered them, I felt that my stories of Coral and the man in the jeep sounded preposterous, the lame excuses of someone who didn't wish to face the truth. It was ridiculous to believe they had killed her, I realized as I watched the nonplussed expressions of my audience. There was no clear motive and no evidence, just my muddled account of a shrine, a stolen money belt, and a young woman traveler who was not everything she seemed. The real facts were these: poor Gemma, who had never traveled before and was so famously unable to cope, had been suffering from fever. For whatever reason or post-hoc justification, I had left her in the jungle. And there, alone and afraid, she had met a terrible death. There was no point in telling stories or putting the blame on others. I'd been responsible for her, and now she was gone.

THAT autumn Steve and I moved to London together. Steve had a placement at one of the big teaching hospitals, and there was no reason for me to stay at home. We found a one-bedroom flat on Holloway Road and when I could motivate myself I managed to go to work: temping, useless PA jobs at faceless multinationals, a stint selling advertising space for a trade magazine, all the crappy low-paid jobs one is supposed to do in one's early twenties before moving swiftly on. The years slipped slowly past. Not better, but surviving. Not forgotten, just processed and stored: my file of regrets. Gemma was gone for good, that much was clear. And me? I was found, but still lost.

23

Five Years Later: Heathrow Airport

AND so here we are, almost full circle, only a small part of my story left to tell. This part I remember in perfect detail, for it was only four days ago. Once more I was about to embark on a journey, but instead of imminently landing, I had not yet boarded the plane. And this time, rather than being with Gemma, I was accompanied by Steve. And of course I was no longer Esther the intrepid explorer, who always got what she wanted and whose life was so charmed. I was just another Thailand-bound tourist, Esther Waring (age: nearly twenty-nine; interesting passport stamps achieved in last five years: nil; number of crap jobs resigned from in last five years: eight) about to go on her holidays.

"IF you wait here with the gear, I'll go and ask."

Steve put down his bag and looked enquiringly into my face.

"What do you think?"

He lingered awkwardly on the blue airport carpet, on the verge of leaving, not sure how to proceed. He was doing his best to be patient with me, but his hands had rolled into fists and a furrow of perplexity had appeared between his eyebrows.

"Whatever."

"It'll be just some stupid air-traffic thing . . ."

He stood for a moment more, waiting for some sign of encouragement, but I tutted and looked down at my feet. I know I should have been more responsive but his hovering attendance was making me feel worse.

"Shall I get you a coffee?"

"No. I'm fine. Just go and find out what's happening and stop going on about it."

"I'm just trying to help . . ."

"Well don't."

Tossing my head, I peered across the Departures lounge at the nearest TV screen. Nothing had changed since I'd last looked: while its peers on either side flashed braggingly that they were boarding, about to depart, our flight, BA307, was still delayed. I sighed and looked back to the row of seats beside me, already regretting the terseness of my voice.

"Steve?"

But he had gone. I scanned the crowds for a moment, my eyes drawn as effortlessly to his departing back as to my own name in a telephone directory. He weaved slowly across the milling airport: a tall, slightly stooped young man with a fleecy top and jeans, walking hesitantly toward the check-in desk. Although only just thirty he'd reached that disconcerting male moment when muscle tone is no longer maintained simply by getting out of bed. The gradually accumulating years were beginning to weigh down on his frame, I now noticed; his shoulders seemed more hunched, his gait a little less assured. His hair was thinning at the back, too. In an effort to stay one jump ahead he'd been cutting this increasingly short, the floppy locks which he had sported in the late eighties long swept away from the barber's floor. Five years ago, hair this suede short would have made him a Stevenage skinhead. Now he looked like just another not yet middle-aged, middle-class young man, with his token earring and not yet middle-aged spread, enquiring politely at the British Airways desk the fate of our flight.

I kicked off my shoes, pulled my feet up on the seat, and rested my chin on my knees. I should stop being such a bitch, I thought unhappily; he didn't deserve to be treated like this. Clasping my arms around my legs I pinched nervously at my calves. Unlike Steve, and his encroaching flab, I've grown even skinnier in recent years, not out of a desire to be thin but a chronic inability to eat. I cut my hair short too, soon after returning from India. The curls no longer seemed to match the way I felt; they were too extravagant, too bouncy for who I had become. Now, when I bother to look into a mirror a face I no longer own stares back: the eyes are too large, the features too gaunt, and the expression too blank for the girl I used to be.

I closed my eyes. I hadn't slept well the night before, perhaps in anticipation of the journey ahead, and had ended up lying on the sofa-bed in the small front room of our flat in an effort to escape Steve's snoring. In the end I'd taken two of my yellow eggs, only to wake clogged and nauseous with chemicals a few hours later. Now, as the sound of the PA system and piped Vivaldi merged into one monotonous background drone, I began to doze.

"TECHNICAL problems. They're trying to fix them. Have a cappuccino."

I opened my eyes to find Steve standing in front of me, a "Traveler's Fare" bag dangling from his fingers.

"Thanks."

Pulling a polystyrene cup from the bag I lifted its lid and licked at the bitter, chocolate-flecked froth.

"You've been gone for ages."

"I was looking around the shops."

"And?"

He tossed a copy of *Marie Claire* on my lap. "Keep your mind off things."

I glanced at him dully. "Great."

"Try not to sound so enthusiastic."

The magazine slid slowly from my lap onto the floor.

"I'll read it on the plane."

We were quiet for a while, sipping at our coffee and gazing uninterestedly around. Once I'd have amused myself by matching my fellow passengers with the destinations on the screen or batting my eyelids at the least attractive men, just to see their reaction. But now I stared listlessly at the assorted backpackers and businessmen and distracted families who milled around the Departures lounge. I cannot say exactly when it started, but in recent months I have been falling into an increasingly zombie-like stupor, a thick fog of indeterminacy in which the only thing I'm certain of is how much I dislike myself.

"So."

I shifted my position, stretching out my legs and placing the empty cup which I'd been grasping between my knees onto the floor. Steve was reading the *Marie Claire*. He looked up, smiling at me mildly.

"So."

"You still think this is a good idea?"

"Yes, I still think it's a good idea."

"It's too far."

"It'll only take ten hours. Then we'll be there."

I was silent for a while, staring ahead and chewing my lip. All I really wanted to do was sleep. Next to me, Steve chuckled and turned the page.

"I don't see why we have to go anywhere."

"Essie . . ." He glanced up in exasperation. "We've had this conversation a hundred times."

"Meaning what? That you're right and I'm wrong?"

"No, just that what we both really need to do right now is go to Thailand, just like we planned."

I stared at his calm, reasonable face. He was always so rational, I thought with a jab of irritation, so forbearing.

"Well, I've changed my mind."

"It's too late for that."

"No, it's not. I'll tell them at the check-in that I'm not going, then they'll have to get my bags back."

He turned back to the magazine, his face implacable. "The break will do you good."

"How do you know what will and won't do me good?"

"I'm guessing. I'm allowed to do that, aren't I?"

"I just . . ."

I stopped, looking disgruntledly at my feet. Steve took another sip of his cold coffee and, licking the tip of his index finger, turned a page, a habit which I found irrationally infuriating. If a minute or so passed without further eruptions he would change the subject, pretending nothing had happened, just as he always did. It's his way of "dealing" with me. After a while he put out his hand and laid it on my knee.

"It says in here that the average *Marie Claire* reader has sex three times a week and fakes an orgasm fifteen percent of the time."

"Ah."

I couldn't even try to be interested. I folded my arms and glanced away from him, toward the flickering screens.

"Can't you try to lighten up a little?"

"Not really, no."

"It's going to be fine."

"That's what you always say."

"Well, it is. We've got this far, haven't we?"

I shook my head bitterly. "I can't keep just walking out of jobs."

"They were arseholes, you said so yourself. And you can't spend your whole life answering phones."

"So what am I going to spend my whole life doing?"

"Look, let's stop going over and over it. It's time to move on. What you need is a nice holiday and then . . ."

I could suddenly bear it no longer. Snatching my hand away, I jumped up.

"Stop talking to me as if I'm mentally retarded! I'm not one of your care in the community cases!"

"For God's sake . . ."

"Why can't you stop pretending everything's normal?"

I'd been trying to keep my voice quiet, but it kept slipping out of my control and now I was shouting. A few seats down a middle-aged couple glanced covertly in our direction.

"Just calm down . . ."

"I don't want to calm down!"

"It doesn't have to be like this, you know . . ."

"Yes, it does!"

"Christ, you're impossible . . ."

"I know! That's what I've been trying to tell you for years!"

Opposite, a man looked up from his book. Catching his curious gaze, I glared at him and stuck out my tongue. The man looked quickly away.

"Jesus!" muttered Steve. "Why do you have to make such a scene about everything?"

"I'm not making a scene!"

I groped under my seat for my bag, retrieved it, then stood up.

"Where are you going?"

"I don't bloody know."

Flinging the bag over my shoulder. I stomped quickly out of the waiting area toward the duty-free. I knew I was behaving like a brat, but increasingly I could no longer control my moods: they descended like thick, rain-filled clouds and soaked anyone caught in the vicinity with my vitriol. Steve should just get it over and finish with me, I thought glumly. He was just prolonging the agony.

I passed the shelves of bottles and perfumes and Armani specs, and began to calm down. As always, Steve was right: I should get a grip, try to think positive. I tried on a hat and bought some suntan lotion and aspirins in the chemist's. It was like he said. We should go on holiday, relax and enjoy ourselves, then start life at home afresh. Wasn't that what normal people did? I passed the Disney Store, wandered around Next, and finally glanced up at the departures screen. Two hours later than its advertised time, Flight BA307 had made it to the top of the list and now was urgently flashing its final call.

STEVE was in the newsagent's, standing disconsolately in front of a stack of bestsellers.

"Hello, handsome."

He didn't even twitch.

"Steve?"

I stepped closer to him, putting my hand on his arm.

"They're boarding the flight. It's the last call."

"Right."

Very slowly, he reached out and picked up a book, turning it over and pretending to study the blurb on the back.

"Friends?"

No answer.

"Look, I'm sorry. I was completely out of order."

He flicked the book over and gazed at the cover. It's a game we've played countless times, our little dance: me sorrowful and repentant, him martyred and eventually forgiving.

"I'm a total bitch, I know, but I'm going to change."

Still he didn't reply. I reached out and grabbed his hand. "At least say something! I can't stand it when you go all silent like this."

He turned and stared steadily at me. "I don't think I can do this for much longer, Esther."

"It's going to get better, I promise."

I squeezed his hand, willing him to respond.

"Please, Steve, let's go and get that flight."

He sighed, closed his eyes for a brief second, and then suddenly opened them wide as if willing the world to be transformed.

"Okay then," he said. "You're on."

24

HALF an hour later we boarded the plane, squeezing into our seats and leafing through the in-flight magazine as the safety video played unobserved on the aircraft screens.

"Look, we're going to be flying right over India."

I pushed the map of flightpaths at Steve. He squeezed my hand: calm and patient, the way he liked to be.

"It'll be dark."

"So what?"

After another long wait the chocks were taken away and the wheels rolled forward. We stood in line for ten minutes more, then suddenly the engines roared and the plane accelerated down the runway. I stared through my small square of Perspex at the rushing tarmac and landing lights. As the aircraft finally lifted and the ground gave way to the night sky I reached for the warmth of Steve's hands, entwining my fingers in his, and resting my head against his shoulder.

The plane climbed steeply over London, leveling out as it turned toward the Channel. After a few minutes the seat belt sign was switched off and people began to stretch and open their papers and look around. A little while later the stewardesses served us gin and tonic in plastic beakers, which I gulped quickly down, and a hot meal which I didn't touch. When Steve went to the toilet, I swallowed another two of my yellow eggs, then stored the plastic cutlery, bread rolls, processed cheese, and perfumed napkins in my bag, my backpacker's habits dying hard. A little later we were handed earplugs, and the cabin lights dimmed. On the screen ahead, the opening credits of a Whoopi Goldberg film rolled. I closed my eyes.

EVENTUALLY the screen flickered soundlessly as its audience slept, their bodies flung awkwardly across their seats, their heads lolling uncomfortably on the armrests. I dozed, then woke, then dozed again, the hum of the engines lulling me into uneasy dreams as regularly as the snap of overhead lockers awoke me. The skies were choppy now, the plane rising and rolling like a ship on high seas.

"Since we are now entering an area of turbulence, please return to your seats and fasten your safety belts."

I'd thought he was asleep, but from out of the darkness Steve's hand squeezed my knee.

"It's okay, it's normal."

I leaned across and pecked him on the cheek, the sensation of his skin against mine so familiar that I hardly noticed it.

"I'm fine, Steve, honestly."

"Not scared?"

"Not scared at all."

More hours passed. The seat belt sign was finally switched off and the aircraft cruised toward the dawn. When I glanced at my watch I saw that we had been in the air for over seven hours. In Britain, it was still the deepest, darkest part of the night, but we were racing eastward, jumping time zones as we crossed the Asian skies. Peeking under the plastic shutters I saw that a pink line had appeared above the clouds. Many thousands of feet below were fields and villages and towns connected by fragile networks of rivers and roads. In a short while we would be even further east and I would finally glimpse the sun, the people below stumbling from their beds to light their fires and say their prayers.

I studied my watch once more. By now we must be over India, I kept thinking. Gazing down at the clouds, I searched fruitlessly for clues. Somewhere, all those thousands of feet below, my life had come apart.

"Gemma," I whispered, the name I had not spoken out loud for so many years coming thick and unformed to my lips. "What in God's name happened to you?"

There, I'd said it. I blinked, shaking my head in an effort to loosen the memory of Gemma's pale face staring back accusingly at me from her bed. After all the time we'd been friends—a whole childhood shared together—it is this alone that sticks in my mind. There has to be more to remember, yet as I try to recall all the other times the image doggedly returns, the one fading and distorted photo I retain: Gemma, sick and angry, and me, about to walk out. Unable to bear it any longer I squeezed my eyes tightly shut.

"It should have been me," I was thinking, but the words refused to come.

It was then that it happened. Suddenly, from a foot or so below my window there was a loud bang, a sighing, puttering noise from somewhere deep beneath us, and then a second, even louder explosion. The jumbo jolted violently to one side, juddering uncontrollably as locker doors swung open and bags were tossed into the aisles.

I started, looking around in surprise. It had sounded like a small bomb buried deep within the underbelly of the plane. All around me passengers were rousing, sitting up, and looking around in alarm; a few people cried out, a murmur of high-pitched, querulous fear rolling down the aisles like a breaking wave.

"What the *hell* was that?"

Steve, too, had opened his eyes and was leaning over me in an attempt to peer out of the window. From the rear of the plane the blasé stewardess who had handed us our tin-foiled dinner was running toward the cockpit, her British Airways hat askew.

"What's going on?" a passenger yelled as she passed. She hurried on, ignoring him: her face not calm and professional and reassuring, but gray with terror.

"I don't know . . ." I whispered.

"It was like we were hit by something!"

Steve was gripping my hand so tightly that it hurt. Behind me, I could hear a woman screeching: "Jesus God, we're on fire!"

I turned, studying Steve's features with interest. His normally smooth forehead was wrinkled with anxiety, his eyes distraught. All around us people were standing up, craning their necks to see what was happening. Somewhere to my right one of the people who had shouted out in shock at the initial explosion was sobbing gently; closer to the front I could see a middle-aged woman with her head between her knees. Mostly, however, there was silence, the plane cast into white-knuckled, breath-holding terror.

I turned back to the window in interest. From the engine flames were spurting into the freezing, dawn-lit air. They were like cartoon flames, I thought blankly, a parody of fire, dancing as orange and bright as a child's drawing. For a moment I gazed at them, unable to speak. I should have been in a state of panic, gripping at the armrests, crying or muttering my prayers like the other passengers, but all I can honestly say that I felt was relief. It was like watching a film, I remember thinking dispassionately, one that I didn't much care how it ended. After all, this was what should have happened to me all those years ago. It was what I deserved.

"Look," I said lightly. "We're on fire."

As I spoke the aircraft turned, the wing above the stricken engine tipping in the direction of the rising sun, which had instantaneously burst from its silver ledge of cloud. Suddenly the plane was filled with light, the rays splashing through the windows and across the seats. We were moving in an arc, for now the sun was coming through the windows on the other side, too. My gaze instinctively following the light, I turned, and shielding my eyes with my hand, gazed across the aisle to the front of the plane.

It must have been a distorted reflection, a play of light on steel and Perspex, but for perhaps two or three seconds I imagined I saw a figure standing there, the dark outline of a man's body surrounded by an aura of dancing color. I squinted at the light, momentarily confused, and in that briefest moment he seemed to take a step forward, his hands folded Buddha-like in front of his face, his head bent forward as the rainbow lights played around his hair. I gawped at him, my heart pounding so hard I was almost unable to breathe. Then suddenly the plane tipped to one side again, and the illusion was gone. Then all I could see were the acrylic curtains separating World Traveler from Business Class and the backs of people's heads.

"Jesus!"

I felt as if I was about to suffocate. I tried to stand, but the safety belt was still fastened and I was pinioned to my seat.

"It's okay," Steve was murmuring. "It'll just be the engine. It'll be fine. They've got other ones . . . It's all going to be . . ."

He stopped. From the intercom came the light, regretful sigh of someone with news of a minor inconvenience

"Ladies and gentlemen," said a male voice. "This is Captain Dubow, your pilot . . ."

In the seats around us, people were frowning and staring ahead, their faces rapt.

". . . As some of you may have already noticed," the voice continued, "one of our engines has gone out of action . . ."

The pilot paused, choosing his words carefully. No doubt it was a spiel he had rehearsed in training. "Although this is an unusual event, I must assure you that we are in no immediate danger. The remaining three engines are perfectly well equipped to fly the plane, but as a safety measure I have just this moment requested to the traffic controllers at Delhi, that we make an emergency landing there . . ."

There was an almost tangible intake of breath from the passengers, a mixture of annoyance and fear.

Captain Dubow cleared his throat. ". . . Whilst I must confess that I have never been involved in an emergency situation such as this before, I can only reassure you that my crew and I have carried out these procedures countless times in training . . ."

"Great! Well, that makes me feel a whole load better."

I tried to return Steve's smile but my face was frozen, my features unable to respond.

". . . So now, as I am sure you will appreciate, we have work to do in getting the plane down, so please stay calm and I shall let you know of any further developments." Click. The announcement was over.

As if awoken from a spell the other passengers were shifting in their seats, looking around the plane, and smiling reassuringly at each other. At the back a man laughed, and somewhere to our right I heard a woman say, rather too brightly, "Perhaps we can all go and see the Taj."

Leaning over, Steve touched me on the arm. "Are you all right?"

I nodded stiffly.

"Like he said, it's all just standard procedure."

"Yeah."

Slowly the plane dipped to the west and began to turn. I

stared through the window, my arms folded tightly across my chest. By now the flames were extinguished and thick smoke was wafting from the blackened remains of the engine. I closed my eyes. For as long as I could remember I'd been terrified of flying, rigid with fear during takeoff and landing and spending the entire time in between concentrating on every sound of the engines, certain that without my total attention they would fail. Yet now that what I'd dreaded had finally happened, I realized that I didn't care.

Everything had suddenly changed, you see. As Steve patted my hand and muttered his reassurances I was hardly listening; all I could think of was what I'd just seen. Of course it was an illusion, a momentary brainstorm brought on by allowing myself to think of Gemma, or the mixture of temazepam and gin, yet try as I could I couldn't erase the image of the Buddha-like figure and its halo of light. I gazed out of the window, wrapping my arms around myself as we descended over the early morning plains of North India. It was the same stale airplane air, but I kept taking great gulps of it, like a person who has nearly drowned. As the plane silently drifted through fragments of wispy cloud and I saw the brown fields and scattered villages emerging below, I could feel myself slowly come alive. I *had* seen something, I thought; whether he was real or not, it had appeared to me for a reason. It was a sign, a wake-up call from the gods.

Above us, the seat belt sign flashed on. The plane was hushed again, the more vociferous passengers quietened by a collective intake of breath, a silent prayer. At the front the stewardess took her seat. Her mascara was blotted, I noticed dispassionately; she must have been crying.

Yet I was not scared, not even a tiny bit. I knew that our crippled plane would land safely, for the flames were there for a reason. It was so obvious, so simple. If I was to carry on, I thought as the roofs of the Delhi shanties finally came into view, I had to stop living in this numb and dumbed-down way. It had taken me five long years to face it, but finally I was going to return to India and discover the truth.

25

THE plane landed ten minutes later, chased down the runway by a precautionary fleet of fire engines and ambulances, their alarms jangling redundantly across the tarmac. As we finally halted in front of the airport buildings there was a brief, vaguely embarrassed flutter of applause from the more demonstrative passengers followed by another announcement from the pilot. The terms "hotel" and "alternative aircraft" were met by sighs; the faces which only a few minutes earlier had been tight with fear were now clouded only by irritation.

"Actually, I think I'll walk!" There was a ripple of laughter at this, people turning and smiling at the speaker: an old American bloke in jogging pants and a T-shirt. Then everyone was standing and reaching for their bags and shuffling companionably down the aisles. If previously they had been afraid, now they were shrugging and smiling at each other, their shared experience melting away the usual barriers of English reserve.

I joined the line. A few steps ahead of me Steve was reaching for the bags of an elderly lady; he kept turning and smiling at me but all I could do was grimace. When I reached the front of the plane I began to descend the stairs. As I stepped into the gray dawn air I shivered, wrapping my arms around myself and looking around uneasily. The airport was still largely empty; a few Air India Boeings waited on the tarmac, but with the exception of the black crows perching on their railings, the viewing decks were deserted. All that remained of the night was a fast-fading sliver of moon.

"Brr," Steve shivered, crossing his arms tightly over his chest and stamping his feet. "You'd have thought it would be a bit warmer than this."

I pushed past him, barely able to glance at my surroundings.

"It's six A.M." I muttered. "And the middle of November."

We filed into the airport, a straggling crowd of pale-faced, bleary-eyed Brits who had hoped to be landing in Bangkok in a few hours and now were doomed to be stuck in Delhi for at least a day. I straggled far behind, my eyes fixed to the floor. I was scared, you see, of the memories that would be lurking in the place, the ghosts I might discover. When I tentatively glanced up I half expected to see me and Gemma standing in the line ahead: two young English travelers, at the start of their journey, but all I saw were the backs of my fellow passengers. In fact, I realized as I looked around, the airport was quite different. I remembered scuffed linoleum and stained, betel-splattered walls, but now I was standing on shining marble slabs and the walls were decorated with brightly painted murals.

"They've rebuilt it," I murmured at no one in particular. "It's all changed."

Ahead of us, an official was signaling that we should wait in a glassed-in area on one side of the hall.

"Something tells me we're going to be here for a very long time," muttered Steve.

"Right."

I flopped to the floor, leaning against my bag and staring with growing despondency around the transit lounge. There must have been about five hundred people in all: some were dozing, their bulky European frames squeezed uncomfortably into the plastic bucket seats; others read or simply gazed into space. On the plane I'd convinced myself that all this was happening for a reason, but now that I was actually in India, my bottom resting on the cool airport floor, my eyes gazing through the windows at the rosy dawn sky and waiting planes, my resolve was seeping quickly away. The engine failure was an inconvenience, nothing more, the strange shadows on the plane a simple trick of the light. Nothing would ever change because I did not have the strength to let it.

I closed my eyes, willing the time to pass more quickly. Steve was asleep now, his head resting on my lap, his mouth hanging slightly open. I stared down at his blank, handsome face, the one I'd betrayed my best friend for, and felt nothing. We had been together for years, I thought flatly, and I no longer knew why.

I began to doze, time moving unevenly as I slipped in and out of muddled dreams, my legs growing numb beneath Steve's head.

"Esther, wake up . . ."

I opened my eyes. On the other side of the transit lounge something was happening. Around us, people were standing and stretching and picking up their bags, a large crowd already formed around the doors.

"Looks like they've finally sorted another plane."

We joined the line, waiting for another twenty minutes as we slowly shuffled forward. It was not actually a plane we were moving toward, the woman in front was saying, but a hotel somewhere near the airport. They would not be able to get another aircraft out for at least twenty-four hours.

"So you'll be seeing India again after all," Steve whispered, gripping my lifeless hand. "Perhaps it won't be as bad as you think."

I shook my head, unable to reply. I felt weak, my legs wobbly, my palms sticky. We were passing through the Arrivals hall now, the baggage carousel empty, the huge hangar of the building virtually deserted. This was more how I'd remembered the airport: the aroma of hot plastic and incense, the barefooted sweepers in their brown uniforms, the twitter of birds trapped in the roof. A group of bored-looking customs officials watched us march past their desks, and then suddenly we were being herded through a fenced-in area marked "exit." My chest was almost exploding with fear as we stepped through the doors, past the crowds of people crammed tightly around the glass, and out of the airport into the Delhi morning.

I took a deep breath, finally daring to look around. The car park was larger than I'd remembered, and at the bottom of the access road a new motorway had been constructed. This was where it had all started: where I'd gone to find a bus and Coral and her friends had first appeared. I tried to picture the scene which over the intervening years I have recalled so many times: Gemma sitting on the rucksacks, Zak, the yellow-haired hippie squatting beside her, and the two women leaning on the railings: one skinny arsed, with her long fake braid, the other bulky and apparently upset. Yet now that I was actually here it was impossible to grasp, the details vanishing like shadows exposed to light. I had imagined Gemma leaning against the airport's doors, but now noticed a low concrete wall dividing the pavement from the glass where luggage trolleys were stored. And with the jostling people and piles of baggage it now seemed unlikely she would have been sitting at the side of the road. Could it be that in the misery and regret of those five intervening years I'd remembered the whole thing wrongly?

I stared across the car park. We were being directed toward a line of coaches waiting on the other side of the road, our fellow passengers already filling the first. From behind me someone pushed past and I realized that I had not moved for several seconds. Steve was pulling at my hand now.

"Come on, Ess, let's go and get the bus."

"I don't want . . ."

But I could not finish the sentence for what I'd suddenly seen made me freeze, my eyes widening in shock. About a hundred feet away from our line, standing purposefully around the Arrivals doors, was a group of Europeans dressed in purple robes: a couple of thin, droopy-looking women and a young man with a shaved head and clunky sandals. They were handing out leaflets, I saw now, pulling them from the cloth bags which they had slung over their shoulders and offering them earnestly to the few Westerners who were trickling through the airport doors.

And there, standing less than fifty feet away from me, was the plump girl who I'd seen all those years ago in almost exactly the same spot, standing at the railings with Coral. I was sure it was her: I'd recalled the scene so many times that her lumpy features and flushed complexion were engrained in my memory. And now, as I watched her step up to a backpacker who had just emerged from the airport doors and was blearily fumbling in his money belt, I suddenly knew for sure that despite what everyone had told me, I'd always been right. It was not just a foolish story, embroidered by denial and self-delusion. All these years I'd been too stifled by guilt and grief to admit it, but beneath the facile surface of my memory I'd always known that Gemma had not died in an accident. It did not make sense and never had. *That* was why I'd never been able to accept what had happened, and that was why I was now so trapped. No, Gemma's death was something to do with this group of people. The missing money belt, Coral's lies, and her strange manic state at Agun Mazir were all connected. She and her accomplices had spotted us at the airport; for some reason they had stolen our money and tickets then pursued us all the way to Agun Mazir. Now Gemma was dead and after all this time the only way I could carry on living was to find out why.

"Essie, for God's sake. *Come on!*"

I shook Steve's hand away impatiently. He was saying something about how we should try and get seats together, but I hardly heard him. My heart leaping, I took a step toward the girl. I didn't know what I was going to do, only that I could not get on the bus with Steve and watch her disappear, taking my past and my future with her.

"Can I have a leaflet?"

At the sound of my voice she turned, her eyes fixing onto my face as she smiled and reached into her bag. I'd broken away from the line of transit passengers now and was walking away from Steve across the pavement toward her.

"Hi," she said softly. "You want one?"

She was older than I'd originally thought, less of a girl and more of a late thirtysomething woman, her round face lined and tired, her hair stringy. On her forehead was a yellow bindi; her arms were covered in what were either track marks or mosquito bites. I stared at her, unable to reply. There was a long pause, which seemed to grow increasingly loaded. I was standing opposite her now, unable to respond.

"Be at peace," she said gently. "And let me help you."

It was just what Zak had said to me that morning in Agun Mazir. The world swayed again. I gasped, my legs nearly crumpling, but she extended a steadying hand and now I gripped at it tightly, her cool fingers the only point of stability in my heaving world. When finally I regained my balance I let go of her and stood shakily. It was my last chance, I thought wildly, and whatever the consequences, I had to take it.

"I just want to know where Coral is," I whispered.

The woman shook her head. Suddenly I remembered the stupid cult name, the one she had told us was part of her transformation.

"Santi, that was what she was called. Do you know her?"

Like a flimsy cloud passing across the sun, she frowned. Over by the road I could sense Steve staring at us. I took a deep breath, fighting to get the words out.

"What are you all up to?" I gasped.

She beamed, her face swamped with happiness. "Our guru's work. Sai Baba, the new Messiah? It's like a miracle. All we do is spread the joy."

Any minute now and Steve would take a few steps across the sidewalk and pull me back into the line, I thought with growing panic. Then I'd be forced onto the bus with him and the other passengers and I would never discover the truth.

"Have you ever heard of someone called Gemma?" I blurted.

Our eyes met. Almost imperceptibly, the woman nodded. For a moment I thought I might hyperventilate. I sucked at the air, the edges of my vision darkening again. All around, people were climbing in and out of cars, loading their bags onto trolleys, and pushing past. Steve was folding his arms now, and had started to walk in our direction. I grabbed the woman's hands.

"What happened to her? Where's Coral now?"

She shrugged and almost seemed to laugh.

"She's with us. Well, I mean, back at our base in Manali."

She pushed the red pamphlet into my hands.

"Take this," she said eagerly. "It'll tell you everything you need to know."

I glanced down, seeing only a muddle of letters and an indecipherable picture. It was a statue of Shiva, the pamphlet advertising some kind of course or yogic retreat. Then suddenly Steve had reached me and was grabbing my arm and pulling me back toward him.

"What are you *doing*, Ess? *Come on!*"

I swung round; trying to break free from him.

"You don't understand, it's Coral's friends. They're *here!*"

He gazed at me, his face hot and confused. Finally he let go of my arm.

"What are you going on about?"

I shook my head. I was feeling so panicked I could barely speak.

"Look, just give me my passport and some money."

Fumbling in his bags he pulled out his money belt and handed it slowly to me.

"I don't understand what's going on."

I was jumping from foot to foot now, overtaken by the urgent desire to get away from him and the waiting buses. Pulling out my passport, a credit card, and a clutch of fifty-, twenty- and ten-pound notes, I flung the money belt back at Steve.

"Coral's here! I've got to find her!"

Still he stared at me blankly. Why was he being so obtuse?

"I don't have a clue what you're talking about."

"It doesn't matter . . . look, just wait for me in Thailand . . ."

"What do you mean: 'Wait for me in Thailand?' " His voice was ominously low. I looked quickly away from his face. I was yearning to be moving now, to be reaching the end of my story.

"I don't know what's going to happen, I can't say . . ."

"Esther, for God's sake . . ."

I took a step away from him.

"Steve," I hissed. "I have to do this!"

"No you don't. You've just got yourself into a state, that's all . . ."

"It's not *all!*" I shook my head impatiently at him. "How can you say that? You don't have any idea how I feel!"

He frowned. "That's funny. I thought that was the whole point."

At the time I did not understand what he meant. Turning sharply away, I peered across the road. Nearly all of the other passengers had boarded the coaches now. In a minute or so one of the airline officials was going to notice we were missing.

"Look, Steve," I pleaded, "I don't have time to discuss this properly. I just have to find Coral."

There was a long pause. Steve blinked sullenly up at me.

"I'm warning you, Esther," he said slowly. "This is the last time you're going to do this to me. I can't take your histrionics any longer. You've got to move on, otherwise I . . ."

But I didn't hear the rest of the sentence, for although it sounds cruel and hard, I'd turned away from him. It was a split-second decision, but I was convinced it was right. Even if it meant leaving Steve adrift, it seemed like I had no choice. I had perhaps sixty seconds left before they started counting the seats filled on the bus.

"I'm sorry," I breathed.

Then, not glancing back, I darted across the road where a line of black-and-yellow taxis waited. Behind me I could hear Steve shout "Esther!" but he was too late, for I'd already slammed the door behind me and told the driver to pull away.

26

It was not until the taxi had joined the motorway that I dared sit up straight and look out of the window. Glancing over my shoulder to reassure myself that no one was following me, I stared blankly at the flat brown landscape, trying to calm down. The cab was traveling through the scrub of the North Indian plains, just as Gemma and I had done that first magical night in India, but it was morning rather than late at night and the road was filled with juggernauts that rumbled endlessly past, their horns blaring. A line of camels plodded elegantly along at the side of the road, their haunches swaying. I glanced at them for a moment before looking away.

I stared down at my shaking hands. I could not believe where I was or what had just happened. Any minute now, I kept thinking, I would jolt awake and find myself on the plane, Steve's arm securely around me. But as I clenched and unclenched my fingers I could feel my nails digging into my skin and the sticky heat of my palms, and knew it was real. Somehow—for whatever reason—I'd ended up in India, and now I was halfway to Delhi, Steve was no longer at my side, and lying on my lap was a shoddily printed red pamphlet which seemed about to propel me into something momentous.

I gazed at the pamphlet once more. On the front, under a crude depiction of Shiva, were the words: "Sai Baba Ashram:

your path to enlightenment." On the bottom right-hand corner someone had handwritten an address: "House number 2, Kulu Road, Manali, Himachal Pradesh." Inside was a lot of guff about spirituality and "God-power," exactly the kind of crap Coral would have been into. She was there all right, I suddenly thought. If I really wanted to find her, it would not be hard.

We had reached the traffic lights and the ostentatious mosque which had reminded me of an over-iced cake all those years ago. I looked quickly away, unable to bear the memories. I didn't have the courage to do this, I suddenly thought. Searching for Coral and the truth about Gemma was the kind of thing the old Esther would have done, but she was different from me. She acted without thinking; she was brave and brassy and foolhardy whilst I, in contrast, had shriveled into something weak and bitter and incapable of action. Who was I fooling? I should tell the driver to turn the taxi around and return to the airport. I would wait for Steve there and when he reappeared I'd somehow make it up with him, just like I always did. Then we would go to Thailand, have a holiday, and I'd forget everything, just like he said I should.

But I did not move. The taxi sped on, entering a wide boulevard of large, luxurious villas, the city center growing ever closer. I glanced down at my watch, a habit I had picked up from work, where each minute past seemed a small achievement. It was getting on for nine. Steve would be at the hotel now, thinking God knows what. He would inevitably be angry and hurt and when I saw him again I'd be apologetic and repentant, willing him to understand, knowing that he never really could.

That was it. He would never understand, and until I'd proved to him that I was not simply hysterical, there was no going back: not to him, not to London, not even to myself. I glanced out of the window, noticing that we were passing the high-walled compounds of what looked like the British High Commission. I stared at the Union Jack fluttering from the roof and the guards lounging by the heavy metaled gates. Whatever happened, I realized, I could not return to the life I'd been living, to that stifled malaise where increasingly all I wanted was to be left alone, for events to wash over me, as painlessly and as unobtrusively as possible. Ever since I had lost Gemma, I'd been sleepwalking. I looked down again at the pamphlet, then folded it decisively, tucking it into my bag. Finally, I was about to wake up.

THE taxi dropped me outside the British Airways office on Connaught Place. I gave the driver a ten-pound note and climbed out of the car, gazing across the radial road as I struggled to get my bearings. Like the airport, everything had changed. I was clearly nowhere near the hostel where Gemma and I had stayed five years earlier; rather than the restaurants and small travel agents I recalled, the shops behind me were grand affairs, dealing in gold jewelry, expensive books, and posh silk saris. The Circus seemed smarter and cleaner than I remembered, too, the traffic moving past in an orderly stream, the as yet unopened shopfronts gleaming. It was true that in the doorways and alleys leading off the wide sidewalks there were sleeping bodies, their heads covered by thin blankets, but there were no more beggars here than in Central London.

In the center of the road, where the traffic paused at lights, a handful of kids were attempting to sell flowers to the waiting cars. I watched them for a while, remembering the children at Old Delhi Station and how I'd so primly reprimanded Gemma for giving them money. I must have been insufferable, I thought grimly: an unbearable mixture of know-it-all arrogance and naïveté. Why on earth had I presumed to understand so much about India after just one day in the place? Even worse, what right did I have to impose my narrow, ill-informed views on poor Gem?

In an attempt to halt the inevitable flow of thoughts, I turned back to the British Airways doors, noticing for the first time that two backpackers were waiting in front of it. They must have been there a while, for they were sitting on the ground, the girl—whose dirty dreadlocks obscured her face—apparently asleep and the boy buried in a book. They were a couple, I saw with a pang of unfamiliar loneliness, for the girl's feet were nestled into the lap of her boyfriend, his ringed fingers absentmindedly kneading her toes. As I approached he roused and put down his book, looking up at me with a smile. His eyebrow was pierced and he had a quasi tribal tattoo on his lip.

"It opens at ten," he said, in the perfectly enunciated tones of an English public schoolboy. "We thought it was nine so we've got another bloody hour to wait."

I cleared my throat. It seemed a very long time since I'd a normal conversation.

"Going home?" I said hoarsely.

"No way. On to Hanoi."

"How long have you been here?"

He shrugged. "A month or so. We were going to spend the whole winter in Goa, but it was totally ruined, you know? Like, there's all these package tourists and people coming from India just to see, you know, white women's tits and the police everywhere . . ." he trailed off. "How about you?"

"Just off the plane."

For a brief, imperceptible moment, he raised his eyebrows, his eyes flicking quickly over my crumpled T-shirt and the tracksuit bottoms I had planned to swap for a sarong once we reached Bangkok.

"Yah?"

I smiled at him again, this time more perfunctorily. "Yeah."

"And you've had enough already?" He jerked his chin questioningly at the British Airways logo behind his back.

"No, no, it's not that. I just wondered if you knew where I could change some money."

"Well, there's a cash machine next to the Air India office, if you've got a credit card or whatever . . ."

"A cash machine?!"

"Sure. This isn't Outer Mongolia, you know." He smiled condescendingly, his status as the more experienced traveler now fully established.

"Last time I was here it took virtually a whole day to cash a traveler's check."

He shrugged. "Well, I guess times move on."

"What about getting trains?"

"You should check out the railway office on the other side. It's all been changed." He sniffed and picked up his book, his interest in me fading.

"Thanks, then. Good luck with Hanoi."

"No worries. Catch you later."

To my amazement he was right. I withdrew one hundred pounds' worth of rupees from the cash machine and waited in line for no more than five minutes in the swish, air-conditioned first-class railway reservations office on the north side of Connaught Place. If I wanted to go to Manali, I was told, I should take the overnight train to Chandigarh, then catch a single-gauge train into the hills to Simla. Flying was out of the question, as the planes were booked for weeks. In under an hour I was standing back on the sidewalk, a train ticket dated for that evening tucked into my passport.

I stood inertly by the road, watching the traffic. Perhaps it was the delayed effect of shock or that I hadn't slept or eaten properly for so long, but my thoughts kept zooming in and out of focus as if, just like all those years ago in the forest, I was stoned. I kept trying to galvanize myself into action. There were preparations to make, I told myself: I should buy some clothes, a toothbrush, and some provisions for the train. But when I turned toward Janpath, I felt suddenly giddy, the light blotting out alarmingly at the edge of my sight. Staggering back to the arcade of shops which arched behind me, I leaned my hands on my knees, fixing my eyes to the sidewalk in an effort not to faint.

It was different, yet completely the same, that was what knocked me off balance. There was the same hot sweet smell of jasmine and latrines; the same fuming rush of Ambassador cars and scooters and Tata trucks; the same street stalls with their paan leaves and sweet tobacco, their one paisa bidis and cheap reproduction prints. Yet everything was transformed, for the person that I'd been before had disappeared. When I'd walked toward the railway reservations office I had marched straight past the hostel where Gemma and I had stayed, not noticing it at first and only spinning around and gawping at the neon sign a few seconds later. For a moment I tried to picture Gemma walking up the steps, her pristine rucksack on her back, so ignorant of what lay ahead. But her ghost had vanished; all I could see was a small group of travelers smoking and chatting on the steps. Back then I would have aspired to be included in their group, to have joined their conversation and proved my credentials for authentic backpacking travel. But now I felt only a tetchy alienation. They had no idea what things were really like, I thought dismissively; they pretended to be so street-savvy; but just as I'd once been, they were innocents abroad. After all, who cared if they could travel around on some First World "budget" that still exceeded the annual incomes of most of the world's inhabitants? What did it prove, beyond their unwillingness to put anything into the places which they passed through so superficially?

I stood up, looking back across the bustling road. The whole backpacker scene was utterly irrelevant; the only thing that mattered now was that I find Coral. And that was what I was going to do. I had allowed five long years to pass as I sank into a mire of guilt and depression, but now I had been sent a sign. Of course I was scared: of what I would learn and the people who might try to stop me, but anything was better than not knowing. Folding my arms tightly across my chest I started walking in the direction of the Underground Market.

27

WITHOUT requesting it, I had been booked into the ladies only compartment in the first-class carriage. As I heard the guard's whistle and the train lurched forward I saw to my relief that the berths opposite remained unfilled. Swinging my feet off the bunk I swayed across the compartment and pulled the metal window blinds down with a clatter. It was already dark outside, but I did not want to see the passing lights. I wanted to be cocooned in my bunk, gently rocked by the train into senseless sleep until it was morning and I had traveled so far north that I was in another country altogether and my memories of me and Gemma were hundreds of miles behind.

Since my fainting fit by the side of the road I'd spent the entire day focusing on the immediate tasks of acquiring a set of warm clothes for the mountains, eating a vegeburger in an ice-cream bar on Connaught Place, and finding a taxi to take me to the station. Yet despite my efforts to keep calm I had found the emotional effort of trying to forget where I was exhausting. Gemma's ghost may have disappeared from the steps of the hostel in Connaught Place, yet my own twenty-three-year-old shadow had trailed around with me all day: a foolish, arrogant slip of a thing who thought she knew it all and who only slipped away when I stood in front of the mirror in the ice-cream place and looked directly into my nearly twenty-nine-year-old face. Esther Waring, the grown-up: with my prematurely lined eyes and too-thin face, who now knew nothing at all.

Locking the compartment, I climbed back onto my bunk, pulling the insubstantial railway blanket around my shoulders and closing my eyes. I had not slept properly for over thirty-six hours and now sleep came quickly and thickly, muffling my thoughts and then blotting them out. I pictured the shops at Heathrow, so many light-years ago, and the rattle of the train turned into the drone of aircraft engines. I was flying now, in a plane without a roof, the planet stretched blue and white and green beneath me. Steve was there, too, his hand on my knee, his breath warm and comforting in my ear.

"Don't worry, Essie," he kept saying. "It's just the engines, nothing to worry about at all."

Then suddenly there was a bang, followed quickly by another, just below my head. I sat bolt upright, my heart hammering. From somewhere across the compartment there had been a sharp rap.

"Who is it?"

There it was again, the sound of a fist bashing on the door. Swallowing hard, I called out: "Hello?"

But there was no reply, just the shake and rattle of the train. Swinging my legs off the bunk I tiptoed across the dusty floor, opening the door an inch and peering out. No one was there, just the long empty stretch of the corridor.

Slamming the door hard, I bolted it as securely as I could and leaned against it, my eyes closed tight, my chest pounding. It was nothing, I was telling myself; just a guard, checking that the doors were properly locked. There was no need to be alarmed.

I double-checked the lock, then swayed unsteadily across the compartment to the window and pulled up the blinds. Beyond the tracks the quiet night fields were illuminated by a full moon, the sky crammed with stars. I sat down, hugging my shoulders for comfort. I was too wired now for sleep, and there were no little yellow eggs to help me on my way, but it didn't matter. Soon—before the next day was over—I would reach the mountains.

OUTSIDE Chandigarh the train finally stopped, and gathering up my few belongings I climbed wearily out. In the chilly half light of six A.M., I was cold. The other passengers had wrapped Kashmiri shawls around their shoulders and were stamping their feet at the morning chill; some wore gloves and scarves. Blowing on my hands for warmth, I wandered up and down the platform, regretting the Punjabi kameez and light trousers I'd bought for three hundred rupees in Delhi. I had badly misjudged the situation, I realized. If I was too cold now I would freeze further north. I was numbingly tired, too; as I waited for the Simla train my eyelids kept fluttering shut and my legs were wobbling precariously. I was, after all, still in British time, and had been on the edge of sleep when the train had stopped.

After about five minutes a narrow gauge train shunted onto the opposite platform and showing my ticket to the guard I was directed to a carriage at the front. This time I was not alone. As I settled into my seat the door opened and a porter loaded with bags and cases staggered into the carriage. After a moment he was followed by a safari-suited man and three little boys in descending order of size. These were dressed identically in gray shorts, knitted jumpers, and sandals, as if on their way to prep school. Finally a woman in a rustling stiff silk sari and elaborately embroidered wrap appeared, her face hidden by a large pair of sunglasses. When the bags were finally arranged on the luggage racks, with the children sitting in a neat row and the woman organized with her handbag and tiffin tins, the man kissed each child on the cheek, nodded at his wife, and jumped dashingly off the train, just as it moved forward.

The platform jolted slowly past. Perched on the wooden bench next to their mother, the children stared at me in silent awe. I looked down at my feet, not wishing to meet their eager, innocent gaze. By now it would have been two A.M. in Britain, and I could feel sleep closing around me, a heavy, all-obliterating unconsciousness. As the train began to gather speed I leaned my head on my bag and closed my eyes. Somewhere in the distance I could hear the children giggling and feel warm sunlight falling on my face, but it already felt far away. I was being rocked to sleep like a baby.

I don't know how long I slept, only that some time later I opened my eyes to the wheeze of brakes. The train was slowing and finally stopping. Sitting up, I gazed blearily from the window. We had halted at a small hillside station and all along the platform people were jumping down from the train and stretching in the chilly morning air. From up the line I could hear shouts and the clank of doors; a few carriages down a chai wallah was moving slowly along the platform, a scarf around his head, a huge urn of tea dangling from his forearm.

I remember rubbing my eyes and reaching into my money belt, thinking only of tea and biscuits. Then suddenly I gave a muffled gasp, jumping back into my seat as if I'd been scalded. What I had just seen made my heart turn over.

On the platform, just a short distance down the line, was Zak, the man I had seen with Coral in Agun Mazir. He looked older than I remembered, his shaved hair grown out sandy gray rather than yellow, the hippie robes replaced by middle-aged slacks and a shirt, but there could be no doubt at all that it was him, for my memory had traced his face so many times in the last five years that I knew each and every contour by heart. I stared at him in stunned silence. His checkered shirt was so old that in places it had been darned with tiny, intricate stitches and the red bag he had over his shoulders was patched and stained with ink. On his feet were plastic flip-flops, their soles worn so thin that his feet might as well have been bare. He was buying a newspaper and had turned slightly away from me to pay the small barefooted boy who squatted next to a pile of Bollywood fanzines and *Time* magazines, but even though his back was now toward me, his erect, self-satisfied posture and short, tufty gray-blond hair were unmistakable.

And then, almost as if he could sense someone watching him, he glanced round. For a second his eyes squinted in the slanting morning light, but then he seemed to focus on my face, and looking directly at me, with those cold blue eyes that I'd never forgotten, he smiled. And as my gaze met his I was suddenly overcome with a terror so raw that the rusty train window seemed to tip forward, the edge of my vision darkening. For the few seconds that our eyes locked I remembered Coral's hunted mania in Agun Mazir, the fear I was now convinced I had seen in her face as she had stood before him on the sidewalk that hot morning of the mela. She had been taking orders, I was sure of it now. And when, a few minutes later, he had surprised me by the jeep he had stared into my face as if programming my features into his memory. If he was after Gemma, he must have been after me, too, I thought with a sick dread that rose and rose inside me like a river about to flood.

"God, no . . ."

Shrinking back into my seat I only stopped myself from screaming out loud by biting my lip so hard that I tasted blood. What was he doing on the same train as me? Had he heard from the others at the airport that I was on Coral's trail? Or was it a simple coincidence? Sliding down into my seat as far as was possible without falling off it I swiveled around so that my back was facing the window, my eyes fixed now to the floor.

"Is there anything the matter?"

Opposite me the woman had taken off her sunglasses and was gazing across the compartment. I blinked at her. I felt sick, my guts dissolving with the shock.

"No, I . . ."

Daring myself to look out of the window again I peeked through the glass. In the moment or two that I'd turned away Zak had disappeared. I goggled for a moment at the newspaper boy, trying to catch sight of a tall male European frame, but saw only an Indian man turn away from the line, a paper under his arm, his hand in his pocket. Perhaps Zak had not seen me after all, I thought desperately. Even if he had, he would surely not recognize me, not after all this time.

"Are you perhaps unwell?" said the woman.

I gazed at her dumbly. Now that she had taken her sunglasses off and I could see her unlined, rosy face I realized that she was no older than me, perhaps even younger. She was watching me closely, her eyes filled with concern. Pulling a flask from her bags she unscrewed the top and started to pour out a cup of tea.

"Here," she said, offering me the plastic cup, "Have some."

I nodded and took it, trying to prevent my trembling hands from spilling the steaming brown liquid. Zak would never have recognized me, I kept telling myself, and nor would there be any reason for him to follow me. In my anxious, sleep-deprived state I was letting my imagination run wild. I gripped at my beaker, trying to breathe more normally.

"Perhaps it is your tummy?"

"No, really, I'm fine."

I forced myself to smile, taking a sip of the sweet strong tea. When we reached Simla I would wait until everyone was off the train until disembarking, I decided, just to be sure. Finally I could hear the doors of the train slamming shut and it started to chug forward.

"And where are you heading?" the woman was saying. "You are . . . on holiday?"

She nodded at me expectantly, her eyes taking in my cheap plastic rucksack and the clothes I'd bought so hastily in Janpath Market.

"No, no, I'm not on holiday."

"So you are on a tour of duty? Do you perhaps work for a voluntary project?"

"No." I shook my head, wishing the questions would stop. "I'm just visiting a friend."

"How lovely!"

"Yes."

"And your friend . . . she is Indian?"

"No, no, she's not . . ."

I swallowed uneasily, gazing away from her face to the three small boys, curled up beside her. I knew I was expected to say more, but could no longer bear her kind curiosity. All I could think—over and over again like a neurotic obsessively washing her hands—was that Zak was on the train and had seen me. And now he would do whatever he could to prevent me from reaching Coral.

No, I was being ridiculous. I smiled wanly at the woman and asked if she had been to Simla before. She was saying something about her birthplace and her sons needing to see their grandparents but all I could do was gaze blankly back at her warm, attentive face. When I suddenly shivered, rubbing my hands over my arms at the cold air which was now rushing through the window, she stopped in the middle of her sentence.

"You are cold. Please, accept this." She held out her shawl.

"No, no, I couldn't possibly . . ."

"Please. I insist. I have a hundred such."

She pushed it into my lap, making it impossible to return.

"If you refuse I shall be hurt."

Finally I took it, draping the soft warm wool around my shoulders.

"Thank you . . ."

"Please, you are a guest in my country. And I think you are in some kind of trouble. You must keep it."

I glanced at her, my eyes hot with tears.

"It's beautiful," I said.

We were both quiet after that, as if words were no longer necessary. After a while the sun slipped through the window and the train began to climb, the track meandering around countless hillside bends. I stared fixedly out of the window, trying to remain calm. Something was waiting for me in the hills and I was moving closer to it. It was the end of my story, the grand finale.

28

WHEN the train arrived in Simla I pretended to the woman that I was meeting a friend and so would not need to share her father's car to the town center. Busying myself needlessly with my passport and tickets I hung back as she gathered up her children and finally swept out of the compartment. I watched from the window as they hurried across the platform. I did not even know her name, let alone the finer intimacies of her life, but during those brief moments I would have given anything to have swapped my position for hers. We were about the same age, yet she seemed to be in a world which for me seemed forever consigned to fantasy, a kind of settled certainty about who she was and what her life was for. Perhaps it was easier to be in a culture where marriage and children were more or less taken for granted, I thought as I saw a large man in a white uniform take her bags; perhaps I'd always had too much rather than too little choice. And I'd made such a hash of it. I was no longer a very young woman on the brink of her life; I was nearly thirty, for God's sake. I should be at least edging toward some loosely defined state of attainment and maturity. Yet I had no plans, desire, or ambition. I could as much imagine myself being a mother as having a career.

After a while the platform emptied, and gathering up my few belongings and what was left of my courage I climbed off the train. There had been no sign of Zak, just a rush of Western tourists and Indian holidaymakers. It was safe, I told myself as I scuttled toward the last remaining taxi; Zak was nowhere around.

SIMLA reminded me of the Lake District, although in reality it was nothing like it at all. The hill station spread along a steep mountainous ridge: a mass of wooden houses which dwindled down the hill into a periphery of muddy clapboard shanties. On the horizon I could see the outline of the Himalayas, their jagged, icy profile stretching into the illusion of infinity. Yet as I wandered down the central Mall the next morning I could not shake off the sense that I'd been transported into a strangely skewered version of Edwardian Britain, with its neat churches, tearooms and oddly reminiscent English architecture. Perhaps that was what the Empire was all about: the transplanting of little bits of fossilized Britain all over the world until it seemed completely normal that the locals use words like "spiffing" and "opine" and every transaction was wrapped around with a creaking, Byzantine bureaucracy that served no purpose but to reinforce a dusty colonial ideal of hierarchy and order. Even the middle-class Indians promenading the Mall looked like 1950s English tourists, the ladies with their gloves and heels, the gents with their cameras and sheepskin coats.

I turned down an alley of steep steps and began to descend the hill. At the bottom, the cheery lady in the tourist information office had assured me, I would find the bus station. From there I could catch a tourist bus to Manali: it left every day at ten A.M. The journey took about eight hours, depending on the condition of the roads.

I shivered, running my fingers through my wet hair. The day before the sky had been clear, but this morning a thick mist had descended from the hills, covering the town with a light gauze of drizzle. I'd bought a heavy cotton shalwar kameez, a button-up cardigan, and a thick pair of hiker's socks, all of which I was now wearing, but I was still cold. I shuddered again, pulling my shawl around my shoulders.

I found the bus stand easily: my eyes immediately picking out the handful of Westerners waiting by the side of the road. They were the usual traveler types: a young guy wearing a Nepalese cap and flip-flops over woolly socks; an Australian couple who sat clumsily on the sidewalk with their arms proprietorially around each other, and an older, white-haired woman in a kagool and climbing boots. After checking that they were waiting for the same bus, I stood a little further down, staring determinedly at the drain so that even the woman, who kept glancing in my direction in a friendly way, was unable to make eye contact.

I did not want to exchange travelers' information, to tell her where I'd been and where I was going. For ever since losing Gemma I have fallen out of the habit of easy chat. At work, when the other girls eat their sandwiches in the park or pop out for a fire-escape smoke, I remain alone; I cannot pretend to converse in the open, empathetic style of other women, swapping intimacies as casually as travelers compare the places they've been. My story is different: no one can offer the comfort of another, similar tale; when I do try and tell it people look horrified or embarrassed. Even worse, they tell me they know how I feel. I don't need friends, I tell myself; not anymore.

When the bus arrived I found myself a place at the back, wedging my bag firmly on the next seat so that the kagool-wearing woman would not be able to share. As we finally pulled away I slid down in my seat, resting my head against the steamy window and closing my eyes. Locked safely into my hotel room in Simla I'd begun to feel better but now a tight, nervous feeling was starting to build in my gut. I was hurtling toward Manali as if all I needed to do was locate Coral and discover "the truth," but now that I was growing close I was becoming increasingly anxious. Supposing she was not there? I clutched at my knees, my fingernails digging through the cotton trousers into my skin. Supposing that she was?

The bus progressed through the fog, the looping road climbing ever higher until the mist furled below and above the mountains the sky turned icy blue. Since Simla the road had been clogged by a line of lumbering trucks, their flanks painted with pictures of planes and plump film stars, their perilously high loads held down with tarpaulins. Now, as it narrowed and folded into a series of ever tighter bends, the flow of traffic seemed interminable. I shivered and wiped at the window with my hand. We had been on the move for three and a half hours and still all I could see were steep-banked hills and trees.

The bus turned another bend, its gears grinding laboriously as the truck behind accelerated noisily past. It was a miracle that there were not more accidents, I thought hazily as it narrowly missed a crowded car suddenly appearing in the opposite direction. In the old days I'd have spent the entire journey gripping the edge of my seat, unable to tear my eyes from the road as if somehow my watchfulness was necessary for our safe passage. Now I looked away from the scene with disinterest.

Resting my head against the plastic seat, my thoughts began to jump ahead. If Coral, or Santi, or whatever she called herself, was in Manali, would she ever agree to talk to me? And if she did, what would she say? I tried to imagine what she might look like after all this time but all I could see was her crazy bridal gear in Agun Mazir, the restless twitching of her hands. She had not been on drugs at all, I realized, she was ill—just like the crazies who drifted around London, or the pathetic, lost patients Steve administered to. Why had I not recognized it before?

And if she had been ill then, what state would she be in now? Would she be coherent and recovered, with memories that could save me? Or would she have vanished into the depths of the ashram, a ranting devotee, unable to convey a thing? I shivered and rubbed my hands together, the doubt seeping through my previous certainty with increasing force. I'd pictured myself knocking on the door of what I now thought was a badly imagined version of the Buddhist Center in East London, and Coral answering. Then—but I had not thought any further than this. What was I hoping that Coral would tell me? That she and Zak had plotted to murder Gemma? That her death really was some kind of accident, that it was nothing whatsoever to do with me? If I wanted absolution, I realized, I would not find it. No, a total reprieve was not an option; the most I could hope for was some different version of the truth.

Outside the window the road was becoming increasingly mountainous. On one side was the rock face, the road scattered with scree and the occasional boulder and on the other, just a short distance from the wheels, a sheer drop of some five hundred meters or so to the valley below. I peered through the grimy glass at the breathtaking view, noticing with voyeuristic horror the battered remains of a bus lying on a ledge halfway down the cliff.

I tried to picture Gemma the last time I had seen her alive, but while in Britain I'd been unable to escape her image, ever since I had gone through immigration in Delhi I'd been unable to summon it up. As I tried to recall how she had looked in Bhubaneshwar, or later, in Agun Mazir, all I could muster was a blurred picture of the back of her head as she walked down the forest track. The more I tried, the more the memories, slipped and slithered away. Even the image of her face when I'd finally and irrevocably stormed out of the bungalow disintegrated. Anyway, it would have been impossible for me to have seen her expression, I saw now, for as I had left the room she would have been behind me. As for Coral, I had no idea how she looked.

The person I did remember, however, was Steve. Each time I thought of Gemma his image shoved its way assertively into my mind. I pictured his face at the airport as I'd been leaving him, the distressed droop of his mouth and the way his hands had dropped helplessly at his sides. He had worked so hard for that holiday, planned it for so long, and I'd ruined it, just like I ruined everything. Poor Steve, he deserved so much better. What would he be doing now? Would he have continued, alone, to our prebooked hotel in Phuket? Or would he have gone home, back to our small, untidy flat in Archway? And when I eventually saw him again, what would he say?

I blinked, forcing the thoughts away. I would sort it out when this was all over, I told myself. It would be okay; he would forgive me. Yet suddenly I wanted to cry. I missed him, I realized, with a rush of regret and longing. I thought that I didn't need him, but I was not used to being alone. It made me feel out of balance, vertiginous even, like a rock climber whose partner has fallen. And now, stretching above me, my supports clattering in the valley below, was this vast mountain.

29

THE bus reached Manali in the late afternoon. I checked in to the nearest hotel: a large characterless block just after the bus stand which charged five hundred rupees for a soulless twin room overlooking the hustling street below. The management claimed there was hot water, but when I ran the tap it spurted icily over my hands. I waited for a few minutes then turned it off. I did not care; I could shower and rest later. I tucked the pamphlet and my cash into my money belt, dumped my bag on the bed, and walked out into the cold, early evening air.

There must have been a recent fall of snow, for despite the heavy traffic the central Mall was white, the fine powder under-laid with treacherous slicks of ice. I trudged across the road, my feet stinging with cold. The place was thronged with people: tall, pale-skinned men with ponchos and woolen caps who warmed their hands on clay pots of smoldering coals; Buddhist monks, in red robes and sandals; Tibetan women with long rainbow-colored pinafores and heavy, clanking jewelry. The road was lined with stalls selling Kulu shawls and Ladhaki caps to the hip-pies and innumerable hotels and cafés, their windows steamy. Whenever I passed a backpacker I scurried on, my face averted.

As in Connaught Circus, I was feeling increasingly light-headed. I kept trying to block out my anxieties, to close down what remained of my rationality and simply go ahead and find the ashram, but each step I took felt more and more surreal, as if I was watching someone playing myself in a movie. It was for Gemma I was doing this, I whispered to myself, for our friendship. Yet as I plodded through the crowds I was increasingly overcome by an unease so visceral that I could taste it in my mouth, feel it tingling in my fingers. It was madness to come here, the voice in my head kept saying; I should have contacted the police in Delhi, or simply walked away when I saw Coral's friends at the airport. What on earth did I think I was going to achieve?

And yet I carried on walking. The ashram was supposed to be on the Kulu road and from the map I'd glanced at in the hotel foyer I was sure this was in the north. I turned off the main road, glancing over my shoulder as I cut down a narrow lane. Ever since leaving the hotel I'd had the prickling sensation of being watched, and now it was growing stronger. There was no one behind me, but I began to walk faster, my heart jumping.

The shops and restaurants were thinning now, the road crossing a river and then climbing steeply. As the light dimmed the air was growing progressively colder. Ignoring my aching feet I marched away from the town center and up the hill. On my left was thick woodland, on my right a precipitous fall. At the summit I could see a hotel set back from the road among the pines; beyond that were more trees. I was getting closer, I was sure. I carried on walking, trying to ignore the shadows which danced in the corner of my vision. When I heard soft steps behind me, I spun around, panting in alarm, but it was just snow, falling from the trees.

Beside me, the occasional car slushed slowly past. The sun had set now and grits of ice kept blowing in my face. Stamping my feet, I tried to blow some warmth into my hands. I would get to the top of the hill and then return to the hotel, I thought. I did not want to be walking alone like this in the dark, not surrounded by these crowding, petrified trees.

I took another few steps, my breath billowing white. I was surrounded on both sides by firs, the only sign that I was on the outskirts of a town the large placards advertising hotels, airlines, and family planning campaigns which dotted the sides of the road. I glanced down the hill to the zigzagged road and buildings below and suddenly felt a hand land heavily on my shoulder. I shrieked, leaping around in horror, my heart exploding into a thousand, palpitating fragments.

There was nothing there, just the low branch I had brushed against. Yet as I peered frantically into the firs I saw something else. Standing a few meters away from me, his body almost hidden by the dark trees, was Zak. He had been waiting for me, just as I had always known, and now was looking straight at me and smiling, his arms slightly outstretched. Around his body, flames flickered: golden snakes, writhing around his torso, ruby tongues, licking at his face.

I gave a strangled cry and leaped back. My instincts were right all along, the voice inside me screeched; he had been following me and now was waiting in the trees, that same cold smile twitching on his lips. I should turn and run, I knew, but I could not move. My legs were frozen, my feet stuck to the frosty ground. I was nothing, all my plans and fears and memories reduced to this frigid, numbing terror.

All this took place in less than two or three seconds. Then I must have blinked, for although I was still staring at exactly the same spot, he had disappeared. There was nothing and nobody in the trees: just the overhanging branches, stirred occasionally by the breeze and the last fiery rays of the setting sun, dazzling brilliantly through the tree trunks.

I peered at the wooded hillside in confusion. I had seen Zak standing there, I was so sure. He had smiled at me and held out his hands, like an angel or a demon. And I'd stood transfixed before him, the world turning on its axis. And then suddenly he was gone and it seemed that I was wrong, that it was an illusion, like the strange apparition on the plane. I was raving, a madwoman who could no longer distinguish fact from fiction, who had become lost in her own fanciful narrative.

I sobbed, turning and running back down the hill, my feet splashing through the sludge. It was all a terrible mistake, the voice screamed now. I should never have come here; it had unhinged me and now it was not Coral who was crazy and deluded but me.

By the time I reached the hotel I was shaking so violently that my teeth knocked together and my shaking fingers could barely grip my key. I dragged myself to my room, placing the "Do Not Disturb" sign on the handle before diving into the bed and pulling the thick brown blankets over my trembling body. I was frozen, so chilled that I instinctively rolled into a tight fetal ball, digging my tingling fingers into my armpits. I had lost contact with my feet long ago.

Slowly, from the deep core of my belly, up into my arms and down my legs, a weak glow of warmth began to spread. I shifted slightly, feebly extending my feet an extra inch and spreading my hands out from under the blanket and over the cool cotton pillow. But even as the heat reached my fingertips and my toes began to thaw, I could not stop shaking.

It was fear, I realized as I lay there: a freezing terror which had gripped me since Delhi and now was holding me against the bed with icy, probing fingers. Alone here in this wintry place I was going mad. Without stopping to think what I was doing I'd marched away from Steve, dumping him as unceremoniously as the aborted dates I used to have. And now I was wrestling with demons which, it seemed, came not from some macabre plot that I was about to heroically discover, but myself. Steve was clearly the only stable force in my life, the only thing which held me together. Without him I was lost.

I turned onto my stomach, wrapping my arms around my waist as I tried to stop shivering. I had not let myself think of him since breaking free at the airport, but now I longed for the firm grip of his arms, his reasoned calm. What would he say if he was here now? That I'd made the whole thing up? That it was just as everyone else said and Gemma's death was nothing whatsoever to do with Zak and Coral? Was my grasp on reality really so slippery?

Whatever the truth, I could not face it. I was too weak, too much of a failure. Perhaps it was true that I could no longer bear the life I'd been living, but I simply did not have the strength to change it. Sure, the other Esther would never have been so defeatist, but she was gone. All that remained was for me to return to Archway and beg for Steve's forgiveness.

I snuggled deeper into the bed, my thoughts finally blurring. He had been right all along, I decided as I began to forget where I was, some things were best left alone. It was not too late to change my mind; first thing tomorrow I would leave this place and go home. Steve and I would pick up the pieces, just like we always did. We would make it up and I need never think about Zak or Coral or Gemma ever again.

WHEN I next opened my eyes it was morning and my face was wet with tears. Dabbing uselessly at my slimy cheeks with the backs of my hands, I rolled over, staring around the room as I slowly remembered where I was. Diffuse light filtered through the thin hotel curtains; outside my door I could hear the sound of the floor being swept. Sniffing back the snot, I sat up, looking through the small boxy window to the white wintry sky beyond. I'd been dreaming of Steve, the memory still so vivid that for a moment I was confused, unable to distinguish between reality and the dream. I'd been in a phone box desperately trying to call him, but could not remember our number. When eventually I got through, the phone just rang and rang. He had left, and I didn't know where he was.

My relationship with Steve was over, I realized as the dream disintegrated, and that was why I was crying. There was no point in returning to Britain to seek his forgiveness, for I'd ended everything the moment I turned my back on him outside the airport. He was my best friend, my only friend, who had stuck by me through everything, offering the only support he had: consistency; patience; a solid, unquestioning kind of love. And I had tossed it all away, without even knowing what I was doing. I loved him, I really did. But we could not continue as a couple; we had passed that point without even knowing it and now we had to continue our lives alone.

I stared down at my unringed hands, my fingers white and wrinkled with cold and suddenly missed him so much that it hurt: a dull ache, deep in my belly, a longing for the reassuring bulk of another body pressed against mine. But as I blinked back another glut of tears I realized it did not mean what I first thought. It was true that I was lonely but it would not be Steve who could stop me feeling that way. My yearnings for him were based on fantasy, not on how things really were. Perhaps we had once been right for each other, but over the last few years we had started to bicker continually, a simmering low-level dissatisfaction which neither of us dared to admit. When he touched me these days I felt irritated, impatient, wanting instinctively to move away.

Reaching for the roll of toilet paper I had tucked into the top of my bag I tore off a piece and blew my nose. God, I would miss him, but the truth was that I'd chosen to leave him behind, chosen to come here, chosen to be alone. It was not just an unfortunate accident; it was what I'd wanted. I splayed my fingers, clicking the joints and wiggling them as I tentatively swung my feet onto the hard stone floor. There was no point in being afraid about what was going to happen today. It was my fate, my dharma. And now it was time to find out what it was.

30

This time I took a taxi to the top of the hill, stopping it outside the hotel I'd passed the evening before and walking the final kilometer. I felt strangely calm now, the terrors of yesterday receding into what felt like the distant past. It was quite simple, I told myself. I was going to visit an ashram at an address on the Kulu road in order to find and speak to someone about an incident which had taken place five years earlier. There was nothing to be afraid of, not even my own untrustworthy mind. I'd had an uninterrupted night's sleep, a breakfast of banana pancakes and yogurt in a backpackers' café on the main street, and the paranoid illusions of yesterday were forgotten.

I started to walk up the last part of the hill. Yesterday in the dusk I had seen only the towering shapes of the dark pines. Now, as I shuffled through the hard packed snow I saw that while the road zigzagged sharply up the woody hillside, a panoramic view of orchards and terraced fields opened out below. The scene was so pretty that I stopped for a while, gazing across the green brown valley and listening to the birds like any other tourist. Beneath me two small goatherds in long brown capes and bare feet were scrambling through the trees that clung to the hillside.

I watched them chase the straggling goats back to the herd,

their shouts and laughter only dimly resonating in my mind. Despite my attempts to block it out I was beginning to feel afraid again, my thoughts skidding nervously, my mind unable to concentrate. What would I find at the top of the hill? If Coral was there, what would she say? It was too much, I suddenly thought; too terrifying. I should return immediately to the café where I'd eaten my pancakes an hour earlier, spend the day reading month-old newspapers and drinking tea. I did not have to do this thing.

And yet of course I knew that I did. After everything that had happened, how could I turn back? I stared up at the meandering, icy road. Just before the next bend was a turning into the trees. That would be it, I was sure. My heart was starting to beat a little harder, my palms to get clammy. Taking a deep breath I turned and started to climb the final stretch.

As I approached the turning I saw a small wooden sign with the number two painted on it. When I reached it I stepped quickly off the main road, not looking back. After the exertion of my climb I was hot and now I pulled the shawl off my shoulders, transferring it to the crook of my arm. At first there was no sign of any building, the road progressing through thick, dark firs. Then suddenly there it was: a large, two-story house built in timber with a red pagoda roof. Leading to the front door was a flagstone path which someone had recently cleared of snow, piling it neatly at its sides; flower beds and what looked like rose bushes stretched beyond. On the far side, set back in the gardens, was another concrete building, perhaps an extra dormitory or a storeroom; at the back of this I could see more grounds, falling steeply away at the side of the hill. Sitting in a bed of gravel just beside the front door was a large bronze Buddha, his fat belly and beatifically half-closed eyes sprinkled with snow.

This was it, I was sure. Ignoring my swelling queasiness, I strode through the garden toward the front door, fixing my eyes to the bamboo wind chimes that hung from the porch. It had started to snow again and all I could see were the crazed patterns of falling flakes. I took a deep, calming breath, but my heart was banging manically against my ribs. All I had to do, I told myself, was to knock at the door. After that fate or destiny or whatever one wanted to call it would take over.

When I reached the door I stopped, staring blankly at the heavy wooden knocker as if I'd forgotten why I was there. I inhaled and then exhaled, tasting snow on my lips, my thoughts and feelings frozen, my heart so still it seemed temporarily to have stalled.

"Just do it," I whispered. Then, trying to steady my quivering hands, I placed my fingers around the knocker and lifted it. "I'm looking for Coral," I said out loud, and it fell with a heavy thud against the door.

My chest was hammering so violently now that I could hardly breathe. I clutched at my trembling hands, too terrified to even turn and run. From somewhere inside the house I could hear the indistinct shuffling of footsteps approaching. I wiped my hands across my face and nervously tried to smooth my hair. Just as I noticed that my shawl had been trailing in the muddy snow, the door clicked open.

And there, standing before me, was Zak. This time it was not an illusion. There were no flames, no shivery shadows to claim him back, just the reality of a middle-aged ex-hippie in jeans and a thick Punjabi shirt standing in the doorway before me. He looked at me quizzically for a moment, and then an expression almost of relief passed across his face.

"Hello there, Esther," he said quietly. "We were wondering when you were going to show up."

I'm not altogether sure what happened next. I think I might have screamed, and I certainly stumbled, for Zak reached out and caught me, pulling me up and inside the house as I flailed at the air. Perhaps we stood like that for only a few seconds, or perhaps it was longer, yet as I clutched desperately at his arms I felt my whole history wash around me, each and every story I'd ever told myself swept over by a wave of something else.

When I had finally regained my balance I stepped away from him. I'd gone beyond terror now, to that numb place where in a strange way, nothing mattered anymore.

"I saw you on the train," I croaked.

He blinked, almost humorously. He had once suffered from acne, I noticed, for his neck was pocked with scars.

"I thought it was you," he said.

I gulped. My heart had started to pound again. I wished it would stop, for it was preventing me from breathing properly, let alone speaking. I took another deep inhalation of air, as if I was suffocating.

"Is she here?" I stuttered.

He nodded. Then, before I had time to realize what was happening, his strong hand gripped mine and he was leading me outside. He was a man, not a devil after all; as my shaking hand was encased by his I could feel the pulse in his fingers, his roughened palm. He had a pen tucked behind his left ear, I noticed now, and a small blob of red sauce smeared down the front of his shirt. I stared at it, momentarily unable to focus upon anything else. Did evil cult leaders really spill ketchup down their tops?

"Come on then," he said, smiling paternally at me. "Let's go and find her."

Taking my arm, he guided me silently along the icy path that skirted the side of the house. I followed him trustingly, my feet obediently moving one in front of the other. There was nothing left to resist, I kept thinking, nothing left to decide; all I had to do was what I was told.

At the end of the path was a tall wrought-iron gate which stood between the main building and the outhouses and led to the grounds behind. Unlatching the gate, Zak stood aside.

"She's at the bottom of the garden," he said. Very gently he squeezed my shoulder. Then he turned and walked back up the path. For a moment I was unable to move, my legs too heavy with shock. Then, taking another deep breath, I stepped through the gate.

The first thing I saw was a large, snow-covered vegetable plot, the green tops of carrots or perhaps potatoes peeking through the expanse of white. Beyond this were a mass of bushes and trees and an area of icy earth that must have recently been cleared. Coral was not there. I started walking across the flagstones which led around the vegetable plot, gazing distractedly across the garden. To my left were more bushes and rough grass, to my right a small orchard of fruit trees. Perhaps this was where I was meant to go. My feet crunching on the frosty grass, I hurried through them and found myself facing a small enclosed lawn leading down the side of the hill. At the bottom was a newly planted arbor of trees, a makeshift shrine to another huge stone statue of Buddha.

And there, squatting on the ground in front of the Buddha, was a robed woman, her hair wound into a long braid. I stared across the silvery lawn, unable to move. My heart had started to pound again, very, very loudly. Although she had her back toward me I immediately knew who she was, for I had learned the slope of her shoulders, the shape of her neck by heart. She was lighting a candle, I saw now, her hands cupped around a tiny flame. Leaning over she placed it on the stone pedestal, her head bent as if in prayer.

I opened my mouth to call out her name, but nothing came. For a moment my whole life—everything I had ever believed and thought myself to be—revolved before me. Then pinching at my arms through my thick woolen shawl I took one and then two steps across the lawn. The woman stood, hoisting herself up as if her body was stiff, and slowly turned around.

I stared into her face. Of course I'd always known who I was really searching for, I realized as I gazed at the small, slightly pointed nose, the still stubborn chin, the devastatingly familiar gray eyes; that was what I'd been waiting for, the real reason I had come all this way.

"Gemma!" I shrieked, and then I was holding out my hands and crying and running across the grass to meet her.

31

Agun Mazir, 1989

She had always thought of herself as a coward: her grip on life too weak, her fear of failure overwhelming. But lately something had changed; she could feel an imperceptible shift within herself, a gradual edging toward the unexpected. As Esther slammed the door, clattering noisily down the wooden steps and out of her life, Gemma turned over and sat up. She had been feeling better all morning, but now the fever and pain had completely vanished, replaced by an unfamiliar exhilaration, every inch of her body shaking with suppressed triumph. For four long weeks she had been holding back, waiting and watching as Esther's confidence was gradually replaced by invasive, needling doubt. She thought she was so in control: the one who knew it all, but she was so wrong that it made Gemma want to laugh out loud. She had always known about Esther and Steve, from that very first night in the pub. And now, after so many years of being ordered around, of being the friend to be pitied and taken in hand, the repository of so much useless and thoughtless advice she had finally had her say.

"Give thanks to Kali, the Destroyer! Give thanks to the Great One—the Day of Judgment comes!"

On the other side of the room Coral was pacing in a circle, her eyes down, her hands folded and pressed to her forehead like a Hindu bride. As she walked, her sari was unraveling from her thin body like silk from a bobbin.

"What are you doing?"

"Soon you will understand, sister. Soon they will carry me to my pyre!"

Gemma glanced at her with irritation. She had stopped pacing around now, and was standing in the middle of the room, her eyes fixed to the ceiling. It was hard to imagine that only a week ago she had been in awe of her. In Calcutta she had been so empathetic, so understanding of everything, her hints of a knowledge yet to be revealed irresistible. But ever since their visit to the shrine something else had taken over. She was losing control, her postures and costumes becoming increasingly fantastic, her thoughts all tangled up. Coral was sick, that was what Zak had whispered to her the night before. She suffered from delusions, got involved in mad, overelaborate schemes; he'd been trying to keep up with her ever since she had run off in Delhi and now she needed medicine and to be taken back to the hills.

Zak. The sound of his name was like a prayer. Gemma closed her eyes, allowing the joy to wash over her like a sweet cool breeze. He was her angel, with his calm blue eyes and hands that touched her like a blessing. That first evening in Bhubaneshwar she'd been so nervous that she had hardly been able to speak, but still, she had understood. She had sat down soundlessly at the table in the coffeehouse where he and Coral were waiting for her and he had reached out, right there in the jostling, noisy restaurant, and traced his finger down her cheek. And as he touched her she felt a volt of pure static pass through her, a shock so real that her heart flipped over.

That was when everything changed. She looked from Zak to Coral and then back again to Zak, and suddenly knew there would be no return. This was to be her new reality; these people— with their freedom from doubt, their liberation from all the *fears which so oppressed her—her new family. Steve meant nothing now, the affair with Esther was an irrelevance. They were the past, her history, something to be overthrown.*

"So where's your mate?" Coral said.

"She's sick," Gemma had said with an easy smile. "She said I should come alone."

It was only a week ago, but it seemed like much more. She lay back on her pillow, suddenly tired. The fever was starting to slowly spread over her again, a deep flush of heat which reached into her joints and blurred her thoughts. All she wanted was for Zak to return. Then he would take her and Coral back to the place he had described, where it was cool and quiet and she could spend all day watching the clouds pass across the skies and need never, ever think of home again.

He had promised, and she believed him. He said he was going back to Delhi to do some business; that when it was finished he would fetch their things from the locker, then return. She had given him her key without telling Esther. Why should she? After all, Zak was her secret, and if Esther found out she would ruin it, just like she had with Steve. So she told Zak that Esther was a hedonist, unwilling to do little more than party, and did not want to come. They planned to leave that night. She would return Esther's plane ticket and travelers checks to her wallet and then be gone. But now Esther had made her own mind up, slamming the door behind her, just like she always did, and Gemma need not tell anymore lies.

"Wake up, sister. The ceremonies are about to begin."

Gemma opened her eyes, her head throbbing. Her forehead and cheeks were unnaturally hot again, her skin slimy with sweat. Hoisting herself up on her pillow she looked around the room in disappointment; she had been hoping that Zak would be here by now, but Coral was alone, sitting on the edge of her bed and peering anxiously into her face. She was still dressed in the sari, but had painted thick kohl lines around her eyes and splodged pink rouge on her cheeks. With her fake braid hanging lopsidedly from the back of her head and the plastic tiara perched on top she looked like a little girl playing at dressing up.

"What ceremonies?"

"For the wedding, of course."

Leaning across the bed, Coral picked up Gemma's floppy hand.

"But I need a ring?"

Gemma snorted, half in laughter, half in contempt.

"Well, you're welcome to this piece of shit. I don't need it."

Twiddling at Steve's ring, she pulled it off her finger. It really was a piece of crap, she thought as she glanced down at it: mass-produced plate silver which she had to use all of her cunning to get the pathetic sod to buy. He was a jerk, just like his darling Esther.

"There you are, you can wear this."

"Jesus, Gem, that is like, so beautiful . . ."

Gazing down at the ring as if it was a twenty-four-carat diamond, Coral slipped it onto her finger. She was nuts, as screwy as a brothel, but Gemma didn't care. Let her play out her fantasies, she thought. So long as Zak returned in time to rescue her.

"So," she said, trying not to laugh. "Who's the lucky guy?"

Coral exhaled and ecstatically flopped back on the bed, her eyes druggy with bliss.

"You mean you don't know?"

"No, of course I don't. Go on, surprise me."

"Well, it's Zak of course. I wasn't going to tell you, but we, like, did it last night."

Then, as if in a Victorian peepshow, she smirked coyly and pulled the sari away from her chest.

And there, right in front of Gemma's eyes, were two purple love bites, one above her right breast, the other almost on top of her small brown nipple, an obscene warning, a portent of everything that Gemma dreaded. She stared at Coral's tender, bruised skin in shock. How could this have happened? Every time they met it was her *eyes that Zak gazed into,* her *hand that he squeezed. Yet last night he and Coral had woken her together and—she remembered now with a rush of sick realization—as they had stood by the side of her bed their hands were entwined.*

She shuddered, and looked away, her hands rolled tight and hard under her sheet. She wanted to smash her fists into Coral's chest, to pulverize her until she had reached her splintered, brittle bones. Her thoughts were fuzzing over, her vision misty red.

"He wants us to get married when we go back to Manali," Coral was cooing. "He says I'm his lucky star."

She was making it up, of course she was. Zak would never say something so trite. He was hers, her angel, her love alone. It was her he was sent to rescue, he had virtually told her so, not stupid, loony Coral. She gripped at her covers then suddenly threw them violently aside. She was so fucking hot, that was the trouble, and now her head felt as if a clamp had been placed over her temples and was being squeezed tighter and tighter. Sliding off the bed she stumbled across the room. She suddenly, desperately needed to cool down.

"What's the matter?" Coral was saying. "Are you sick again?"

"No."

Opening the door she took a deep breath of the cool air. She would explode if she didn't escape from Coral, her brain boil over into something she could not control. She flapped her hands in front of her face, her legs wobbling. From down the hill she could hear drums and the amplified sounds of prayer. It was the mela, just like Esther had said.

"So shall I do it, then?" Coral suddenly said.

"Do what?"

"Go to the flames? They're preparing them now. That's what all this is all about. For, like, the ultimate transformation?"

Very slowly, Gemma turned around. Coral was standing naked in the middle of the room, her sari a pool of silk at her feet. She was looking at Gemma expectantly, her confused, innocent face empty of malice, a little girl waiting for a treat. She was beautiful, Gemma realized as she stared at her, with her long willowy body, her tiny stomach and perfect, bitten breasts. So, her eyes were crazy, her face smeared with mud and her hair clumped and thick with grease under the wig, but in her madness she was radiant, her face dancing with hope.

And she was still Gemma, the plain, dumpy one, who the boys never chose. All her life she had been taught that to love was to lose and all her life she had watched other women win. She stood by the door and stared at Coral and she thought of Steve and Esther, of all the discos and parties she left alone, all the patronizing lies she had been told. Even her brother had not cared enough to stay; even her father had gone off with someone else. And she was expected to accept this shit, to take it like a trooper, to smile and say it didn't matter, to still want to be friends. She stared and she stared until she could no longer see and everything that had ever happened rose up inside her in a bloodied, murderous rage and she heard herself whisper: "Yes, Coral, I think you should."

There was a long pause as if it was not what Coral was expecting. She seemed to be thinking hard.

"You mean, he'd like, love me more?"

"Of course he would," Gemma heard herself say evenly. "It's the ultimate sacrifice."

It was almost like a joke, the stupid make-believe games she used to play with Esther. How could anyone take that sati stuff seriously? It was all in Coral's head, her foolish, fucked-up fantasy of India. As she said it she sniggered, but Coral did not get it. Instead, she spun round, her eyes gleaming.

"Well, I've like, got everything prepared."

She gestured to the table. Gemma had not noticed it before, but now she saw a large brown bottle sitting among the fags and water bottles and orange peel. It was petrol, she realized with a thrill, and next to it were two large candles and a box of matches. Turning with a laugh to gather her bounty in her arms, Coral tripped across the room.

The old Gemma would have stopped her there and then. She would have told Coral to calm down, taken the petrol and candles and matches from her hands, tried to talk her back to sense. Perhaps deep down a part of her might have wanted Coral to carry on, but she would have been too scared of the repercussions, too apprehensive of what lay ahead.

But the old Gemma was gone. In her place, the woman she had become took a step back from the doorway and smirked at Coral as she walked through it.

"Good luck," she whispered.

But Coral didn't seem to hear, for by now she had jumped down the steps and was running down the hill.

Grabbing at the window ledge to steady herself, Gemma stared at Coral's disappearing back. For a moment her vision blurred with nausea but then suddenly it cleared and even though she was burning with fever she had never felt so lucid. It was not a joke, of course it wasn't, but still, she was not going to stop what was about to happen. Why should she stand back while others took what she wanted? Lunging for the door she threw it open and ran down the steps.

∽

32

To her surprise it had been raining, and now puddles lay across the path, the steam lifting like breath from the branches of the trees. The air smelled dank and heavy: of warm, damp earth and rotting flowers; mosquitoes were droning in her ears. As she ran Gemma was blasted by the heat; the sweat dripping down her face and back and thighs so that the baggy trousers she was wearing stuck to her skin in damp patches and got caught up around her legs. Somewhere, not far ahead of her, was Coral.

She came to the road, pushing her way past the few pilgrims that milled around, and headed for the track which led to Pir Nirulla's tomb. Everything kept slipping in and out of focus, her surroundings fading and then sharpening as she splashed down the muddy path. Her heart was pounding furiously.

When she reached the first bend, she stared down the track, the sound of drumming thundering in her ears. From where she was standing she could see the crowd, pressing tighter and closer as it neared the shrine. And there, right at the back, where a crowd of men were standing back to watch the spectacle, Coral was dancing, waving the now burning candles high above her head.

It was too late for Gemma to intervene, of course it was. And *after all, it was what she wanted. She leaned forward, straining to see what was happening. Coral was directly beneath her now, her naked hips gyrating lewdly, her eyes closed, and her mouth hanging open as if in a trance. She had shaved off her pubes, Gemma noticed with surprise, and now looked like an oddly distorted child, a small girl who has got involved in the wrong game. As she danced her breasts jigged up and down, her writhing body twisting like a serpent. Then suddenly there was a movement from a group of men standing to one side, and Gemma saw what must have been a stone hurling through the air. The missile hit Coral squarely on the forehead. She staggered backward, her face covered with red, then dropped from Gemma's view.*

The procession carried on: those in the front unaware of the small commotion at the back, the men at the back pressing onward, their anger at defilement by the Western woman's appearance overtaken by their desire to reach the tomb. Somewhere in the trees, Coral must be lying wounded.

Gemma took a deep breath. It had just been a joke, what she'd said, but Coral had misunderstood it, so now she should go to help her. Was that not what Zak would have wanted? But still she did not move. How dare Coral fuck him, she was thinking. How dare she mess everything up?

And then just when she was least expecting it, it happened. On the empty path beneath her, Coral suddenly burst from the trees. For a moment she stood facing the shrine, her shoulders heaving, the blood that poured from her face splattering the ground. She seemed to be fiddling with something in her hands. Then there was a terrible flash and whoosh as if lightning had struck, and Gemma saw brilliant flames reach up in an arc, then settle back into the shape of Coral's body, which shuddered, as if momentarily surprised.

She didn't want to look anymore, but she was transfixed,

staring down the hill as the figure staggered around for a while, the fire leaping boldly from its limbs. She could hear the fizz and crackle of the flames, smell the roasting flesh. Even if she had wanted to help, she kept telling herself, it was too late. Then suddenly the figure crumpled, dropping down on the ground, so that she was completely out of sight.

She almost fell herself then. It was what she had wanted, but not what she'd expected, not the reality of it, not that sighing, screaming hiss of fire, not the sizz of cooking fat. She could have, should have, stopped her, but then she had seen the flash, felt the warmth of the flames from the track, and now she was crying out loud and running down the path to where Coral's body lay. When she reached the place where she had seen Coral dancing she stopped, looking around in alarm. The path was empty: the only sign of the fire a fine layer of ash already settled on the stones. Coral must have tumbled into the bushes. Glancing around she noticed a blackened area of undergrowth to one side of the path, the smoke still rising. Leaping past it, she bashed her way into the trees.

It only took a few minutes to find what was left of Coral. Her corpse was slumped against the buttress roots of a tree as if she had just sat down for a rest, her skin so charred it seemed barely human. Her scalp was coming away, Gemma noticed with disgust, the face which stared sightlessly up melted into a melange of misplaced features: the brow of a nose, a skeleton's jaw, even Aussie teeth, grinning at the trees. The smell was overwhelming: pig on a spit, the meat she never touched. For a moment she almost retched, her throat constricting, her chest heaving, but she fought it back. She was dripping with sweat now, the fever consuming her with heat.

Bending over, she pulled at Coral's body. No one need ever know, she was thinking; why should they? They were in the jungle, where bodies decomposed within hours, where everything *that was dead was eaten up by the ravenous, unstoppable living. Yet however hard she tugged, the corpse was too heavy to move. She would have to bury it instead. Her fingers scrabbling frenziedly at the leafy ground, she began to cover it with vegetation: her breath coming in short, exhausted gasps. She was almost too weak to carry on now, her back racked with pain, her hands shaking with the delirium which was closing down on her like a fire curtain.*

When she'd finished, she stood up, her legs swaying treacherously. She had to make it back to the path, otherwise she would be lost. She took a few more steps, then her vision blurred and, her legs folding beneath her, she fell to the ground.

When she next opened her eyes the odor of burning had dispersed and her angel was there. She saw his face, felt his hand against her cheek, tried to sit up.

"What's happened to you?" he was saying. "Where in heaven is Coral?"

He put his arms around her, and she let him pull her up. She was deeply chilled, her body damp and shivering.

"She's gone," she whispered. "She and Esther took off for the south."

She looked up at his face. For a moment it seemed to change, a flicker of uncertainty or surprise momentarily disturbing the calm glaze of his features. Then it was gone, a fragment of evaporating cloud in a clear sky. He had not noticed the burnt bushes, or the candles and scattered matches, or the pile of leaves a few meters from where she was lying.

Leaning her head on his shoulder she took a faltering step toward the path. She could hear the beat of his heart, sense the warmth of his skin through his thin robes. He was hers now. Nothing and nobody would ever come between them.

"And you waited for me," Zak said.

"And I waited."

"But why are you here? I was looking everywhere."

"It was the mela. I wanted to see it. I got confused."

"And look, you're so cold. You could have died."

And then he was pulling Coral's sari from the bag of their things he had already packed and wrapping it around her and almost carrying her up the hill toward his waiting jeep. When they got there he lifted her carefully into the back, as if she was a doll. She laid her head against the seat as they accelerated away, the breeze rushing against her face. Already her temperature was falling, the sickness fading, her thoughts stabilizing.

After that, they drove and drove, until the road was dark and stars arched over the jeep like signs of hope. Gemma slept and woke and slept again until finally, toward the end of the next day, she was able to sit up and look around. She wound down the window, pushing her face out at the cold, sharp air. On the horizon she could see the mountains.

It was over: the nausea had gone, her thoughts were clear, and the old Gemma had disappeared. The past was finished with now, all those early years of loss and bitter craving and she was someone else entirely: a woman without a history, a woman who was not afraid, who would never look back. She was the person I am today.

That's right. This is my story, and as I stand in the garden looking into Esther's face I know I'll never repeat it to her. Why should she know what happened? What claim does she have over the truth? She's never understood me, despite her protestations of intimacy, never been aware that there may be more than one version of the past. And she could never have achieved what I have over the last five years. She's far too soft and flighty for the hardships I've endured, for the way I've turned away from all those superficial distractions of my old life and found out who I really am, this woman of strength and certainty.

And she would never have won Zak over in the way that I did, either, however attractive she used to be. It took a while, especially when he was so confused about Coral's disappearance. He had been trying to break free of her attachment for months, he told me later, but she was so troubled, she always needed him so much. And now suddenly she was gone and he did not know how to feel. So I waited. And while he tried to work things through, I made sure I was always at his side. It was meant to happen, that was what I told him over and over again. It was kismet, our fate.

And now Esther's here, standing in the garden we dug from the mountainside, crying rapturously, as if I was risen from the dead. It's a shock, however I tried to prepare myself. Zak told me he saw her on the train and I've been waiting for the last couple of days, not sure what I'll feel or how I'll react. Yet she's changed so much that had I not known I might hardly have recognized her: her famous beauty shriveled and diminished, her long hair gone, and her thin face drawn and harried. She keeps clutching at my hands and crying and saying how she's missed me and she loves me. And the strange thing is that I feel nothing. Not even anger.

～

33

AFTER I'd just about managed to stop crying and let go of Gemma's hands she tucked them into the rough pockets at the front of her robe and stepped back, smiling almost politely. She had obviously been outside a long time, for her cheeks were ruddy with the cold, the tip of her nose pink.

"Perhaps we should go inside," she said. "It's freezing out here."

We walked back across the lawn and through a door into the kitchen. I was still too shocked to speak, or to make sense of anything. I kept taking sideways glances at Gemma, still not wholly believing that it really was her who was accompanying me into the building. Yet the calm-faced woman with the long brown braid who strode slightly ahead of me could be no one else. It was the rounded slump of her shoulders which gave her away, the way she swung her arms as she walked, the dimple in her chin. It was like being in a dream: for so many years she had haunted me and now I kept expecting to suddenly wake and find myself lying next to Steve's somnambulant body, the sound of London traffic outside. And yet it was real: she was really here, my fantasies of murder unfounded. Already I felt lighter, the oppressive weight of an imagined history lifting and dissipating into the wintry sky. Wiping at my eyes with the edge of my shawl I glanced at the gleaming pots and pans, the stone sink, and huge oval table already laid for lunch with rows of stainless steel plates and cups. Stacked against the wall was a pile of folding chairs. It was like a youth hostel, I thought fleetingly; so bare and unhomely.

I followed Gemma out of the kitchen into a large whitewashed hall, wincing at the plummeting temperature. Like the kitchen, the hall was empty of comfort or clutter: a functional space for a functional institution. The only decoration was a huge carved Ganesh resting against the opposite wall, a handful of rose petals scattered at his feet. The air smelled faintly of incense.

"Don't worry," she called over her shoulder. "We're going somewhere warm."

Her boots slapping the stone tiles, she hurried across the hall toward the stairs. When she reached them she turned left, down a short dark corridor. Opening a door at the end of this, she stood aside.

The room was lit with candles. I stepped inside, my eyes adjusting to the shimmering light. The floor was covered with a thick Kashmiri carpet; worn silk bolsters were stacked against the walls. On one side of the room was a massage table; on the other was a small bookcase filled with bottles of oil, books on Buddhism and the Tao, and a brass incense burner. Squatting down, Gemma lit a small stove in the far corner.

"It's our therapies room. It should warm up soon."

She sat on the floor, her legs crossed, her back resting against the wall. I stared at her, still too disorientated to speak. Like a much-loved garden revisited after many missed seasons of growth and planting, she was both completely different and exactly the same. Her hair, so long dyed and cropped and spiked now fell in a heavy and loosely tied braid down her back, and without the eyeliner her eyes seemed larger and more alive. Her body had filled out, too, giving her the appearance of strength and substantiality rather than fat. Age suited her; the few lines around her eyes and mouth adding depth to her face, her expression somehow more settled and calm.

And yet she was still Gemma. As she folded her hands in her lap and gazed down at her small booted feet, her eyebrows furrowed in exactly the same way they had done when she was five, her small lips pursing. She still had a mole just above her right eye, and that dimple in the middle of her chin filled me with such nostalgia that I had to bite my lip.

"You look fantastic," I blurted, instantly regretting the triteness of the comment. Five years earlier she would have blushed and snorted in denial or perhaps returned the compliment, but now she simply nodded, her eyes unreadable. There was a long pause. I gulped, my fingers twisting with embarrassment. Since we had sat down my initial elation had been increasingly superseded by a sharper, more uncomfortable emotion. There was so much to say, so many questions and apologies and explanations; speeches I'd imagined reciting a thousand times, but now that a miracle had occurred and Gem was alive and sitting in front of me, her chapped hands so close I could reach out and touch them, her cheeks rosy from the mountain air, I couldn't recall a word.

"Look, I'm sorry," Gemma suddenly said. "I know you've come a long way, but I won't be able to chat for long. I've got to lead the devotion before lunch."

I stared at her.

"I can't believe you're here," I started to say. "All this time, when I thought . . ."

She cut me off, her voice businesslike. "So where are you staying?"

I blinked at her in bewilderment. Why was she talking to me like this?

"Just this crap hotel, I . . ."

"We've been expecting you all day. Poppy said someone had been asking after me in Delhi and then Zak thought he saw you on the train? He said you tried to hide under the window when he caught your eye . . ."

She smiled at me, her lips twitching with what I could only interpret as amusement. I stared at her numbly. An unpleasant pressure was beginning to push down on my chest.

"I was confused," I muttered, glancing down at her white hands, her thick hemp robes and boots, doing anything but meet her eyes. My hands were beginning to shake again, my teeth chattering not with cold, but with something more profound. Gemma was silent, waiting for me to say more. Throwing my arms around my shoulders in an attempt to stop them from trembling, I mumbled, "I just can't believe you're here."

She did not respond. The shaking was overtaking my entire body now. I hugged my knees to my chest, unable to prevent the violent knocking of my teeth, the uncontrollable juddering of my shoulders. She gazed at me detachedly. After a moment or so, she said, "Perhaps we should get you a cup of tea or something."

I kneaded at my hands like uncooked bread.

"I'm fine."

"You've had a shock," she went on. "And now all that pent-up energy is being released. It's part of the healing."

"The healing?" I echoed faintly.

"Isn't that why you're here?"

"I don't know." I took another deep breath, my eyes suddenly smarting with hot, unshed tears. "I was searching for someone, but . . ."

I stopped, unable to continue. Who *had* I been searching for? If only I could stop myself from shaking so badly I might be able to put my jumping thoughts into words, but all I could do was look away from Gemma's smug, closed face, and mumble: "What are *you* doing here?"

She smiled, not in the blissed-out, blurry way of the woman at the airport, but with the condescending patience of someone explaining the basics to a novice.

"It's where I'm meant to be. If you'd wait until our Baba gets back you'd understand. He's the light, and we're the ones who hold him up."

I stared at her, my mind suddenly snapping to attention. It sounded like utter hippie nonsense, not the kind of stuff *my* Gemma would ever have spouted.

"Baba is the *light?*" I repeated slowly, letting go of my knees and sitting up straight. The trembling was subsiding now, my shoulders and hands finally becoming still. "I wouldn't have thought you'd be into something like that."

"Like what?" She smiled at me tightly.

"All this . . . *cult* stuff."

"It's not a cult. It's just an ashram, where we follow our master, and learn how to live." She regarded me with kind sympathy, the way one might look at someone less privileged than oneself. "Unfortunately it's not something most ordinary people are open to," she said. "It's about belief and commitment, and letting the old stuff go."

I nodded, understanding only that she was somehow boasting.

"I have to say though that a lot of what's happened here has been because of me and Zak. I mean, all the followers Baba has now. We've got over twenty sanyasis living here full time and loads more passing through." She tossed her head with what I could only interpret as pride. "It's one of the most successful ashrams in this part of India. Zak runs it for Sai Baba when he's away on his tours, which these days is nearly all the time."

"Zak runs it . . ." I said vaguely.

She snorted, and for a second I saw a glimmer of the old

Gemma, the one I used to know. "He *thinks* he runs it. Or rather, I let him think he does. You know we're a couple now?"

There was another long pause. It was ridiculous, for my mind was crammed with questions, yet something in her face made asking them impossible. It was as if I was a vague acquaintance of hers, someone with whom what connection there might once have been had long since withered and died.

"I knew you'd find me in the end," she suddenly said, and I glanced up at her, my face flushing. "I didn't want you to, but I knew you would."

I frowned. "I wasn't actually looking for you."

"No?"

"I was looking for Coral."

She shrugged, her eyes flicking dismissively to the fire.

"She was a nutcase. Why would you want to look for her?"

She was still smiling, but something in her voice was harder and at the mention of Coral's name she had inadvertently bitten her lip. I stared at her, my resolve beginning to grow.

"I thought she might know what had happened to you," I said. "For the last five years I've thought that you were dead . . ." I stopped, unable to control my voice as I suddenly pictured the blackened stump of hand, the humped, scorched corpse that I had thought was her. Gemma gazed resolutely at the floor. "Well, I'm not dead," she finally said. "I'm more alive than you could ever imagine."

She glanced up at me and in the brief moment that our eyes met I thought I saw triumph. I looked hastily away, my mind whirling. It was too much to take in. I'd been so sure of my story, but now it seemed that a large chunk of the plot was missing, the central characters cut suddenly adrift. On the wall the shadows spluttered and jumped, just as they had done the terrible morning I'd woken to Coral's ring of fire.

"So what are you saying?" I whispered. "That it was *Coral* who was killed?"

She shrugged. "I don't know. Anyway, it's all in the past."

"But I saw her in the jeep. On the road back to Bhubaneshwar . . ."

"No, that must have been me."

"I don't understand . . ."

"It was me. Coral ran off somewhere. She was unstable, a nutter. You said that yourself."

I stared at her. Outside I could hear the thud of a heavy door and the sound of footsteps walking across the hall. The whole story, the one on which I'd based my entire life, was premised on a single factual error. And yet now that the real, living Gemma, with her mottled hands and plump bosom, was sitting before me, I realized that it made complete sense. Of course it was Coral and not Gemma who had died, for in retrospect the former was clearly hurtling toward lunatic self-destruction, while despite all her protestations of fragility, the latter was a rugged survivor.

"But there was a body . . ." I said slowly.

Gemma blinked, her cheeks suddenly red.

"I don't know anything about any bodies."

I gazed at her in silence, my mind slowly filling in the gaps. It was grotesque, an incident in a badly conceived black comedy, but we must have buried the wrong body. It hadn't been Gemma who her family and friends had grimly lowered into the Stevenage soil but a messed-up drifter, an Australian girl who called herself Coral and whose family probably didn't even know she was dead. For an absurd moment I almost laughed, a wave of hysteria rising up within me, like all those times in A-level English when Mrs. Crewe would say something and Gem's and my eyes would meet and we'd splutter with badly repressed hilarity.

And if it was Coral who had died, I suddenly thought, why had Gemma disappeared? Reaching out across the cold room, I touched her arm.

"What *happened,* Gem? Why didn't you let us know you were okay?"

She glanced at me, her face composed once more. "You could cope. I just assumed you'd head off for Goa or somewhere and have a good time. You didn't need me. You only asked me to come with you on your great trip because you felt guilty."

I swallowed, the pressure in my chest tightening another notch. After all that I'd been through, how could she say such a thing?

"But you *disappeared*!" I croaked.

"So what?"

This was more than I could take. How *dare* she sit there like the Queen of the Hare Krishnas and pretend that she was blameless, her only crime not staying in touch? I let go of her arm, sitting up straight and glaring at her angrily.

"Didn't you think that you disappearing might have an effect on me?" I said, my voice rising angrily. "And what about your family? For God's sake, what about your *mum*?"

She looked quickly away.

"She never bothered about me before," she said quietly. "So why should she now? And anyway, it doesn't matter now. All that attachment stuff is irrelevant. What matters is the path ahead."

I gazed at her, so shocked that for a moment I could not think of what to say. She was not going to get away with it, I suddenly thought. She might have changed almost beyond recognition, but she was still Gem, my oldest friend, on whose memory I'd based my entire life.

"What do you mean 'it doesn't matter'?" I cried, feeling the blood rush furiously to my cheeks. "You thought you'd just vanish, just like that?"

"Why not?"

I grabbed at her limp hand. When I squeezed it only the slightest pressure was returned.

"Why did you do this? Was it because of me and Steve?"

She laughed. "It's completely irrelevant."

"Then what was it?" I said hoarsely. I was nearly in tears now. I sniffed them back, determined to carry on. "Did I push you into it, or something? Please, Gem, I really need to know."

Very slowly, she pulled her hand away.

"It wasn't anything to do with you."

"But I took Steve from you! And I left you there in Agun Mazir, with Coral so off her head . . ."

"No, you're wrong."

Tilting her chin upward, just as she had always done when she was feeling particularly obstinate, she stared into my face. "I made you do it," she said. "It was what I wanted."

I stared back at her. She was lying, I was thinking; for some reason she was making this all up.

"What do you mean? How could you have?"

"I wanted you to leave me. If it wasn't Steve I'd have found someone or something else to blame you for."

Now I was shaking my head. I could feel the pressure of tears behind my eyes again, my chest tightening into a sob.

"But why would you want me to leave you, Gem? We were best friends!"

"Best friends? You hardly knew me."

"But that's not true . . ." I could not finish the sentence. From outside I could hear laughter and very distantly, the faint strumming of a guitar.

"It was you that had this big scene about our friendship," she said quietly. "Not me. I just needed someone to help me escape."

I gave a sob, the tears spilling down my cheeks.

"But you've ruined my entire life!"

Gemma shook her head. "No, I didn't," she said. "It was you that did that. I just followed my path."

In the corner, the smoldering wood popped and whizzed. I gazed numbly at the glimmering flames, the tears sliding unchecked down my face. Everything felt so surreal, my brain only dimly taking on what she had told me, yet in a small corner of my mind I could already see that it all made perfect sense. To disappear in such a way was exactly the sort of thing Gemma would have done. It was her style of revenge.

"Look, I don't mean to be rude," she suddenly said. "But I've really got to go."

She stood up, brushing the creases from her robe.

"If you want to hang around until tomorrow Babaji will be back and you can meet him."

I gazed at her. Perhaps five years ago I would have become angry, screaming that she was wrong, that she had misremembered the past, that ours had been the truest, closest friendship, marred by one fatal betrayal; that I would not allow my story to be dismissed so easily. But somehow I no longer had the energy. What would it gain? The only truth which mattered was that once we had loved each other, in the immediate, practical way that little girls do. Now, though, it was over. We were strangers, linked only by the dimly recalled, fragmenting past. I had got the whole story wrong. None of it mattered in the way that I thought it did.

Standing up, I wiped the tears from my face. Suddenly I felt very calm.

"No," I said. "There doesn't really seem much point."

She gazed at me for a moment, as if on the verge of saying something, then shrugged. "Is Steve with you?"

I swallowed, but she was looking at me without any discernible ill will.

"No."

"But you're still together?"

"Not anymore."

"What happened?"

"You know." I turned to the door, not wanting her to see my face. "Stuff got in the way."

"Shame. I always thought you two were made for each other."

I did not reply. Gemma stepped through the door and I followed her into the freezing hall. When we reached the front door she opened it, standing aside to let me pass.

"Looks like it's clearing up," she said, glancing outside.

"Right."

I stepped onto the porch.

"You'll be all right?"

"I'll be fine."

"Esther?"

"Yeah?"

I turned around and saw that her face had softened. For the first time that day, our eyes met.

"I'm sorry. I didn't mean to hurt you." Very slowly, she reached out and took my hand. "It was just something I had to do. I had to get away."

I shook my head. I was suddenly close to tears again.

"So what about your mum?" I eventually said. "Do you want me to tell her that you're here?"

She seemed to shudder, wrapping her arms around herself as if for comfort. "No," she said. "I'll write to her. It's time."

We embraced then, stepping into the warmth of each other's arms for the briefest of moments, then clumsily separating again, our cheeks colliding in a mistimed kiss. When we stood apart I understood that everything had finally changed.

"Take care."

"Yep. You, too."

"See you around then. Stay in touch."

"Yeah, for sure."

I turned, pulling my shawl tightly around my shoulders. In the time that I had been inside the ashram the path leading through the front garden had iced over. I started to walk along it, taking it one step at a time, not looking back to wave at Gemma, just making sure that I did not slip.

34

WHEN I reached the bottom of the track I crossed the road and stood by the side of the hill, looking through the trees to the valley below. Gemma was right; although the temperature had fallen, the sky was clearing: above the trees clumps of cloud drifted apart to reveal a clear stretch of blue.

In the patchwork fields below, I could see the lines of the plow, patches of common land sprinkled with goats and sheep, the thatched roofs of houses, their smudge of smoke rising into the air above. Directly beneath me a shallow river was winding through the fields, its waters still low enough for a wide beach of pebbles and sand. As I looked down I saw that just below the bottom line of trees a group of women were washing clothes, the slap of garments against the boulders blending with the gush and gurgle of the water.

I stood for a while, watching the women below. I felt strangely still, my thoughts suspended in the calm clarity of aftershock, those few focused moments before it all sinks in. And as their chatter rose up the hill it all came back: the Story of Gemma and I, or How I Lost My Best Friend. I thought of our childhood together, of our secrets, and passions, and vows and how it had all gradually changed, ebbing away with each different turn of our lives. I thought of school and how she was meant to be the clever one and I was the one who was pretty. I thought of how I had passed my exams while she had flunked hers and saw how deeply competitive everything was that we did: those Cindy Doll games, those discos and university places and men. How had I ever thought of her as someone to be pitied? I had known her for so long that I'd stopped seeing her as herself. She was not poor, overweight Gem, whose parents had split up, whose hopeless mother spent her life whingeing; not Gem the failure who had fucked up her A-levels and was stuck in a dump. No, she was someone else: Gemma the strong one; Gemma, who made her decisions and stuck to them. It was me who wanted to hold onto the past, me who was scared to let go. And it was me who had always been lost.

So I stood there for hours, watching as the women worked and thinking about everything. And as the sun slowly moved across the sky I began to realize how free I'd suddenly become. And I am standing here still, rooted to the edge of this hill, my story almost over. I have told you everything I know, all that I remember. And now that I have reached the end, I've discovered what I should have known all along. Gem and I loved each other once, of course we did. But then it ended, like most childhood friendships eventually do. It did not matter who did what, it was not about guilt or blame. It was just about growing up.

I take a deep breath, filling my lungs with the cold mountain air. All that time, what I thought I'd lost was never there at all: it was a mirage, a trick of the gods. Later, I may not feel like this; inevitably there will be confusion, and anger and pain. But now I laugh, reaching up at the cold air. It is over, and I am suddenly weightless, soaring above myself, as light and easy as the clouds. I look through the pines to the sky, almost expecting a sign, and with a sudden flash of silver the sun appears from behind a tree trunk, the light glinting off the patchy snow and momentarily dazzling me. It's the real stuff now. All this time I have been so hopelessly lost, but now the journeys and the waiting are finished.

Below me, one of the women has started to sing. Shielding my eyes with my hands, I turn away from the view and start walking down the hill.

Katy Gardner is a graduate of Cambridge University, and received a Ph.D. from The London School of Economics. She is currently a senior lecturer in social anthropology at the University of Sussex. She lives on the south coast of the United Kingdom. *Losing Gemma* is her first novel.